Back Roads to
Bliss

MAIN

Also by Ruth Glover
A Place Called Bliss
With Love from Bliss
Journey to Bliss
Seasons of Bliss
Bittersweet Bliss

The Saskatchewan Saga

Back Roads to
Bliss

A NOVEL

RUTH GLOVER

Fleming H. Revell
A Division of Baker Book House Co
Grand Rapids, Michigan 49516

Published by Fleming H. Revell
a division of Baker Book House Company
P.O. Box 6287, Grand Rapids, MI 49516-6287

Printed in the United States of America

Library of Congress Cataloging-in-Publication Data
Glover, Ruth
    Back roads to bliss : a novel / Ruth Glover.
       p.   cm. — (Saskatchewan saga ; 6)
    ISBN 0-8007-5829-3
    1. Young women—Fiction. 2. Saskatchewan—Fiction. 3. Women immigrants—Fiction. I. Title. II. Series: Glover, Ruth. Saskatchewan saga ; v 6.
PS3557.L678B33 2003
813p.54—dc21   2003009422

Scripture quotations are taken from the King James Version of the Bible.

To Donnybrook School
and the people who
fill my dreams and stir my memories

England, 1898

It wasn't the usual yap of her dog, Fifi, that wakened her, nor was it the muted sounds of the chambermaid as she went about lighting a fire. Neither was it the cheerful birdsong outside her bedroom window, promising spring in England. She awoke with some distant thought nagging for attention; in her half-asleep state it eluded her. Never mind. As a girl—young woman—in a well-appointed bedroom in a handsome mansion, with breakfast on its way up shortly with no effort or worry on her part, with all of life before her and her body throbbing with health and vigor and her future full of possibilities, Allison Middleton had no appreciable concerns.

Accustomed to luxury though she was, she couldn't help but take a moment to admire and appreciate the latest addition to the house as soon as she had made her sleepy way toward it: a room for no other purpose than pampering oneself, an exalted privy—a bathroom.

Stepping into this marvel of convenience, closing the door behind her and locking it, Allison leaned against it and found her satisfaction with life in general mounting, realizing, without speech, *The world is so full of a number of things, I'm sure we should all be as happy as kings.*

Taking her comfort and her luxuries for granted most of the time, occasionally a small sense of gratitude—as in this moment—swelled her heart. And never more so than when, at the close of day, she watched the stream of workers file from the factory, her father's mill, the income from which made all her blessings possible. Seeing their weariness she was sobered, but only momentarily. For no pity of hers, no sympathy, would change their lot. What might have been done for them had she been a son was null and void because of her gender. The mill and its workers would never be any concern of hers. So she enjoyed the benefits of the woolen mill, with none of the worries.

Papa might have his faults, but stinginess was not one of them. Moreover, Papa was driven by a burning ambition to climb the social ladder, and if indoor plumbing was the latest thing being installed in the great houses of England, Middleton Grange should have it regardless of the cost.

Not that cost was any deterrent to Quincy Middleton. If wealth alone could have purchased the standing he wanted, it would have been his in a minute. The Midbury Woolen Mills, while making him excessively wealthy and giving him a certain power and importance, also marked him as a merchant and thus low on the social scale. But there was always the hope that, with care and effort, he might win some honor from the queen or perhaps run for some position in government. As it was, his importance didn't go much beyond the boundaries of Midbury, the village that had sprung up around the mill that supplied its inhabitants with work and housed them, the rent going into the already bulging coffers of Quincy Middleton.

Yes, Quincy was careful to observe the amenities, to make the gestures, to sponsor the causes that would establish him as a man of parts, a man of talents, perhaps even as a gentleman.

Quincy's canny choice of a wife had been the first rung on the ladder to success and acceptance; Letitia was born "quality."

Success, in a business sense, he had attained, and wealth in abundance, but acceptance from the aristocracy, in spite of his marriage, eluded him. But still he tried.

The bathroom was part of that effort. London, of course, had developed sewage and water systems long ago, but they were slow in reaching the outlying areas, small villages like Midbury, in particular.

A spare bedroom had been given over to the project, and Letitia had seen to it that it was lavishly fitted out. Vanity, cupboards, overstuffed chairs—all added to the aesthetics of the room. The ceramic sink was set on graceful pedestals, the cast-iron tub was supplied with a shower ring that could be hung around the neck, sluicing water deliciously over the standing bather. There was no longer any need for water to be carried upstairs from the kitchen, growing cold as it came; a tank in the attic assured an abundant supply, and the new gas line meant hot water at the turn of a tap. Leaning against the door, Allison took a moment to savor the privacy, the cleanliness, the convenience.

But the privacy was threatened—a rattle of the doorknob at her back woke Allison out of her reverie.

Taptaptap—by the gentleness of the sound Allison knew it was her sister, Sarah. Allison herself, if denied entrance, would have banged on the door, called impatiently, demanding entry. But Sarah, at fifteen, two years younger than Allison and in all respects different, was self-effacing, unassuming, modest, and—at least to date—meek.

"Go away," Allison called, stirring from her daydreaming at last. "I just got in here and I'm not going to hurry." She could hear the soft sigh of resignation from the other side of the door and felt a small pang of remorse.

"Give me a few minutes, Sister," she amended, and immediately the sunshine, which had dimmed for the moment, returned to her day. Sarah was such a mouse, it was difficult not to override her. Allison was a person of decided opinions and quick and

9

thoughtless action; to do her credit, she *was* working on these aspects of her character. Not very successfully, she often feared, as she leaped into life and—yes—love with abandon.

Leaning toward her image in the mirror, blinking away the last vestige of sleep that lingered in her eyes, Allison examined her typically British rose-petal complexion for a single flaw and could find none. Sighing with satisfaction, she snatched the frilly cap from her head, impatient with the protocol that demanded it for sleep, and ran her fingers through her dark, springing hair, as resistant to taming as her spirit.

Suddenly wide awake, the import of the day struck her with full force, and the thing that had been teasing at her mind ever since she wakened: *This is my wedding day!* Or, on second thought, possibly tomorrow . . . probably the day after.

Excitement leaped into the vivid face in the mirror and brightened the eyes until they danced to life, sparkling like sunlight reflected from a gray sea. Allison's eyes were that way—deceptively calm and quiet one moment, lit and lively the next.

Across Midbury, in the rooms above his father's shop, was Stephen waking to the same thrilling realization, and were his thoughts full of cautious, secret schemes as were hers? She was sure of it.

Her mind given to breathless intrigue, Allison gave no thought to her parents, seated below in the morning room, except to wonder how to get out of the calls her mother had arranged for the afternoon (it was considered very ill bred to call before lunch, and Letitia was rigidly circumspect in all things). Allison knew the new calling cards had arrived, cards that included her name—as was right and proper for a daughter living at home—and Letitia would expect to be accompanied on her rounds today. Allison was sure her mother would include the Flagle house as a subtle means of displaying her *available* daughter's charms to Norville's mother, and she grimaced with distaste, enjoying the effect in the mirror.

Too bad about the cards; they would go to waste. Glazed, with simple engraving without flourishes or adornment in the best of

10

good taste, they would be carried in a special calling card case emulating the style Queen Victoria had made popular, depicting a castle—Windsor in this instance—and known as a "castle top" case. Allison had been pleased when her mother ordered them, anticipating many sociable hours. Now she dismissed them and their importance impatiently.

Sarah was considered too young for calling, not yet out of the schoolroom, although the real reason was that she shrank from public exposure and begged her way out of such obligations. But Allison—she of the lively temperament and supreme self-confidence—had no such excuse; and with the new cards in hand, Mama would be counting on her accompanying presence today.

But in view of the things she had to do, like sorting and packing, an afternoon of calling was out of the question.

Moreover, her excitement was so extreme she was sure she could never conceal it from her mother. To be ladylike, restrained, polite, chatting inanely with the mother of Norville Flagle, whom she despised, while her heart beat fast and her head whirled, would be an impossibility. Some alternate plan must be put into effect, and quickly.

Looking at herself in the mirror, Allison noted her high color and bright eyes and decided she would make them work for her: a fever, sick with a raging fever—that would be her excuse. Allison pinched her cheeks, already rosy, and was gratified by the heightened color that could surely, if accompanied by moans and perhaps a few ready tears, indicate an illness that would keep the sufferer to her room for the day. Mama, though disappointed, would sympathize, apply a damp cloth to her daughter's forehead, send the housekeeper up with some nostrum or other, and carry on with her scheduled calls for the day.

Below, in the great house called Middleton Grange, Letitia, in perfect morning fashion in her loose robe of fine cashmere (never of silk, which was reserved for gowns), looked uneasily at her husband concealed behind his newspaper and set her teacup aside. Letitia rarely let business interfere with the pleasure of her morning tea. So important was it, and the proper brewing of it, that her household retained the old-fashioned system of blending its own tea, making it to her specifications. After considerable experimentation over the years, it was narrowed to China tea with a precise measure of Hyson and Congo leaves. The resulting blend was stored in a chest under lock and key. The staff—cook, personal maid, chambermaid, kitchenmaid, parlormaid, laundress, needlewoman, butler, valet, coachman, groom, two gardeners—who loved their tea and their teatimes, must settle for a brew made of the cheaper Common Bohea or Common Green leaves. And count themselves lucky to have it.

Letitia was reluctant to give up her morning tea while there was still some in the pot. But knowing Quincy well, she sensed a storm was brewing.

"It's . . . it's Allison, isn't it?" she asked falteringly, having sat through her husband's silence long enough.

Quincy, after a long moment, a moment designed to punish his wife for not attending to his mood earlier, peered around his newspaper. "You must admit, Tish, she acted most unacceptably last night when the guests were present. Especially toward young Flagle. Dash it all—when will she learn to behave properly, as a young female should!" His jowls quivered, and his mouth, under his mustache, was pinched in a mix of fury and frustration.

Letitia was reluctant to admit it, but Allison had indeed been too flip, too restless, too casual with the languid young man who might have, if handled properly, had his latent interest fanned to the point of romance. An alliance with the Flagle scion would give Quincy the "in" he coveted. For were not the Flagles third cousins to the Earl of Shrewton? Surely Allison had been unwise last night. But there! The child knew little about and cared less for social standing. Her father's absorption with it and her mother's constant attempts on his behalf had made no impact on her.

"She still retains a little of her childish enthusiasms, I'm afraid, and her girlish fancies." Letitia offered the only excuse she could come up with, which was no excuse at all and a very poor explanation. "And if they don't include courtship . . . at the moment—"

"At seventeen," Quincy said quenchingly—strong on Scripture, and as usual appropriating it incorrectly—"it's time to put away childish things."

"She *is* doing better, I think." Letitia's assurance wavered under the reproachful look in her husband's eyes, a look Letitia guiltily identified as accusing her personally. *With your background and social standing,* it said, *you should be doing better.*

Letitia was not deceived concerning herself, and she fully understood why Quincy had been a suitor for her hand in marriage. That he had a chance to win her was due to the inability of one of her eyes to track with the other (commonly and crudely called being "cockeyed") that had lessened her choices among the wellborn, perhaps finicky, young gentlemen of her acquaintance. It was not she who attracted him; he was drawn like a magnet to the fact that her father was a baronet and her family was of high social standing. Moreover, her dowry was considerable and had, when invested in the mill, assured its success.

Letitia had married Quincy, the mill owner, with her eyes wide open and had not regretted it. They lived well: Quincy, though careless and thoughtless, had provided generously for her; they were of some importance in the backwater that was Midbury; and she had two lovely daughters who would, one day, make advantageous marriages.

Quincy couldn't complain! The marriage had elevated his status considerably. If only—Letitia mourned again silently—there had been a son. Her connections would have meant so much to a son, making it possible, through her relatives, to meet the best people, attend the best schools. But in this—she was reminded occasionally—she had failed miserably; there had been only daughters.

Quincy considered himself a patient, forgiving man, making the best of a bad situation, such as two daughters who pleased him not all that much. Allison he considered hoydenish, Sarah too timid. Quincy—when he considered them at all—looked at his daughters with jaundiced eyes.

Allison *had* expressed interest at times in the mill and had an insight into business that, in a male, would have been gratifying. As it was, because Allison was a female and therefore unfit to participate in the business world, Quincy was frustrated because the child wasn't a son. It was as if he said, "It's all wasted—this cleverness, these brains, this ability."

Secretly, it was a great comfort to Letitia that this same child showed all the feminine graces and wiles necessary to make a brilliant marriage one day, gaining a place in Midbury society, perhaps London society. Letitia took pride in her child's beauty, her perfection of face and form. And her eyes were not flawed!

But, Letitia often sighed, the child was too outspoken, too much of an individualist, too impatient with protocol. She needed to curb her tongue, particularly when faced with standards and etiquette that she thought silly and pointless. The queen, for instance, who should be honored and revered, was *old-fashioned* according to this outspoken daughter. Who but an old person, she asked, would submit to the wearing of the heavy, clumsy Balmoral petticoat—so named for the queen's favorite residence? Who, with a speck of pride in herself and her appearance, would submit to the Balmoral boot in place of Morocco slippers? Who would pull mohair stockings over slim legs, no matter if the weather were freezing? Allison flouted the tried and true, the wise, the sagacious, the sensible. "It's time for the Edwardian era," she declared. "Or for the queen to get herself out of Balmoral."

Letitia, shocked and pale of countenance at such audacity, pled for silence on the subject. All in all, Allison's unpredictability kept her mother uneasy . . . what would she come up with next? It was important to instill adult values and viewpoints in the child as quickly as possible. Letitia was counting on the rigid protocol of afternoon calls to curb Allison's impetuous nature, to restrain her heedless speech, to shape her into an acceptable Victorian mold, a mold Letitia adhered to and admired above all else.

14

While Letitia exhibited patience, Quincy, a man with an overweening desire for advancement, had no patience whatsoever.

"Norville Flagle," Letitia said now, "will not be the only opportunity for Allison, by any means. She's pretty enough, heaven knows—"

"But does she care a fig for that?" Quincy complained. "Young Norville has been making sheep's eyes at her for ages, but she ignores him. Ignoring him in spite of the fact he's from a prestigious family. His uncle's an earl!"

"Third cousin," Letitia added automatically, having worked out the connection, "twice removed."

"Once . . . twice . . . three times—no matter, the connection is there! What's the matter with the girl? Doesn't she understand *anything?*"

Quincy was well familiar with Patrick Colquhoun's *A Treatise on the Wealth, Power, and Resources of the British Empire.* Though the book was outdated, things had not changed all that much in British thinking, and rank and prestige still played a powerful part in British society. One legacy of the Victorian era would be the sharp contrast between High Society and what were clearly regarded as Lower Orders. You were one or the other, and you knew where you belonged. If Quincy had any doubt, he painfully located himself in Colquhoun's *Treatise* as Third Class.

Third Class (Quincy knew it by heart) included clergy, doctors, bankers, merchants, and manufacturers of some importance.

Second Class was made up of the exalted and envied baronets, knights, and those having large incomes and estates.

Highest Orders included lords, great officers of state, peers above the degree of baronet, and, of course, the royals.

Blessed, favored Classes One and Two! Quincy was sometimes tempted to gnash his teeth and curse the strict codes that consigned one to a certain class and made it so difficult to get out of it. Might as well be in India's caste system, he deplored, for all the good his money and toil did him. The aristocrats looked down their long noses, bought his factory's goods willingly enough, and flouted his presence at their tables and in their clubs.

With Quincy's money and flourishing factory, it might have been possible for a son to move into Class Two—if he were selective of his friends, emulated the aristocracy's behavior, spent money lavishly (which Quincy would gladly provide), showed no inclination to soil himself with work, and chose a wife a little above him in class (if he had to settle for one with some blemish, such as being cockeyed, so be it).

It was useless to continue to bemoan the absence of a son; he had two daughters. And one, Sarah, Quincy thought sourly, had no ambition whatsoever. But Allison, with her considerable graces, her wit, and her beauty—and with the large dowry he would offer—would make a marriage that would, once and for all, lift the name of Middleton from the plebeian to the peerage.

Quincy, of a sudden, found hope springing up in his heart. Norville Flagle, with his thrice-removed connection with the aristocracy, was the key to Quincy's ambitions. And Allison was of marriageable age.

"I think," Quincy said before he returned to his paper, and striking his wife speechless, "I'd like you to plan a ball of spectacular dimensions for Allison's eighteenth birthday."

B eggin' yer pardon, Mum . . ."
"Yes, Becky," Letitia said, turning her head to look at the
little maid, "what is it?"

Becky, not long in service and only recently advanced from
scullery duties to chambermaid, twisted her red and callused
hands, directing her words to Letitia while casting anxious
glances toward her lord and master. But Quincy, having delivered his startling request for a lavish birthday celebration for his
oldest daughter, had retreated behind his newspaper, leaving Letitia to grapple with his surprising announcement. From being a
most careless, unconcerned father, Quincy was now showing
remarkable interest in Allison.

There had to be more to it than goodness of heart. Knowing her
husband well, Letitia was aware of the reason: Quincy had come
to the realization that Allison was a . . . well, a *pawn* in the game
he played. With a father's authority, he could command what her
future should be; his whim could decide her destiny, the destiny of
all of them. His caprice could change the course of their lives.

Some small flicker of resentment, long thought to be dead, struggled to life momentarily. With a shrug of realism, Letitia snuffed it out; wasting time on what would never be was useless.

It seemed clear, from their conversation, that Quincy had only just realized what a treasure he had in his daughter. And to think she had been right here, available for his using, all along. The fact of the matter was that Allison's marriage to the right man would work the miracle Quincy had dreamed of, connived for, and almost despaired of.

And it had taken the magic name of Norville Flagle to open his eyes. What possibilities! Quincy's small eyes gleamed like burnished coins; the corners of his mouth twitched in a way Letitia knew meant satisfaction. Allison, like a goose ordered plucked and prepared for the table, was fated to be offered on the altar of Quincy's ambition.

Still—Letitia comforted herself in her helplessness—Allison would love a sumptuous party given in her honor. Whether or not she bowed readily to the inevitable assignation with Norville Flagle remained to be seen. Perhaps if it were made attractive enough . . . a large settlement, perhaps. Letitia sighed, realizing it would take some sort of miracle to turn the spiritless, foppish Norville Flagle into a man who would appeal to her imperious daughter. Allison would never settle into marriage as compliantly as had her mother. Letitia automatically lowered her lashes over the offending eye that had shaped her own decision, and another small sigh escaped her lips, to be heard by Quincy.

His eyebrows raised. "A ball doesn't meet with your approval?" he asked. "I thought you'd be delighted—a chance to invite all those relatives of yours, let them see that you live far better than most of them do. If you need help, you could hire Miss Hotchkiss—"

"That's not necessary," Letitia said stiffly. After all, she was fully capable of doing what was required to entertain so august an assemblage. Immediately names and faces of long-neglected relatives rose in her mind, only to be jarred into oblivion by the maid Becky's hesitant interruption.

"Well, Mum, it's Miss Allison."

"What about Miss Allison?" Letitia asked, fearing the worst where this headstrong child was concerned.

"Her's sick, Mum."

"Sick? What do you mean, sick? And where is she? And how long has she been indisposed?"

"Her's in her room, Mum, and I expect her's been sick all night. Her's tossin' on her bed, moanin' somethin' fiercelike." Becky rolled her eyes dramatically, as though to describe the symptoms of the afflicted Allison.

"All right, Becky. I'll go up. Thank you very much; you may return to your duties."

The little maid made her escape, to repeat the story in the kitchen, dwelling importantly on her part in the small household drama. "There I were," she described breathlessly, "come into Miss Allison's room jist to do the fire, an' coo—I heard this groanin' and moanin'. Like a banshee, it were—"

"That's enough, Becky," cook said sternly. "When will you learn that what happens above stairs should not be bandied about below? Now get back to work, my girl."

Allison's "moanin' and groanin'," abandoned in the interim, resumed when the door opened a bit later and her mother appeared. Letitia hastened to the bedside.

"Allison! What's wrong? Are you sick, dear? Do you hurt somewhere? Is it your stomach?"

Allison groaned and put a hand feebly to her forehead. Her mouth sagged weakly, her eyes stared in a blank manner, her head rolled from side to side. Perhaps she went too far, for Letitia's concern seemed to cool considerably.

"Lie still, dear. Let me feel your brow," she said. But Allison's tossing head made it difficult to determine whether there was a fever and just how high it might be. The cheeks were red, however, and looked feverish. But cheeks could be pinched.

"Water," Allison croaked.

Letitia spoke soothingly to her daughter and promised to send up a cold drink, all the while studying her with some skepticism; she'd been through these charades with Allison before, usually timed to escape something she didn't want to do.

"Your stomach's not upset, then?" she inquired, and she was assured that only the head hurt; food, as well as drink, would be acceptable.

"And medication," Letitia pronounced, and noted that, in spite of the supposed headache, Allison's fair forehead wrinkled with distaste. Positive Headache Cure it would be. For did it not guarantee relief within fifteen minutes of the first dose, with a second rarely necessary except in obstinate cases? No matter what the cause of the distress, whether from headache or stomach or a severe case of neuralgia, Positive's guarantee covered it.

Feeling considerably relieved (Positive Headache Cure had worked a miracle more than once, getting the malingerer on her feet before even a teaspoon was swallowed), Letitia turned to depart.

"I'm afraid it's toast for you today, my dear," she decreed, adding, "unless, that is, you are up and on your feet and able to go calling. Then you'd want to partake of teatime, of course . . ."

Allison's moans increased. Letitia could see it was going to be one of the protracted bouts, enduring the entire day but probably "cured" by the following morning when whatever was aggravating the child should be over and out of the way. She was able to leave with little or no concern for Allison's welfare.

"Well," Quincy said impatiently when his wife joined him again, "what's going on up there?"

"Just a little malaise, dear," Letitia reported. "Perhaps she indulged in too many cream buns yesterday. She's at that age, you know—part child, part adult. Or girls that age," she added delicately but implying much, "can have certain ailments—"

"Well, it's time she grew up and acted like an adult. Did you tell her about the birthday celebration?" Quincy asked, folding the newspaper, gulping one last swallow of coffee, and preparing to rise from the table.

"I thought," Letitia answered rather dryly, "I'd save that exciting and stimulating news for—when she's feeling better."

"Tell her—that though there's 'a time to break down,' " Quincy quoted and felt the better for starting the day with Scripture, "there's also 'a time to dance.' And now is that time. No doubt the news, had you shared it, would have gotten her up on her feet and out of these missish vapors in a hurry."

"She was hardly in a condition to consider dancing, Quincy. And there's plenty of time. We have three months, you know," Letitia said a little huffily. After all, didn't she know the genteel thing to do—when to act and how to act?

As was correct in society at the height of the season, Letitia would see to it that invitations went out, in paper form as was right and proper, three weeks before the occasion, and not sent by post but delivered by a servant. One-third more invitations would be sent than the rooms would hold; if they were crowded, so much the better. Though uncomfortable, the guests would be impressed and would refer to the evening as a *crush*.

She would need to arrange for a cloakroom for the ladies, a hat room for the gentlemen. Arrange, too, for one of the men servants to fasten a brush to one foot and put a soft slipper on the other and dance over the ballroom floor for several hours, dance until a reflection could be seen. Care with the lighting must be taken—wax candles could drip onto the dancers below. As for the music, four musicians would be best—a piano and violin, perhaps a viola . . . certainly a flageolet would be less blaring than a horn. Fortunately, the waltz was no longer frowned upon, Queen Victoria herself having given her stamp of approval.

And so ran Leititia's thoughts.

The village of Midbury, of course, did not boast an assembly room; the great hall at Middleton Grange would have to do. In spite of everything, "class" would be very much in evidence. To flout or disobey the unwritten laws of society would be a terrible breach of etiquette. Still—Letitia determined even now—no cord would be stretched across the ballroom as at some country balls, the upper end of the room being appropriated by the aristocracy, and lesser personages being relegated to the lower half. How embarrassing for Quincy, to be corded off from those he wanted to impress, and at his own gala, too. Unaccustomed perspiration beaded Letitia's upper lip, though winter was far from over and the house was plagued by drafts in spite of its coal fires in every room.

Moreover, Letitia wondered now, increasing her agitation, should the ball be preceded by a large sit-down supper, or would light refreshments be sufficient? Bother! This was more anxiety-laden than she had realized.

"Better get that needlewoman of yours onto the job right away—" Quincy, having made his wishes known, prepared to go off to his day in the mill's offices with a pleased expression on his rather heavy features; money could accomplish so much! But as yet, it had failed to get him what he wanted most of all—recognition by the aristocracy.

"I will, Quincy. Everything's under control," Letitia said with a confidence she didn't feel. "There's no need for you to fret about a thing." That was all she needed—Quincy puttering and fretting the entire three months.

⁍═══⁋

"What's the matter?" It was Sarah, opening the door to Allison's room, stepping in, coming to the bedside. "I saw Mama coming out of your room and I knew something was wrong. Are you sick, Allie?"

"Am I ever sick?" Allison enjoyed marvelous health. Marvelous health, high spirits, a vivid imagination, and boundless energy.

Sarah, not so endowed, was carried along on the tide of her sister's enthusiasms many times and admired her greatly. Younger, milder, more colorless in looks and in personality, Sarah had not a single jealous bone in her thin, childlike body. But neither did she have the slightest smidgen of passion in her entire makeup and, consequently, observed her sister's zeal for life with constant amazement mixed, at times, with trepidation.

Now she asked cautiously, "So why are you in bed? Why did Mummy come up here?"

Allison's toast arrived at that moment, carried by Becky, now so caught up in the little drama as to be almost visibly vibrating with excitement.

Allison looked at the tray with distaste. "Go back, Becky, and bring me a decent breakfast, eggs—" Allison loved coddled eggs, as Becky well knew.

"Oh, no, Miss," Becky gasped. "Missus told me this's all I was s'posed to bring. No matter what her begs for, her said—"

Allison muttered a word that would have turned her mother's eyes cold. Sarah put a hand to her mouth; even Becky, accustomed to such exclamations, pursed her lips and looked severely disapproving.

"Allison!" Sarah said. "And in front of Becky, too." Becky managed to look properly affronted.

Allison spluttered but restrained any further outbursts.

Her day, having started out so well, was disintegrating into something aggravating, not filled with the fuss and frenzy that should happily mark wedding preparations. But then, no one knew, not even Sarah. Consequently, everyone went their usual way, fixing fires, carrying trays, dressing, eating breakfast as if nothing momentous were happening.

"I'm sorry, Becky," Allison, repentant, said now. "Just leave the tray, please."

Becky, mouthing the surprising word the young mistress had muttered in her frustration, scurried off down below, there to dare once again—in spite of cook's stern glance—to embellish the account of life as it existed above, so different from her own as to seem magical.

"I suppose you realize they'll all hear about it downstairs," Sarah said.

"It'll liven up their lives," Allison said airily, flinging back the covers.

"When did this sickness rise?" Sarah asked. "You seemed all right earlier."

"I told you, I'm not sick!" Allison said. "It's just a smoke screen, for Mama's sake."

"What are you up to now?"

"Who said I was up to something? Can't a person take a day off without being accused—"

"Oh, come on, Sister. Why are you trying to fool Mama?"

Allison was dressing herself casually. Later, when everything was in order and the time was right, she would dress with care. Glancing through the window, she shivered. Frost sparkled on the ground, and, yes—it was beginning to snow. Was even the weather going to be against her!

No matter. The plan was made; Stephen, across town, would be working on his final arrangements; she would carry out hers. Now Allison's shiver was from something other than the cold; a delicious tremor of daring, expectation, dreams come true, ran up and down her spine.

Sarah noticed. "You're shivering. Maybe you aren't well, after all."

"For heaven's sake, Sarah, quit acting like an old maid! Now then, I've got things to do—"

"Can I help?" Sarah asked eagerly.

Allison stopped, pondered, and nodded. "Why not? Listen; what I need to have you do is slip up to the attic and try and find a traveling bag of some kind—"

"Traveling! Are you going somewhere, Allison?"

Allison sighed. Little sisters were such a pain!

"Can you keep a secret?" she asked abruptly.

Sarah looked injured. "You know how many secrets of yours I've kept. Why would you have to ask?"

"Because this is something . . . something . . ." Words failed. Allison sat back down on the edge of the bed, hugged her slim arms around her body, and said, eyes dancing and cheeks dimpling, "Sarah—I'm getting married!"

Sarah was silent. Then, hesitantly, she said, "Well, so am I—someday. I hope."

Allison threw herself back on the pillows with a massive explosion of breath. "Not *some* day, silly! *This* day. Or, actually, day after tomorrow."

Sarah's expression froze. "What . . . what do you mean? Oh, Allison, what have you gone and done now?"

Sarah's apprehensive cry rang throughout the room: "Allie! What have you done!"

"Oh, hush, you silly goose! Do you want the whole house to hear you?"

"But, Allie, you said—"

"That I'm getting married. Is that too much to comprehend? People do it all the time."

"But not . . . that is . . . Oh, Allie! How *can* you!"

"How? It's very simple, really. You just declare yourselves married before witnesses—"

"Allison! Be sensible!" But Sarah was a bit relieved; if Allison wasn't serious, if this was her way of teasing . . .

"If you know so much about it, why ask?" Allison responded, tossing her long dark hair not yet fastened up for the day.

"You know what I mean. That type of marriage was banned in England—oh, years and years ago. I need you to answer me sensibly. That is, if you're serious. You're not, are you, Allie?" Sarah verged on being distraught. Such an announcement—

and to be treated so lightly! Such a revelation—and then to tease about it!

"You've read too many novels," Sarah decided when Allison was slow in responding, instead smiling a secret smile. "The marriages you mention—they happen in fiction. They're not legal. You can't get married that way in England anymore."

"How about Scotland," Allison said, slanting a gray eye toward her sister.

Shocked silence. Then, "Gretna Green!" Sarah breathed. "Gretna Green! Allie! You wouldn't!"

There was a trill of delighted laughter from Allison. "Oh, wouldn't I?" she asked saucily.

Sarah was clearly horrified. This, her expression said, must be some sort of low joke. Allison had done some foolish things in her life, but this was, beyond all, the most madcap. Gretna Green indeed!

Nowadays it was the custom for couples to walk up the aisle of the churches in their respective parishes and exchange vows before the altar. Banns must be published beforehand, or in some cases and for a large fee, a special license could be obtained, making a hurried wedding possible; the practice of standing before witnesses and declaring themselves husband and wife had been prohibited by an act of Parliament in 1745. But as far as banns were concerned and obtaining parental approval—no such law existed in Scotland; Allison was clear on that.

England's runaway couples, eluding disapproving parents perhaps, or deeming it circumspect to be married immediately, were in the practice of fleeing across the border into Scotland to the first place a ceremony could be performed. And that was Gretna Green, a changing post for stagecoaches on the London to Edinburgh route. Here a pseudo priest, rumored to be the blacksmith of the village, called in a couple of witnesses who were ready and waiting and paid well for their services, read the Anglican marriage service, and it sufficed.

That her sister would entertain the thought of such a ceremony was shocking to Sarah. And perhaps frightening. She knew her father's wrath well and never dared rouse it herself, though she had been a terrified observer numerous times when Allison had breached the etiquette of the day or of the home.

"Oh, Allie," she said now. "Papa will be so angry."

"Let him," Allison answered airily. "I'll be a married woman, and he'll have no say over me whatsoever."

"And Mama," Sarah continued, twisting her handkerchief. "How can you deny her the satisfaction of putting on the grandest wedding ever known in Midbury? I'm sure she has it all planned in her mind. The white wedding gown—"

"Silver. I never have liked this switch to white."

"Queen Victoria—"

"If Queen Victoria jumped off the parapet of Balmoral Castle, would you do the same? You and the whole wide world may wear white if you wish, but as for me—"

"As for you, Allie, it won't be white *or* silver, if you run away."

Allison was nonplussed, but only for a moment. "Well and good," she said firmly. "Orange blossoms, veil of satin—they're just popular because Victoria had them at her wedding. Did you know, Sarah, that the cost of the lace on Victoria's dress when she married Albert was one thousand pounds?"

"So?"

"A thousand pounds for lace alone, Sarah! Tell that to Mama and see how quickly she changes her tune about a big wedding. Anyway," Allison said impatiently, "why are we talking about Victoria? I never have been that impressed with her—"

"Oh, Allison!" Sarah reproached her sister for this near-blasphemy and criticism of the august presence who so influenced an entire age that it would henceforth be known as the Victorian era.

"Pish and tush!" Allison said. Sarah's mouth pruned up, but at least the expletive had been milder than the one used earlier.

"There's so much to do!" Allison said, changing the subject, throwing out her arms dramatically and looking around. "Just think, Sister, I'll never sleep in this room again. I'll be a married woman—"

"Living at Flagle Manor. Oh, Allie—"

"Flagle Manor? Flagle Manor? Who said anything about Flagle Manor?"

"But," Sarah stuttered, "isn't that where you'll live? Norville doesn't have a place of his own. Oh, maybe rooms in London—"

Once again Allison fell back on the unmade bed, this time breaking into peals of merry laughter. "Norville Flagle! That witling? That dullard? He'd drive me to Bedlam in no time at all!"

Sarah's face was a study. "Not Norville?"

"Never Norville Flagle."

"But Papa's expecting . . . I know Papa's expecting you to make an alliance with the Flagle family."

"Make an alliance? What am I, a political figure on the historical scene or something? This is Midbury, Sarah, not the great courts of Europe."

"That's how Papa sees it—as an alliance."

"Where does love fit in?" Allison asked. "Don't you ever think about love, Sarah? Dream about the one you'll fall in love with?"

"I guess I've thought that Papa—"

"Sarah, Sarah, Sarah. We don't live back in olden days when marriages were arranged. It's almost the turn of the century! Surely females in this enlightened time may make their own choices. I've certainly made mine. And it's not Norville Flagle, I'll have you know."

Afraid to ask, still Sarah wanted to know. "Who then, Allie, who then? Who is this person you've chosen?" Sarah could think of no one in their circle other than Norville Flagle who would be acceptable, and who was available.

Allison sobered, sat up, breathed deeply, and confessed proudly, "Stephen Lusk. It's Stephen Lusk, Sarah. You remember Stephen Lusk, surely."

"Stephen Lusk," Sarah repeated slowly, thoughtfully. "Lusk . . . Lusk. The only Lusks I know live in the village. I remember a boy—"

"That's the one."

"A thin, blond boy. For years I'd see him driving around making deliveries. Allison! His father is a shopkeeper!"

"So? He's honest, isn't he? And thrifty? And well thought of?"

"But . . . but . . . a shopkeeper! You know what Papa will say! And Mama, too, most likely. They'll simply die!"

"They'll change their minds," Allison said, "once they get to know Stephen."

"Isn't he very young to be making such an important, er, alliance? He's your age, isn't he?"

"Older. A year older. Almost a year older. Plenty old enough to know his own mind. He's been away to school, you know. His father insisted on that, wanting his son to be something more than a shopkeeper. I hadn't seen him for a long time until I ran into him one day when I was shopping for ribbons. I just turned around, and there he was." Allison's pert face lit. "You should see him now, Sarah. He's so handsome!"

"And poor." Sarah was matter of fact.

"Papa has enough money for all of us," Allison said. "And Papa has no son, remember. He can put Stephen to work in the mill, perhaps as an overseer at first, then—"

"Allie," Sarah said positively, "Papa will never, never, never accept a Lusk."

"In which case we'll go to London and make our own way," Allison, daughter of affluence, accustomed to opulence, stranger to bare existence, stated firmly.

"Allie," Sarah said, annoying her sister with her persistence, "does Stephen have any money? This elopement that you're talking about—it's going to cost money. The blacksmith charges to perform the ceremony, you have to pay the witnesses, and how about the trip there and back? Will you go stagecoach? You'll have to, because Mr. Lusk has a dogcart and one old horse to pull it, and I'm sure he can't let Stephen take it, even if you wanted to. It's cold out there, Allie, and you'd freeze to death in the dogcart, that is if you didn't jiggle to death over the frozen roads. And it's painted bright yellow and green—"

"I have money," Allison said confidently. "You know Grand-mama keeps giving us money for birthdays and Christmas and all sorts of times, and we never have any need to spend it. Yes, I have plenty to do us until we get back and Papa and Mama set us up in housekeeping. I thought maybe the gatekeeper's cottage, fixed up, would make a darling first home."

Sarah moaned. "Allie, Allie. Please wait and think this over."

Though Allison had trouble admitting there might be any problems whatsoever connected to the scheme, Sarah, without any trouble at all, could imagine the entire escapade coming to disaster very easily. Not an imaginative person, still she could picture, quite vividly, her father's servants overtaking and intercepting the stagecoach, dragging her sister home ignominiously, and Allie—poor, disgraced Allie—doomed to a life of shame forevermore. Because the story would get out; the staff would see to that.

In spite of Allison's confidence, Sarah could not accept the plan with anything but dismay, even alarm. Too late, she wished with all her heart she were ignorant of the entire matter.

But feeling that someone had to talk sense to Allison, Sarah did her best. It wasn't appreciated. Her pleas for common sense, her warnings regarding their father's reaction, her suggestion to wait, to find another way to do this, fell on deaf ears. Allison, headstrong always, brushed aside her sister's arguments.

"You don't know what love is all about," she said, "or you wouldn't say things like that. Great lovers have always risked everything to be together." And Sarah, with no experience at all, had no defense.

"Now, Sarah," Allison said at last, "we've wasted enough time. And you did ask if you could help. When you get to the attic, see if you can find that alligator club bag Mama uses at times. If not, how about that canvas thing . . . you know the one I mean. It's old, but it would do, I think. It's shaped like a small trunk. Whatever you choose, it can't be heavy. I'll have to carry it myself, of course, until I meet up with Stephen. But it has to be large enough to take everything I'll need."

"Will you go out through the window?" Sarah, a dreamer of dreams in spite of it all, asked.

"No, silly. We're on the third floor, remember? And Mama sits down there in the room below when she's sewing or reading. Now scoot."

Sarah dutifully left the room to make her way like a shadow along the hall toward the stairs leading up to the attic area where she and Allison had sometimes played in bad weather during childhood. Frightened, and feeling quite desperately guilty, she scuttled past rooms, climbed stairs, flinching at every creak, peering cautiously around corners until anyone watching would have known immediately she was up to no good. Finally, she gained the attic and slipped inside to pause a moment while her heart slowed its thudding and her eyes grew accustomed to the shadowed interior.

Leaving the door ajar for light, she began feeling her way through mounds and mountains of the accumulation of years toward a distant corner where she seemed to remember trunks and bags and carryalls were stacked.

"I should have brought a lamp," she muttered to herself. With only a few bumps and scrapes, she reached the pile of baggage. The brassbound trunks she could identify easily by touch, and she turned her searching fingers toward other dark shapes, feeling around for something suitable for Allison's need. Dust rose in a dim cloud, and she sneezed—

"Who's there?" The voice came from the half-open door.

Sarah—poor, rabbity Sarah—froze into huddled immobility. *Oh, no!* she moaned silently. The worst possible thing had happened: She was discovered. *Be sure your sin will find you out,* she thought, knowing not whether it was Scripture, Shakespeare, her mother's warning, or her own imagination. She only knew it was terribly, horribly true.

"Who's there, I say! Speak up, whoever you are!" Without a doubt it was the housekeeper, Mrs. Buckle.

And then Sarah Middleton, second daughter of Quincy and Letitia and sister to Allison the beautiful and the bright, had the first flash of creativity, of originality, she had ever shown; it was born of desperation and burst all bonds of training, decorum, and tradition: She meowed.

Folded awkwardly into a dark and dusty corner, draped with cobwebs, her hands dirty and her hair mussed, Sarah parted her trembling lips and meowed.

One meow; she had the wit not to overdo the performance.

"Cat!" Mrs. Buckle spat the word. "Miserable cat!" Then followed a nerve-wracking two or three minutes while she called, first persuasively, then demandingly, for the interloper to reveal itself. "Here kittykittykitty . . ."

All might yet have been well if Sarah had not sneezed again; muffling didn't help. The sound brought instant silence. And then Sarah could hear the heavy footsteps of the determined housekeeper making her way through boxes and barrels and the collection of years until at last she held her lamp high over the fair head of the shaking Sarah.

"Sarah!" Mrs. Buckle said in a terrible voice. "What in the world are you doing here?"

Sarah's moment of inspiration wasn't over. Scrabbling into a box and coming up with the first item her hand touched, she held aloft a long-discarded stuffed toy—a cat of limp and forlorn appearance and once a favorite of hers.

"Ah," she managed to croak, "Miss Mouser—there you are. Do you remember Miss Mouser, Mrs. Buckle?"

The face Sarah raised to her was so guileless Mrs. Buckle no doubt had trouble believing it was guilty of duplicity. Her suspicious look softened. "Why in the world would you be up here rummaging around, and in the dark?" she questioned, wavering in her grim attitude. "And for a toy you gave up long ago. I can't see what earthly reason—"

"For old times' sake, Mrs. Buckle. I'm sure you understand— nostalgia and all that. Now come along, Miss Mouser." And Sarah, still caught up in the glow of inspiration, looked into the soulless shoe-button eyes and meowed again.

It was enough. Mrs. Buckle was convinced. With only a couple of "harrumphs," along with a few words grumbled under her breath, she seemed to feel her duty was complete. At least there was no cat in the attic!

Sarah rose shakily from her crouched position, her face ghastly with the fright she had endured and the dust she had encountered.

"Now, Mrs. Buckle," she said, with a dignity never displayed before, "if you will be so good as to light me to the door, please."

Perhaps it was the sound of authority in the girl's voice, a sound the housekeeper, in service since she was twelve years old, recognized and accepted, but Mrs. Buckle led the way to the door and watched the girlish form march down the hall and out of sight with no further comment.

Once around the corner, Sarah's thin legs threatened to crumple. Her breath came raggedly in synchrony with her pounding heart. She opened the door to Allison's room a veritable wraith—a dirty wraith.

Allison ceased her humming, dropped the armload of clothes she held, and stared at her sister—distraught, wild-eyed, and clutching an old, castoff toy, a cat of dubious vintage and of no importance whatsoever.

"Sarah!" Allison said, annoyed, "where's the bag I sent you for?"

Bursting into sobs, Sarah threw herself across Allison's rumpled bed, clutching the uncomplaining Miss Mouser to her, burying her face in the familiar comfort of the discarded toy as in days gone by.

Allison looked on aghast. Sitting down beside her sister, she put a hand on the dusty shoulder and patted it, making soothing sounds, and soon the tempest of tears abated.

"I'm sorry if the attic was frightening. Was that it?" Allison, an adventurer at heart and rarely faced down by anything or anybody, couldn't comprehend being terrorized by the familiar attic. Still, if that's what had Sarah in tears, she'd go up there herself and find a carryall suitable for her needs.

Once again Allison realized her day wasn't going as well as it might have; she hoped Stephen's was going better. After all, it was up to him to locate a carriage or check on departure times for the stagecoach and take care of numerous additional matters to assure the success of their venture. It was imperative to get out of Midbury, and quickly. Any lingering and someone would see and report them to her father. The trip, one way, would take the best part of two days—there would be food to buy, drivers to pay.

Allison shivered when she let herself imagine what it would be like to be intercepted before ever boarding their getaway conveyance; yes, Stephen's responsibility was a big one. Stephen was not an authoritarian; Allison couldn't help but feel a little anxiety about how he might be getting along on his own.

She, however, was confined to her room as surely as though she were behind bars at Newgate. And with little to do to put in the time. Any unusual activity on her part would alert her mother, and the entire plan might come to an end before it ever got off the ground. She had to trust Stephen.

Their time of meeting would coincide with the darkness that would serve to cover their getaway. In the meantime, Allison found herself wildly impatient, tense with the possibility of detection and the worry that something might go wrong.

Sorting through items to take with her, she had been constantly on the alert for her mother's approach. Cleverly, she had pulled a chair close to the door so that anyone entering would be delayed long enough to allow her to flee to the bed and, once again, feign illness. She didn't know whether to be proud of being such a humbug or ashamed of her deceitfulness. *Desperate situations call for desperate actions*, she consoled herself.

"I'm not afraid of the attic," Sarah said now defensively, uncurling herself, wiping her wet eyes on Miss Mouser and dirtying herself even more in the process. "I'm not so pigeon-hearted as that, for heaven's sake!"

"What happened, then?" Allison asked skeptically. Privately she considered Sarah too timid to say boo to a goose, but now was not the time to mention it. "And where is the carrying case? And why have you brought back this—"

About to say "useless old cat," Allison used rare discretion and changed it to "worn-out toy." Her questions caused a new spate of tears.

Never known for her patience, Allison was fast losing what little she possessed. "Either tell me what's wrong or hush up!" she said, adding pontifically, "Tears never help anything."

How thoroughly she was to learn—firsthand and before too long—the truth of the words so glibly and ignorantly uttered.

"Mrs. Buckle—" Sarah quavered.

"What about Mrs. Buckle? Don't tell me that busybody followed you. Or was the attic locked and she wouldn't open it for you?"

"It wasn't locked," Sarah gulped, getting control. "And I sneaked in. . . . It was dark. . . ."

"Never mind," Allison said, calming her sister lest another fountain of tears burst forth. "You're all right now, and you needn't go back. But what about Mrs. Buckle?"

"She caught me! Oh, Allie—she caught me!"

"Hmmmm, that could be bad. She'll probably run to Mama."

"I don't think so." Sitting up at last and recalling what had happened in the attic, Sarah stiffened her backbone. "That's how come I have Miss Mouser," she explained. "On the spur of the moment I pretended I was looking for her."

"How clever of you, Sister!"

"But, Allie—" Sarah should have felt better, having received a compliment of sorts from her older sister. As it was, her pale eyes suffused with tears once again, and her face was tragic in appearance. "I lied to her. All on account of you and your determination to run away and your need of a bag so you could do it—I lied! And what's more—I sneaked! I sneaked, and I lied!"

Once again Allison had occasion and reason to feel uncomfortable. What had seemed like a lark during its planning had dark aspects to it. And certain people were being hurt, Sarah among them. Allison sighed. Would nothing go right this day?

"Think about it this way," she placated. "All's fair in love and war. Everyone says it, so it must be true, right? And this is both— it's war against Papa and Mama and their unfair decisions, and it's love for Stephen.

"That makes what you did," she pressed on, noting the wavering in the desperation in Sarah's eyes, "perfectly all right. You can see that, can't you?"

Sarah wasn't to be that easily persuaded. "I don't know," she said feebly. "It seems to me that what you're doing is wrong, and I'm doing wrong, too."

Allison had had enough; it was time to move on. Rising briskly, she said, "Trust me, Sister. I know what I'm doing. And just in case you forgot—you begged me to tell you."

She was right; Sarah could only nod miserably.

"If it's too much for you to handle," Allison continued, "then go and leave me alone. But don't forget—you also promised not to tell. If you do," she warned, "that'll be another sin. Lying, sneaking, and breaking your word in one day—tut tut!"

Allison's face was severe as she laid this load on her sensitive little sister.

If possible, Sarah's slender face grew even whiter. She sat huddled on the bed, hugging Miss Mouser and swaying back and forth, uncertain of her next move, already guilty of two sins and trembling on the brink of a third.

"I won't tell," she muttered. "I said I wouldn't, and I won't. But, Allie—you're in for trouble; see if I'm not right!"

Having shown surprising spunk for the second time in one day, Sarah rose from the bed and flounced to the door, Miss Mouser dangling from one hand and trailing behind her and detracting considerably from the dignity she might have commanded otherwise.

Standing in the middle of the room, biting her lips and watching her sister go, Allison was left in turmoil, and oddly hesitant. Bother!

Now was no time for second thoughts; with a toss of her dark head and a shrug of her slim shoulders, she turned back to her preparations. Allison had always operated from impulse, not from reason, and this time was no different.

And after all, wasn't Stephen, without a doubt the handsomest lad she knew, waiting for her? And wouldn't the remainder of her life—after this flurry of recklessness—be the conventional one of wife and mother? Wouldn't she and Stephen settle somewhere in the English countryside as her mother before her had done, and her mother before her, and back and back across the centuries? Allison, in turn, would fit into the mold without fuss and flurry, for hadn't it always been so?

If there was any possibility that adventure, far horizons, new challenges—anything beyond a wild escape to Gretna Green—might lie ahead for Allison Middleton, there was no hint of it in the quiet bedroom, no reason to suspect it. And certainly not with Stephen Lusk.

Though Stephen Lusk had gotten away from Midbury to attend school, he was not a free spirit. Hesitant, cautious, he was seemingly without a daring bone in his comely body or thought in his delicately sculptured head. Allison had to admit it had been her strength of character that had brought them thus far. But what matter! He was so handsome!

As a son of the working class, subservient all his life and with a nature not given to the breaking of new trails, Stephen had agreed with some qualms to the idea of eloping.

"It's the only way for us, Stephen," Allison had pointed out, and he had hesitantly agreed.

Their love had seemed hopeless; Allison's father, if he had so much as suspected what was going on—the secret meetings, the stolen embraces, the desperate plans—would have turned the dogs on the young suitor, would have peremptorily closed the Lusk shop, would have ordered the Lusk family from the premises of business and home. The entire Lusk family would suffer, with no hope of recovering their small degree of comfort and prosperity. Stephen couldn't chance it, not even for love of Allison; on this he was adamant. Allison, though raging against the probabilities, knew he was right.

But marriage. Marriage, with its indissoluble bonds, would settle the problem once and for all. That's why it was imperative to reach Gretna Green before being caught, to have the ceremony performed posthaste. Starting out early in the evening,

Stephen and Allison would have an entire night's travel before their absence was detected and a chase was begun.

Yes, the marriage ceremony would solve everything. Divorces could be obtained, of course, but they were a costly and lengthy business accompanied by considerable disgrace. Quincy Middleton, slave of respectability, though he might gnash his teeth with fury, would be impotent to dissolve the bonds of marriage. What God had joined together, no man—including Quincy Middleton—could put asunder.

At times Stephen shivered, imagining the things that might go wrong and contemplating the fearsome and far-reaching power of Quincy Middleton, and then he would be bolstered and encouraged by Allison's magnificent confidence and her assurance that everything would turn out well in the long run.

"You know what Papa needs?" she had once asked thoughtfully. "He just needs to come up against someone who has a stronger will than his own, and then he'll fold up like an umbrella."

Poor silly child, to think she was the one.

Peeping from behind the drapery, Allison watched her mother leave for her calls. Knowing the schedule well, she was in bed and covered to her chin when—later in the day, back home again and with her wraps removed—Letitia came by to see how her daughter was faring. Sarah, who hadn't been back since she flounced out in the morning, slipped into the room behind her mother.

"A little better, I think," Allison said feebly in answer to her mother's query. "But weak. I can't get my strength back on tea and toast." And all the while her strong young body hummed with energy and an eagerness to be up and moving.

"I'll see that something more substantial is sent up," Letitia conceded, laying a hand on her daughter's brow, finding it cool and hiding a smile. Looking around, she asked, "Why is your room in such a turmoil? You've spent the day in bed, haven't you?"

"It was Fifi," Allison said quickly, blaming the room's disarray on the innocent little dog who had, for the most part, spent the day lying quietly on the bed, eating bon bons from the fingers of her mistress. "She's the only company I've had all this long day. She chewed things and dragged them around. She wanted me to play with her, I'm sure. Maybe tomorrow . . ."

"A good night's sleep is just what you need to set everything right, I shouldn't wonder," Letitia said, satisfied that Allison was malingering, playing a little game, and for a reason known only to herself. Perhaps the child had dreaded a scold concerning her treatment of Norville Flagle the preceding evening. Perhaps it was time she learned of the impending ball; it might be well for Allison to begin to think seriously of the advantages of an alliance with the Flagles and their cherished third cousin, Lord Shrewton.

And there was no time like the present to get things underway. So thinking, Letitia said now, "Allison, you will be pleased to hear that your father and I are planning a ball for your birthday—"

Allison's eyebrows lifted with surprise. Her lips curved with pleasure.

"A ball," her mother said, watching her daughter, "that will launch you into society—"

"Uh—Midbury society?" There was instant scorn in Allison's voice. For a moment it appeared that she would fling back the covers and expose her fully clothed, indignant self.

"—and be a springboard to marriage," her mother continued calmly. "A proper marriage. With your father's money and my connections, you should do very well for yourself. We have high hopes for that, you know, Allison."

Letitia clearly hinted at matters of great import, and though Allison managed to control herself, subsiding and clutching the covers to her, rebellion filled her heart. Was there anywhere in the entire world a woman . . . girl . . . was free to make her own choices? It was narrow-mindedness such as this that was forcing her into the scandalous alternative of a Gretna Green marriage!

"Think about it, my dear, during these hours when you have nothing else to do." Noting a disturbing tightness in Allison's face, Letitia emphasized, "It *is* coming; it *will* happen, in case you have any silly, girlish thoughts otherwise."

Well pleased with the outcome of her visit, Letitia stooped and laid a cool kiss on her daughter's forehead. "I'll see you in the morning," she said and swept from the room. Sarah, quiet throughout the entire performance, remained.

About to rise from the bed, Allison was stopped by the accusing look in her younger sister's eyes. Arms akimbo, mouth tight, Sarah looked the picture of disapproval.

"What's the matter?" Allison asked crossly.

Sarah shook her head.

"Speak up, Sister! Has the cat—Miss Mouser—got your tongue?"

"I was just listening to you, Allie. Listening to you and your lies—"

"Are you back to that dreary subject again? I thought we covered that before. It's all in the game . . . the game of life."

"We talked about my lies; this is about yours. You lied about why you're in bed—sick, you said, when you're strong and healthy and planning to run off. You lied about Fifi, poor little innocent creature that she is."

Allison bit her lip. What a time for Sarah to act like an adult!

"I had to," she defended, shoving back the covers and getting to her feet; fully dressed, she shook out her garments. Bending down, she pulled a canvas bag from under the bed; she had managed, with no trouble at all, to sneak it from the attic. It was bulging, and Allison viewed it with a frown; adjustments in its contents had to be made, that was obvious.

"How can a marriage based on lies turn out well?" Sarah pursued, not about to give up the subject.

"How many marriages start out with lies, do you suppose? Love, honor, and *obey?* I'm certain!" Allison scoffed. But even Allison was uncomfortable with the thought of bald-faced lying. "Sometimes, Sarah, it's necessary to shade the truth."

42

Sarah's accusing eyes, her shaking head, spoke for her.

Tired of the subject and of being accused, Allison said, "You always did pay too much attention to the Scriptures our governess assigned to us. I daresay she'd be so pleased. You need to keep in mind that the verses were meant for memory work; they weren't oracles to live by."

"I don't think so, or why do they keep popping into my mind? And in yours, I'll be bound, if you'd admit it. How about, 'Thy word have I hid in mine heart, that I might not sin against thee'? Remember that one, Allie?"

"You're a spoilsport, Sarah, that's what you are," Allison said crossly. "I'm sorry I told you about my plans. I thought you'd be excited; I thought you'd be happy for me. Now look what you've gone and done—spoiled everything!"

The light had faded as they talked, and shrill and insistent, a whistle was heard, wafting up from the garden below.

"Stephen! It's Stephen! Help me get this bag shut!"

But for the second time that day, Sarah had slipped through the door and was gone.

A llison opened the window and leaned out. Below, a slender, pale face was turned up to her. At the sight, her anxious fears were as nothing; gaining Stephen was worth any effort.

Afraid to speak aloud for fear of being overheard and knowing a whisper would not reach him, Allison gestured her welcome and her excitement as well as she could—clapping her hands together, bobbing her head, wriggling a little, smiling. Stephen, if he felt any of the rapture she was demonstrating, managed only a nervous gesture: *Come on down,* it said, and he made repeated motions with his hands.

With a final wave, Allison shut the window and turned to the hodgepodge that was her room. There was no time to do anything more in regard to the trip, and her bag was stuffed. But there was time to remove her slippers and don heavier footwear. And now she blessed Queen Victoria for her Balmoral petticoat and boots; at this moment they made good sense, promising warmth and comfort. But something in Allison rebelled at the heavy, cumbersome, *ugly* items, and at the last moment, standing in her boots and swathed in her petticoat, she stuffed her fine Morocco slippers into the bulging canvas bag. If she had her way, she'd stand before the anvil with feminine feet!

About to leave the room, she turned back with a gasp, having forgotten the velvet pouch containing Grandmama's contributions and donations and gifts, given on special occasions over the years. The thought of forgetting the money to fund the entire undertaking and finding herself and Stephen stranded somewhere, helpless, sent a shiver through Allison. Hastily she tucked the money away in her bag and turned again to the door.

Once again her hand dropped; once again she paused. A note! Should she leave a note for her parents? *By the time you read this, I'll be Mrs. Stephen Lusk* . . .

But of course she wouldn't be, not when they read it. They would find the note in the morning, and she and Stephen would be well on their way but not yet arrived, not yet married.

The longer it took her parents to discover her absence in the morning, the better. No doubt, first of all, a maid would spend a few minutes looking for her, going from her room to Sarah's, checking the bathroom, eventually making her way to her mistress to report Allison's mystifying absence. Allison could imagine how things would go from there as the household went from calm normality to disbelief, to dismay, to tumult. Letitia, from dallying over her breakfast tea, would make a casual passage upstairs. Here her air of petty annoyance, her sighs at having her daily schedule interrupted, would change to agitation as she searched for her daughter, as she noted the absence of certain articles of clothing and the disarray of the room. She would hasten to Allison's father, who would turn turkey red over his paper, spluttering in his coffee. Finally, Letitia would take to her bed with a headache.

Though there was no one to see, Allison grinned impishly. No, she'd not leave a note. In any case, it wouldn't take her parents long to dredge the truth out of Sarah. Then and only then a search would be initiated.

A pebble rattling against the window woke Allison from her reverie. Still she hesitated. How odd, how wrong it seemed, to leave one's home without a send-off, without a wave, without a kiss. At the last she longed for Sarah's thin arms around her, Sarah's sweet kiss of approval on her cheek. It was not to be. Allison had made her decision and would pay whatever price was necessary.

Still, it was rather wistfully that she whispered, "Good-bye, Fifi. Ta ta."

Fifi made a snuffling noise, opened one eye, and went back to sleep in the swirl of bedding where she spent her days as well as her nights. Fifi, forever on the lookout for her own comfort, would happily move her headquarters to Sarah's room if a bon bon was forthcoming from time to time.

With bulky boots on her feet, a warm cloak over one arm, and a heavy bag dragging at the end of the other one, Allison moved down the hallway toward the back stairs. Once, hearing a noise nearby and startled into immobility, she made a quick decision to put on the cloak. Setting the bag down, she swung the garment into place, fastening it securely, pulling up the hood and tucking her hair inside. It was the nearest she could come to a disguise. If she were noticed and recognized, her garb and her stealthiness would raise immediate questions, of course, as well as her use of the stairs ordinarily reserved for the servants. But she dare not use the front staircase and could think of no other means of descent, aside from the window, which was, as she had pointed out to Sarah, beyond reach, beyond reason.

Once away, no one would know exactly where to look for her or which direction to go to find her. They would check her friends first, she thought, to see if she were with any of them. The name Stephen Lusk—until Sarah broke—would never enter their minds.

The stairs were manipulated with secrecy and safety; no servant had need of them, no one came to investigate the strange bumps and scrapes coming from the narrow stairwell, caused by Allison's bag.

Once through the door and outside, Allison breathed more easily. Eagerly now, though carefully, she maneuvered herself through bushes, around corners, under windows lit and unlit, until—a hand went over her mouth.

Her scream stifled before it was born, for one brief second Allison thought all was lost and that she was discovered. Then Stephen's voice whispered in her ear. "Shh now. No talking. Just follow me."

Turning, Allison allowed time for one quick embrace. Leaning against the slim form, she gathered what strength she could from it, and what courage. Through the dark, Stephen's face was a white oval, and his eyes—so large and moist in the daylight, reminding one of an innocent fawn—seemed filled with something akin to panic on this night. The sight took the adventuresome Allison aback.

Quickly she reminded herself of all that was at stake for Stephen. Far more, probably, than for her if they were caught. She could bear the recriminations; his entire future would be in jeopardy. Quincy Middleton could be counted on for no mercy. So she excused Stephen his natural reaction and his croaked words, "Hurry! The stagecoach is due any moment. We've got to make it!"

Stagecoach. Allison was disappointed. She had hoped for a conveyance of their own, preferably a post chaise. Far more comfortable than the public stagecoach or mail coach, the post chaise was a favored means of travel. But it was expensive to hire. Although holding only two people—which pleased Allison's romantic nature, thinking of two days shut intimately inside with Stephen—it used two or four horses, which must be changed regularly on an extended drive. For so small a conveyance, it required a post boy as well as a coachman and, riding at the back on the dickey, or platform, a groom. Yes, a post chaise was expensive. It was Allison's first experience with straitened circumstances.

Aside from the Lusk cart, not at all suitable, Stephen had made the decision to arrange seats on the stagecoach. Not a vehicle of the rich, like the post chaise, or of the poor, like a wagon or cart, the stagecoach was the transportation of choice for the ordinary person. Not the most comfortable, not the fastest, it was the only way to visit most places. As for trains, Stephen knew nothing of train schedules or routes into Scotland, nor did he have the courage to inquire. And probably not the money.

With Stephen leading the way and Allison stumbling behind, her bag bumping her leg painfully, their feet crunching through the newly fallen snow, they made their way toward the village and the inn. Here a dozen people had gathered, bags and boxes were strewn around, and even as the couple approached, fresh horses were being herded into place.

Someone was flinging baggage to the roof of the coach, shoving it into the boot. Already a satisfied man was firmly ensconced above in the box seat by the coachman, a favored place, perhaps the best of all. Except for the four inside seats.

Four people, four only, would mount the step and ride inside. Crowded, cold, their state was much to be preferred than that of the poor wretches whose purses allowed only an outside seat; their suffering, long before they reached their destinations, would be dreadful.

Now men and women alike, regardless of blowing skirts and flying shawls, were being handed up top, scrabbling for toeholds, settling themselves as best they could, pulling something, anything, around them against the wind and the snow.

Dumbly, Allison turned her eyes on Stephen.

"Inside, *cherie*," he said with pride.

Stephen had studied French at school, as well as Latin, and knew Shakespeare and the great masters of art and literature. Allison was sure he would be an asset to Middleton enterprises. But did he know commerce, trade? Could he handle investments, use funds to advantage? Well enough, it seemed, to arrange a seat inside the coach, and poor, shivering Allison thought it money well spent.

"Oh, Stephen!" she said with relief. "Thank you!"

Their baggage was hoisted above, and at the hostler's urging, Stephen gallantly handed Allison into the rig. Bending, crushing her skirts to her side, she was thrust in, and turning, she fell with a plop into the seat. Fell onto a lap.

From the shriek that erupted, it was a female lap; Allison was grateful for that.

"These seats are taken," a gravelly male voice said.

"Oh! I'm sorry . . . I beg your pardon . . . I couldn't see—"

"That's a' reet," the female voice said faintly. "Just turn around, if you will, and be seated—again. That way you'll get off my toes."

"Gracious!" Allison said, still bent awkwardly, fumbling to turn her massive skirts in the small space. "I'm terribly sorry!"

The couple already seated had the favored location—facing forward. Somehow Allison hadn't realized that they might ride the entire two days *backwards*. And crowded. Stephen's head and shoulders were inside, and he was looking helplessly, in the dim light, at the few inches of seat remaining to him.

Allison gathered up her skirts and her full cloak, pulling them around her, knowing she'd need them for warmth and grimly grateful for the Balmoral petticoat and shoes. A cold wind frisked through the open door.

"Come on in, Stephen," she urged.

"Sit doon, if ye'll be sae kind," the gravelly voice said, more gently than before, "and close the door."

Stephen squeezed his long, thin form into the spot allotted to him, and the door was shut. Both he and Allison turned immediately to the small windows, watching anxiously, willing the vehicle to move, to get underway, to begin the escape from Midbury and Quincy Middleton.

With a shout and a jerk they were off. The sudden movement caused another shift in the seating arrangements, and like coal shaken into a scuttle, the four travelers settled into place, side by side, toe to toe.

Stephen had no covering; Allison could see he was trembling pitifully, from cold and perhaps nervousness; she could feel his shoulder shaking against hers, and she flipped the end of her cloak to cover him a little. The couple across from them were bundled together under a carriage robe.

"We canna see ye verra weel," the man said eventually, "but I'm Crispus McCloud, and this is m'wife, Clara. We've been in Lunnon, and we're headed for Edinburgh, and home."

"I'm Ste—"

A sharp nudge of Allison's elbow brought Stephen's introduction to a halt.

After a moment's silence, Allison said, "Go ahead, tell them our names, *John*."

"Ah, yes," Stephen managed. "We're the . . . the Buckles."

Allison, already tense, barely kept from giggling hysterically— the Buckles!

The housekeeper and butler. Staid, upright, narrow-minded— the Buckles. If there was anyone in the world less inclined to flout the conventions of life, to run from duty and from security, Allison didn't know who it might be. The Buckles!

"And where might ye be headin'?" Mr. McCloud asked, as the carriage jounced over rutted and frozen roads.

"Scotland. Yes, Scotland," Stephen answered, adding quickly before the question could be asked, "but not as far as Edinburgh. Yes, that's it—Scotland, but not as far as Edinburgh."

If the unseen Scotsman's "I see" was a little dry, Allison and Stephen never noticed. Allison slipped her cold hand into Stephen's cold hand and, eventually, let her head fall onto his shoulder, and she slept.

They were all roused, of course, when a changing station was reached.

"This's yer chance to 'op out and warm up," someone shouted and opened the door. The McClouds and "Buckles" took the opportunity to climb out, stretch cramped limbs, visit the necessary room provided for travelers, drink a cup of tea, and board again. Except for one or two men, the travelers up top never moved. Perhaps they couldn't. Burrowed under their tentlike creations, they couldn't take a chance of snow sifting in, of losing the small bit of heat they had generated.

At dawn they stopped again, with more time allowed for the passengers to disembark, walk to and fro, and obtain something to eat. Allison was amazed to find out there had been a small child, just an infant, up top. Bundled and motionless until now, it set up a feeble wail, and the young mother rocked it patiently before the big fireplace in the inn, the Goose and Quill.

"Stephen," Allison whispered, moved to sympathy, "that baby has been up top all along. Maybe we should give our places to that woman—"

Stephen was quick to reject the idea. He was a young man . . . youth . . . who knew his place. And though it wasn't in a post chaise, neither was it on top of a public stagecoach. He was even more aware of Allison's place; if her father learned that she had ridden on top of a stagecoach for a day and more in bitterly cold weather, Stephen would suffer for it, and severely. Never having met the man, knowing him only by reputation, still Stephen showed the deference of his training and his station.

"No, no!" he protested. "She wouldn't thank us for interfering. We'd upset the entire balance of culture."

Sometimes, Allison thought, *maybe Stephen shows too much education, or the wrong education.* Surely thoughtfulness and kindness were more important than maintaining one's position. Maybe it was because she was so tired, perhaps she saw Stephen in a light never suspected before, but at the moment he didn't seem so handsome, so Greek-godlike. At the moment he seemed young, gauche. Funny that she had never noticed how his eyes— as well as being entrancingly doelike—protruded too much; his mouth—those gloriously curved and generously shaped lips— seemed weak.

"Allison," he pursued urgently, "if your father ever found out I let you ride on the top of a public coach—"

He *was* sweet. And thoughtful.

"At least," she said, "go over and order that girl some tea and a little breakfast."

The McClouds proved to be a short, stout couple, now that they were unwound from their blankets and shawls. Their faces were kindly enough, but Mr. McCloud's eyes were shrewd. Allison caught him studying her closely, and when she lifted her chin and gave him a straight look, he nodded politely and turned away.

The day passed slowly, with occasional stops to change horses, rest a little, and eat a bit. Allison found herself more and more watching the road behind them and was not surprised to notice Stephen doing the same. Fortunately, because of riding backwards, they could watch the oncoming traffic without turning their heads. Still, Mr. McCloud grinned a time or two when some rig overtook them and whirled past them and Allison and Stephen drew back into the shadows of the coach.

"He knows," Allison whispered to Stephen, satisfied once again with the blazing blue of his eyes, the tender curve of his mouth, the gentle pressure of his slim hand, and the graceful bend of his slender body.

They swayed and bounced, groaned and muttered, waking and sleeping through another night. It was at dawn the problem arose: A wheel came loose.

The gyrations of the coach alerted them to trouble. Quickly the coachman hauled the rig to a halt. Allison could hear loud voices, felt the lurching of the coach as men climbed down, heard the discussion, the peevishness in the voices.

"All right—everybody out! Everybody out!" Someone with authority issued the command.

Standing in the dim morning light, shivering in the wind, people clustered together at the side of the road, ankle deep in snow. A wheel, loose and leaning away from the coach at a crazy angle, was clearly the problem. A low moan arose from the weary passengers, to be swept away in a swirl of snow.

Mr. McCloud had stepped over to the group of men who had gathered around the wheel, kicking it, shaking it, testing it. He talked earnestly with the driver, motioning toward the huddled passengers, seeming to come to some conclusion.

"The next inn," he said, back with the group once more, "is aboot twa miles doon the road. There's naething tae do but walk."

So saying, he took his wife's hand, placed it on his arm, and turned his dogged steps forward. One by one the others followed.

Allison knew she fared better than most. Warmly clad, young and strong, she actually found a certain exhilaration in being on her feet and moving again. But Stephen—poor Stephen. His thin suit was inadequate protection against the weather, which had steadily worsened the farther north they went. *Where is his Macintosh,* Allison wondered, until it occurred to her that perhaps he had none.

She was in fairly good condition when they reached the warm hearth of the Harp and Trencher, but Stephen was blue and shaking, his hands, claws, his feet, in their light shoes, stiff and lacking feeling.

Hot tea for everyone, a turn by the fireside, warm food, and there was a general reviving of spirits, even some dogged preparations to climb aboard once again and resume the trip, a fresh coach having been provided. There was no choice.

The delay, though taken in stride by others, was agony for Allison and Stephen. Her father's well-sprung coach, his well-fed horses, his determined men could overtake them easily now. Time was ticking away; every minute counted now.

Consequently, it was with almost hysterical relief they finally disembarked at Gretna Green. The young couple—so pressured, so tense, so fearful—had no time to study the hamlet that would have interested them at any other time. They could only look around for some sign of the pursuit they feared. Then, reassured, they made a dash for the smithy.

"God bless ye!" shouted Mr. McCloud. Watching them go, he turned to his wife and said triumphantly, "What did I tell ye?"

The beefy blacksmith, far better dressed than for his apprenticed trade and obviously awaiting business in his acquired profession, stepped forward and greeted them.

"And is it gettin' marrit you're wantin'?"

"Yes. Oh, yes!" The coveted moment, so dearly longed for, so dearly paid for, was within their grasp.

"Good, verra good. Now step this wa'."

And there was the anvil, the anvil over which many a lover had pledged his troth, the anvil of romance, the renowned anvil of Gretna Green. A bedraggled but starry-eyed Allison—in her relief completely forgetting the Morocco slippers in her bag—looked up at a haggard Stephen and whispered, "We made it, Stephen; we made it!"

"Step forward; step forward," someone invited.

"Wait." Allison had the wit to remember her footwear. To everyone's amazement, perhaps amusement, she fumbled into her bag and withdrew her dainty Morocco slippers and, blushing slightly as she removed the Balmoral boots, put them on. Put them on feet cold and stiff, and turned, flushed and sparkling, to her wedding.

"And now," asked the waiting officiant—and the spittle turned dry in her mouth, and Stephen's face turned a mottled green, and the world tilted at a crazy angle—"if ye'll jist show me the papers, provin'—as required by an Act of Parliament—ye have lived the necessary twenty-one days in Scotlan' . . ."

Canada, 1898

Parker Jones chunked another piece of wood into the big range that dominated the "living room" area of his simple home in the Canadian bush. Outside, winter was obviously far from over, though it was April. Chickadees, not finding much to eat in a landscape long picked clean, were eagerly chipping away at the generous slab of suet Molly, on her last visit, had fastened to a tree just outside the window. As Parker well knew, Molly, even more so than the birds, was impatient for better weather. Then and only then would the men of the church begin to enlarge his present abode, transforming it into a parsonage fit for a wife to preside over.

How good it will be to have a proper home again, Parker thought as he looked around at the rough, though snug, cabin. Various church ladies had done what they could, but it remained, at best, cheerless. His glance rather sourly settled on the ubiquitous pot of beans on the back of the range, and he thought dismally of another skimpy supper scraped together and eaten alone. After all, one could only drop in, unannounced and hungry, on one's parishioners so many times—gracious though they were and willing to add another plate to the table—without becoming a nuisance.

But winter was no time for building, though the logs for the enlarged house were even now stacked in the yard, cut to size, and weathering, a constant reminder that better days were ahead for him.

Though Molly would have done so gladly, there was no way he could ask her to settle into a cabin and from there carry on the ministrations of a bush pastor's wife. She had been a small girl when her parents had come to Bliss from Scotland. Her family had been accustomed to a life of deprivations while they were bringing their land to production, and Molly had declared herself ready to live in a dugout, or house of sod, and happily, if it meant sharing it with Parker Jones. But dugouts, Parker thought with a shudder, were places of last resort; soddies, however, were plentiful, dotting the prairies by the hundreds, perhaps the thousands, and many a wellborn lady lived in one, having followed her man to his claim of free land. But here, in the northern bush country, soddies were replaced by cabins built from trees on the settler's own land—an abundance of trees, a veritable shroud of bush, a tangle that intimidated some folks and turned them back from the massive task of clearing enough land, in enough time, to satisfy the Lands Office.

Trees for building, trees for burning; Parker Jones opened the draft, and the fire flared to life, roaring up the slim stovepipe and throwing out a blast of heat into the room.

He automatically stirred the beans, replaced the lid, and turned, with the enamel coffeepot in his hand, to the slop pail beside the door. Into it went the remaining dribbles of his morning and noon coffee and, after a vigorous shake, the meager grounds. With more care than usual, he measured new grounds, dipped water into the pot from a nearby pail, and set the coffeepot on the hottest lid of the stove to boil.

Next, he turned to the open-shelf cupboards, clearly of the handmade variety, and contemplated his crockery, a mismatched conglomeration of castoffs gleaned from the homes of his congregation. He congratulated himself on having washed his dishes earlier in the day and felt something akin to a housewife's satisfaction in what seemed to be, to his uncritical eyes, a neatly ordered cupboard. No board member should go home shaking his head over the pastor's disgraceful housekeeping practices, to have his wife look at him with accusing eyes and remind him that the "poor man" needed a wife and was only waiting for the board to do something about it.

Parker figured he would need five cups but could not, for the life of him, match them up with the proper saucers. At last they were set in a neat row on the round oak table that graced the center of the room and was covered with an oilcloth of Molly's choosing and ordered from the catalog.

Unfortunately, he thought with some regret, there was not so much as a cookie crumb left from the baking Molly had delivered the day before. The men of his board, cold when they arrived, would welcome a cup of hot coffee and would understand his lack of baked goods. Perhaps, sympathizing with his pathetic limitations, they would be spurred on in their avowed plan to enlarge the cabin so that he and Molly could marry.

Parker Jones, not long a pastor, felt himself blessed to have ended up in the Saskatchewan Territory among the good people of Bliss. No better people existed, he was sure, certainly none who would have made him feel more needed, more welcome. They felt keenly their lack of sufficient monetary support and regretted it—Parker existed on the offering that was placed in the basket each week, usually egg and cream money, and some weeks it was pitifully small. But in the fall, when the crops were harvested, the faithful would bring in the tithe. And if the crops were good, so was the tithe. Cash might be sparse, but there would be bushels of garden stuff, shelves of canned goods, sacks of flour. The enlarged parsonage would need a roomy cellar—he must remember to mention that today; picking up a pencil, he jotted it down.

Feeling at last that things were in order, Parker seated himself in a rocking chair at the stove's side and picked up his book. A man of medium height, with a shock of dark hair, a sensitive face often grave but capable of breaking into an infectious smile, Parker Jones was clearly a man of good breeding and obvious gentility. He exuded masculinity in the same way a spring crocus exudes sturdiness.

His hands, not accustomed to the plow or harrow, were fitted to the pages of a book.

Regardless of all else—no matter the season, through meals of beans, bannock, rabbit stew, and pancakes, enslaved by the endless feeding of wood into the stove, sidetracked by board meetings, engaged in courting—sermon preparation had first priority. It was as though—when he pledged himself to the ministry—he had taken a vow as solemn as the wedding vow and much like it: for better, for worse, for richer, for poorer, in sickness and in health . . .

Therefore, the amenities completed and all things prepared for the monthly board meeting, Parker Jones returned to his studies. With the cabin cradled in a blanket of snow and silence, the only sounds now were the popping of the fire and the occasional creak of the hand-me-down rocking chair.

Here, in the backwoods (also termed the bush), in this place rather incongruously called Bliss, an outpost was burgeoning to fruition and vigor, a colony marvelously free of the bondage of the old world. Here, men and women enjoyed opportunity and freedom such as they had never known, gladly paying the price and embracing the struggle. Here, though it seemed a most unlikely reality, dreams came true.

Most of the civilized world thought of Canada as a wilderness. An idyllic wilderness, perhaps, with a charm that beckoned the adventurer, but a wilderness nevertheless. And they were not far wrong; wilderness it was, for the most part. Such a huge land and so few adventurers.

But that was changing; they were coming. What had begun as a trickle was to become a torrent as men and women—downtrodden, poor, hopeless—turned their shabby shoes and beaten wills westward.

On the frontier, one of the most important figures was the preacher. His presence supplied one of the only antidotes for the loneliness of the isolated lives of the hardworking pioneer. His bodily presence—being there with them—was a tremendous encouragement; his messages, much needed: God loved them; God was with them; they could never get beyond His care. The preacher performed their marriage ceremonies, buried their dead, baptized their believers.

At times revival meetings were announced, and emotion ran high, stirring dry-as-dust spirits and warming the hungry hearts of those needing the strength, the encouragement, the peace offered. Attendance was good; the warning against sin and unrighteousness was powerful, the invitation to turn from such ways was fervent. The Church of England, more formal, popular in larger cities, was not widely popular on the frontier. The rugged, the real, the tried—that was what satisfied.

Education and religion went hand in hand; schools invariably sprang up where churches went. It was a Methodist minister who set into operation a province-wide system of government-controlled primary education. The new Canadians were serious about education; even those whose broken English kept them tongue-tied managed to make themselves understood: There should be schools for the children.

Schools and churches often shared the same building. This was true of the hamlet and community called Bliss.

Bliss was named to honor the first settler in the area, George Bliss; by and large, the people of Bliss were satisfied with it. "What's in a name?" Herkimer Pinkard had been known to quote philosophically whenever the subject came up, adding, "That which we call a rose, by any other name would smell as sweet."

With no dissenting voice across those first years and no better suggestion, in time "Bliss" became the name of the schoolhouse. And when the church was established, the name seemed particularly suitable, the worshipers maintained.

George Bliss himself had drawn together the first circle of believers. They met in his home, eventually outgrowing that and welcoming the opportunity to conduct services in the schoolhouse. Having become a real congregation, a real church, they contacted a Bible school in the East for a pastor.

Parker Jones was that man.

And to think, he sometimes marveled, that it was here, back of beyond and far, far from the madding crowd, he had met the one girl in the world for him. Walking into the Morrison home, the first place he was to board—the initial arrangement the church had made for a pastor—he had walked directly into Molly herself. And heaven's gate, and—bliss.

Molly Morrison was a treasure. Vibrant, full of life and love she was, slender as a willow withe, with black hair that tumbled in lively disarray around a face both angelic and magical. Best of all, Molly loved the Lord and loved Him best of all. This arrangement—with him, Parker, being second best—was satisfactory with Parker Jones.

The coffee was burbling, filling the air with fragrance, when the first rig pulled into the yard. Before Parker had welcomed his prospective father-in-law, Angus Morrison, a man of tremendous standing in the community and a worthy father of the matchless Molly, Herkimer Pinkard arrived. Herkimer of the wild orange beard and a gift of coming up with quotations, jokes, bits of choice wisdom or humor from the inspirational to the downright ridiculous. A bachelor, if he wanted a wife, Herkimer had not been able to find one among the few, very few females available on the frontier. "He scares them off or they die laughing" was the opinion of Bliss's sympathetic populace. Everyone loved him; no one wanted to marry him. Herkimer managed very well by himself and never complained of his single state.

Stomping the snow from his boots on the porch, coming into the house through the door Parker held open for him, Angus greeted his pastor warmly and handed him a box, his blue Scottish eyes twinkling in his rugged face.

"From the womenfolk of my hoosehold," he explained unnecessarily, and suddenly Parker's supper took on possibilities: The fragrance of roast beef wafted enticingly into the room.

"Lift oot the pan and set it in the oven, laddie," Angus directed. "Those're the instructions given me. When you're ready to eat, supper'll be ready and waiting."

The others, when they came in, were equally generous. Parker realized, with gratitude warm in his soul, that he should have expected it, might have known, could have counted on it. But then, he reasoned, if he had taken it for granted, he wouldn't have been so wonderfully surprised, so blessed, so appreciative.

Bly Condon brought butter and eggs; Brother Dinwoody (so called not because of his position or dignity or spirituality but because his name, Adonijah, fractured the speech of anyone trying to pronounce it) proudly set a chocolate cake on the table. And even Herkimer, bachelor though he was and no cook according to all who had occasion to eat his food, brought a jar of fresh, sweet cream—Parker Jones could almost see it swirling in thick, golden richness over a piece of the Dinwoody chocolate cake at suppertime. All these items had been carefully wrapped and arrived unfrozen and savory.

"Lay aside your wraps, gentlemen," Parker invited, and coats were hung on the nails by the door, overshoes set in a row beneath. Protocol for this procedure was the same in every Bliss home. There was, usually, one entrance: It was a kitchen door and was used for everything and by everyone.

All four turned as one man to the stove, huddling around it and holding out cold hands and rubbing them, until Parker ushered them to chairs around the table.

Cautiously holding the metal handle of the coffeepot with what he had been informed by Victoria Dinwoody—the child who made it—was a hot pad, Parker poured the steaming brew into each cup. Silence reigned as this rite was performed, the men watching, then reaching, then wrapping work-hardened, icy hands around the comfort of the cup. Setting the pot back on the stove, adding water, and recklessly throwing in a few more grounds—sometimes Parker got tired of endless scrimping—he paused, hesitating before sitting down to the table and his own cup.

His eyes went to the Morrison box, as yet divested only of the pot roast, and then sought Angus's face with an unspoken question.

Angus nodded. "You'll find oatcakes in the box, laddie."

Gladly Parker dug into the boxed treasures and passed around the plate that bore the treat.

"No doot aboot it," Angus said, with more than a touch of the accent that had been largely muted for years, "we've got to get the mannie a wife."

The others grinned and nodded and ate and drank and eventually sat sipping as the meeting was called to order.

The minutes of the previous meeting were read.

"Seems, Angus," Bly Condon said, "you made the same remark about the mannie needing a wife a month ago."

"He needed her then, and he needs her now," Angus said, unabashed.

The minutes were approved.

The treasurer's report was given, briefer and skimpier than ever; with some shuffling of feet and a few chagrined sighs, it was accepted.

"A short horse is soon curried," Herkimer said thoughtfully. And that about summed it up.

Old business was called for, and the enlarging of the parsonage was discussed.

"We'll need to time things exactly," Brother Dinwoody said, having given the plan considerable thought. "We know we need to start on it as soon as the first chinook blows and the logs are uncovered, in order to get it up and finished before the land dries enough to put in the plow. We all know what that means . . ."

There was silence as the men contemplated the end of the still and quiet season and the burgeoning of the time of sixteen-hour days of hard and unrelenting labor. The long days and short nights would make it possible to reap a crop in the one hundred frost-free days Mother Nature might allot them—if she were in a benign mood. If she were to be capricious, as she so often was, it would be survival only, the tightening of belts and "making do" for another year.

"We can mend harnesses now," Bly Condon said, "and grease machinery and such things, if we haven't already done so." Winter was filled with harness mending, furniture making, whittling, the chopping of wood, busywork to keep a man from going mad, and his wife, housebound with him, the same.

Out came the rough plans, and the men passed them around and could find no improvement to be made in them. Since the logs were already cut, there was no possibility of changing the concept originally decided upon; they simply needed to fix the plan more firmly in their minds and renew their interest and determination. And of course, they assured Parker Jones, a fine, generous cellar would be included.

About to adjourn until the following month, Herkimer remembered that he had mail to distribute, having been to the post office that morning. Parker Jones took the one item addressed to him and looked at it, interest sharpening his eyes. Mail was always a high point and in the winter months was all too often delayed for one reason or another.

"Please excuse me, gentlemen, while I open this."

"Of course . . . go right ahead; don't mind us."

Bly, Angus, Herkimer, and Brother Dinwoody prepared to push themselves back from the table, to put on their heavy garments once again, to pull on their overshoes and leave for home. Already dark was descending. It would be chore time when they reached their own homesteads.

Their general comments were interrupted by a strange sound from the seated Parker. Turning as one man to their pastor, they were startled by the shock in the dark eyes raised to them.

"What is it, Parker? Something wrong?" Angus asked.

Parker Jones gripped the letter, obviously deeply affected by something in its pages. "Perhaps," he said, "you should sit down again."

Surprised, the men turned back to their seats and looked expectantly toward their spiritual leader and friend.

"Give me a moment," Parker said in a faltering voice. "I have an idea this—" he indicated the letter, "might change everything."

7

Without a word, Parker's board members seated themselves once again at the table, their eyes fixed on the face of their pastor. Not knowing the problem, yet sensing one, their kindly faces were anxious.

"What is it, Parker?" It was Brother Dinwoody who asked this time, but there was a question in all eyes.

A question and a dread. None of them had been immune from the miseries and agonies—often swift and deadly—that marked the life of the pioneer.

Even those who arrived with money and possessions—pianos, silver tea services, fine china, canaries in cages—were not exempt from brokenness. Even they knew the defeat of overwhelming despair, being driven out by drought, bankruptcy, hopelessness.

Most of them, however, came with nothing, except perhaps a change of clothing wrapped up in a bedroll and hoarding in their pocket the required ten-dollar filing fee that would put them on their own land. Holding on by their broken fingernails, surviving grimly, if at all, working themselves to death—that was how it was.

They lived by the hard work of their hands, endured by the strength of their wills. They gritted their teeth against all odds—hunger, cold, disaster—and endured.

Death, capricious and merciless, was a stalker that followed each lonesome trekker across the prairie or into the heart of the bush; cemeteries were staked out before school lands.

Their experiences were the same; they knew what their neighbor was going through. And they were bonded as perhaps no generation had been before them or would be again.

Parker saw the instant concern in the work-worn faces of the men gathered at his table and felt a surge of warmth for each of them: Blystone Condon, who with Beatrice, his wife, had known better times, better ways, before giving it all up and coming west to live in a cabin and start over; Brother Dinwoody, a fussy little man, learning to overlook the inconsequential, concentrating on the overall need for survival; Herkimer Pinkard, that rare individual with the courage to be himself, keeping his corner of the world refreshed, and always greeted, wherever he went, with smiles. Herkimer took his good times along with him.

These three, and Angus—and Parker knew he could call on a dozen more, if need be, who would lay aside personal needs and problems in a heartbeat to come to his side—turned their attention on this one needing them, regardless of chores awaiting and a cold trip home through the gathering dusk.

Parker clutched the pages of his letter, crushing them in the intensity of the emotions that gripped him. "It's my father—"

"Yes, laddie?" Angus, already sure of the answer, asked it anyway.

"The letter," Parker said, "is from my mother. She's written to tell me that my father . . . my father . . . has died."

"Ah, laddie . . . Ah, Parker . . . I'm so sorry."

Four pairs of hardened, callused hands stretched across the expanse of the oilcloth to touch Parker's hand, his arm, his shoulder, as gently as a mother. Or a father. Three voices murmured sympathy, comfort, consolation. Parker had the distinct feeling of being a tender sapling in the woods, tossed by winds, held straight and true by the sturdy trunks around it. Reaching for the sun. The Son.

"Let's pray," Angus said, and as one man they rose and came around the table. Three grizzly, rough, home-cut heads of hair bowed over their pastor's bent head as they looked to the One who promised, "I will never leave thee, nor forsake thee." Each could personally testify to the truth of it; each could witness to the strength of the sustaining Presence.

"Thank you, my friends," Parker managed through tears.

Still there was no rushing off. Seated again, they waited for Parker's explanation, Parker's decision. For had he not said this might change everything?

"My mother writes," Parker said eventually, returning to the pages in his hands, running his eyes down them, "that it was sudden. His heart, apparently. It seems so odd . . ." Parker's voice trailed off, and his eyes raised to stare off into space—a long, long way.

"Odd?" someone prompted. Sad, they might have expected, or painful, or grievous, but odd?

"So odd, that while I've been going about my work, talking, laughing, eating, doing all the normal things, my father has been in heaven. In heaven, and I didn't know it." Parker's gaze lowered, and he looked at the men around him. "He was dead and buried, and I was living a happy, fulfilled life."

Parker seemed to ponder for a moment or two; the men gave him time.

"So why should I," he said, struggling with a new thought, "having heard about it now, go into a spasm of grief? I believe the Lord is showing me something here." Parker was silent again.

"It'll be something I'll study on and pray about," he said finally. "Perhaps it's similar to what we read in Second Samuel 12:23 about King David, who prayed and fasted for the life of his child but went back to normal living when the child died. 'Wherefore should I fast?' he asked those who questioned him about what they saw as a casual attitude. 'Can I bring him back again? I shall go to him, but he shall not return to me.'"

"A blessed way to look at it," Angus said thoughtfully. "I'm sure you're reet."

Again Parker Jones's eyes gazed off as at some unseen horizon, some distant shore. It was almost with a start he came to himself, looked around almost blankly for a moment, and then said, "There's not much more to say except that my mother needs me now. Not only for comfort and strength but to advise her in the matter of my father's business. He was in the building trade and had a partner. There will be certain affairs to work out—whether the partner buys the business, what my mother is paid, and so on. Though this is a fine man, someone needs to be there to protect my mother's interests, perhaps just to shield her from the headache of it all."

"You have no brothers, I recall?" someone said.

"No brothers. One sister, and she's an invalid. Rather, she was injured in a fall as a child and has never been strong since. Not strong enough to marry, at any rate, or have a family of her own. She and my mother will have each other. But they need me at this time."

"Of course . . . we see your point . . . that's understandable." The voices chimed in with approval, with patience, with concern.

"My mother asks me to come," Parker pursued, as though needing to persuade his listeners. Perhaps he needed to settle his own turmoil of spirit. After all, he had a job, a calling. And there was Molly—

Molly. There had been a time, not long ago, when he had been unsure of his future, had struggled with his "call." Faced with the opportunity to leave Bliss for a teaching assignment in a Bible college in the East and broaching the subject to Molly, Parker discovered that she believed her future, for the time being, was here among the people of Bliss. Thankfully there had been an eventual positive solution to his uncertainties; God had clearly convinced him of his call to the ministry of the gospel of Christ and to a pastorate in the bush country of Saskatchewan.

What would Molly's reaction be to another delay, to more uncertainty concerning their longed-for life together?

Parker looked at Angus and indicated the letter. "I'll need to talk to Molly, Angus, break the news to her myself, if you don't mind."

"Of course, laddie. I'll say nothing. But won't you come along wi' me? Just put on your coat and ride over wi' me to the hoose. Then, after a good supper, ye can talk wi' Molly."

Angus's suggestion was a good one. After all, Parker had no rig of his own, and with no barn as yet, it was impossible, in winter, to keep a horse. The roast in the oven would keep.

"I need the evening to myself, I believe. To think about it, pray about it, come to some peace about it, before I talk to her. But I can't see any way I can get out of going to be with my mother." Parker Jones was caught in a loving web—Molly, or Mother?

"And we'll all pray with you," was the last assurance of the men who now donned their outer garments and proceeded out to their rigs, heading home and leaving Parker Jones standing in the doorway, more alone than ever, it seemed to their sympathetic eyes.

Adonijah Dinwoody and Bly Condon, married men, separately and perhaps wisely came to the decision to say nothing to their wives tonight. Separated by miles of snow and ice from their nearest neighbors, still they had no confidence in keeping anything secret in the bush. How news got around was often a wonder and a marvel—yet get around it did. "A little bird told me," might indeed be the mysterious method of transportation, and were there not the ubiquitous chickadees at this season when most feathered creatures had wisely flown away? Perhaps the partridge's drumming, like the Indians' drum, signaled more than was known; perhaps the owl's hoot, disembodied in the night, passed the news from house to house. At any rate, the men wisely decided to delay passing on the bit of news that would have caused a ripple of excitement in each shuttered home and given food for thought and speculation: What would Parker do? What would Molly do?

Tomorrow would be time enough to stir the pot of excitement and interest. Even in the face of a wife's hungry quest for news, Brother Dinwoody and Bly Condon determined to withhold the pastor's news. Molly should be the first to know, and she should hear it from Parker Jones himself.

Shutting the door, returning to the fireside, and picking up his mother's letter to read it again, Parker realized there was no reason for immediate action. He would write his mother and assure her he was coming. Then when the chinook came and the roads opened, it would be time to leave for Ontario and the town where he had been born and raised. His mother, he noted with a faint smile—for she knew his circumstances—would send the money needed for his transportation.

Parker breathed easier for the moment as the pressure for immediate action regarding his time of departure was lightened. His pressure regarding talking to Molly? Heavy indeed. If her longing was anything like his, and he believed it was, it would be a bitter blow to hear she would need to wait—again.

Rising, he laid aside the letter and went about supper preparations, blessing the dear ladies of the Morrison household for the simple meal ready in his oven. Taking the hot pads in hand, Parker turned toward the roasting pan and was struck—suddenly and for no reason that he could see—by the realization that his concern had been all for his mother, Molly, himself. But there was the church and his responsibility to it.

God had called him to Bliss. Until God indicated a change of plans, Bliss would remain his field of ministry. If the board agreed, he'd ask for a leave of absence, coming back to the pulpit and parish of Bliss. But there was no one available to take his place during his absence, which, he could foresee, might be a period of six months or so.

There was only one thing to do: The board would need to write the eastern school for an interim pastor.

A ye," the burly blacksmith confirmed, no doubt prompted by the blank faces of the young couple before him. "Ye knew not the law, I can see that. Many dinna. They coom dancin' in here, thinkin' we're going to say a few words ower them, an' they'll live happily ever after. And then they find oot about the required residency."

The man sighed massively, his wide shoulders heaving. He shook his head, looking at Allison and Stephen with sad, baggy eyes. Condemning eyes, blaming eyes. *Here I am,* they said without words, *ready, willin', and able, and ye've got me here for naethin'.* Perhaps he hoped for some remuneration in spite of the failed wedding plans.

"Yes . . . yes; I understand," Allison managed to stammer, digging for a few coins and pressing them into his hand. "We dinna . . . didn't know. Is there no place one can apply for a special license—"

"Na, na," the man said, kindly enough, putting away the coins, folding up the printed ceremony, and beginning to turn away. The two witnesses, with long-suffering faces—they'd apparently been through this before—disappeared as quickly as they had appeared, and as mysteriously.

Left alone at the side of the anvil, Allison and Stephen gaped wordlessly at one another.

Finally, dazed and stumbling, they turned and made their way from the dim interior of the smithy to the yard. Here people from the stagecoach were milling around; there was shouting back and forth as the horses were exchanged, as various pieces of baggage were shifted, as people prepared to climb aboard and move farther into Scotland. And life went on normally, for some people.

The sun had come out, the wind was gone, and the snow was melting; the yard was a churned-up sea of snow and mud. Allison and Stephen, standing ankle deep in the wet mass and watching the activity with unseeing eyes, gave no thought to their feet.

"What will we do?" It was Stephen who asked, who looked to Allison for some answer to their predicament. And it was a serious one.

Allison, usually so decisive, had been stunned into silence, into immobility. Her mind, usually so quick, so resourceful, seemed as muddy as the ground.

"I don't know. I don't know," she whispered through stiff lips, lips that, as they loosened, began to quiver, her teeth to chatter.

"Well, *think*," the thin figure at her side urged.

His voice seemed to break the spell. Allison looked up at Stephen, noting with sudden contempt how he was standing there like a scarecrow, limp and lifeless. Her sympathy for the white-faced, stricken-eyed, helpless youth faded. "What do *you* think we should do?" she blazed, driven by the despair and dismay she was feeling.

Stephen gaped, startled at the question, at the responsibility thrust upon him.

"How should I know?" he managed, gulping.

"Do *something!*" she demanded, stamping her thinly clad foot into the wet snow and being rewarded by an icy surge into her shoe, which she neither cared about nor felt.

But Stephen, rather than shouldering the dilemma and finding a solution, looked as though his main desire in life at the moment was to flee the premises never having heard the name Gretna Green, never having seen the historic anvil or, perhaps, the girl at his side.

"Well," he said slowly, helplessly, "I don't—"

"Oh, hush!" a distraught and disillusioned Allison ordered, near to tears and shaking with anger, disappointment, and uncertainty. In her eyes, Stephen's classic beauty was disappearing as his face settled into lugubrious lines.

"Now see here," he offered feebly.

And then, defensively, he said the words that once and for all ruined himself in the eyes of his chosen love: "This was all your idea, you know."

It was a definitive moment. Allison's eyes grew wide. For a moment she was shocked into silence. The portent of his words, his meaning, finally reached her.

Those who knew her best would have been dumbfounded at the maturity of her reaction, the control in her voice. Expecting a quick and contemptuous lashing out, they would have applauded the brief and taut response.

When she could trust herself to speak, she said, "I've given it some thought and come to a good conclusion, I believe, since you don't have one. I think it would be well if you boarded the stagecoach, Stephen, and proceeded to Edinburgh. Perhaps Mr. McCloud will take you under his wing; he may have some clerical work you can do in the export business he told us about." It was a subject that had helped fill the long hours of the journey.

Before Stephen's mouth could open and he could utter another word, good or bad, Allison added, "I'll talk to him," and she hurried to the side of the Scotsman who, with his wife, had been watching, highly curious, the small drama being played out before them.

"Mr. McCloud," Allison said rapidly, reaching his side, "is it possible that Stephen—his name is Stephen Lusk—could go on with you?"

"Go on?" the man asked, taken aback.

Allison was at her best. She dared not fail; Stephen's future, perhaps his life, hinged on her. Having led him, willy-nilly, into this disaster—as he had so humiliatingly pointed out—it was up to her to get him out.

"Yes," she said, her face flushing prettily and her eyes damp with emotion, an emotion not lost on Mr. McCloud. "You see, I'm going back. But it would be a dreadful decision for him to do so. I'm sure you understand.

"It would be such a . . . a boon if you could take him on to Edinburgh with you, put him to work. Could you, Mr. McCloud?" Allison's gray eyes pleaded. Mr. McCloud had to feel he was her champion, the solution to her problems.

"He's educated, Mr. McCloud," Allison added persuasively. "I know he could be an asset to your business." If she had laid aside, once and for all, her dream that Stephen's education would make a way for him in her father's business, it was not apparent as she outlined Stephen's abilities now.

Before Mr. McCloud could utter the refusal that could be read in his face, Allison opened her bag and withdrew the purse—her grandmama's contributions—and held it out.

"Would this help?" she murmured, hefting the coins in her hand, bringing a gleam to the Scotsman's eyes. "This would pay his way and keep him until he could become a help and an asset. *Please,* Mr. McCloud!"

In spite of himself, Crispus McCloud's hand was reaching for the coins Allison was jangling before him. "Weel . . ." he said, and Allison caught the change of tone, the assent, perhaps grudging assent, in his voice.

"Oh, thank you! You won't be sorry. I'll see to that."

And Mr. McCloud, sharp businessman, who knew and recognized a kindred spirit, believed her.

"A' reet, then, lassie," he said, pocketing the money. "But what'll ye do?"

"Don't worry about me," Allison—without a farthing to her name—reassured him with more confidence than she felt. "I'll be all right. I'll go home, of course."

For the single, unemployed, untrained girl of the day, there was no choice. Allison knew it and bowed to the inevitable. Mr. McCloud knew it and agreed.

"Weel, guid luck to ye then, lassie," he called after Allison as she sped through the muck back to Stephen.

"Mr. McCloud has work for you, Stephen," she said brightly. "Think of that! He's waiting for you over there now, ready to get back into the coach. You just have time to join them; they're about to take off."

"I'll not," he said stubbornly. "I'll not go to Edinburgh. I'll not work for that man. Why," he asked crossly, "didn't you give *me* that money, Allison? I could have gone on myself; the money would have kept me very nicely—"

Allison heard him with disbelief. How little she had known him, after all. She shook her head sadly as, for a moment, she had the distinct feeling that her young love, her first love, crumpled and fell soundlessly into the broken earth at her feet.

Still, she spoke with common sense. "He's a good man, Stephen, with a good business. And just think of it—you'll be working at a profession—"

"I'll not," Stephen repeated, unmoved from his refusal. "Nothing will change my mind—"

"You might like to know, Stephen," Allison interrupted quietly but tensely, "that those are my father's horses about to turn in at the gate. That's my father's carriage, that's my father's coachman driving, and that's Buckle—the real Buckle—sitting there beside him. I don't know who's inside—"

Like a bolt of lightning or as though shot from a cannon, with no word of farewell, Stephen Lusk's cold feet took him across the churned-up yard, thrusting past anyone in his path, to the open door of the stagecoach. He barely touched the step as he dove into the dark interior and disappeared.

S itting down on a bench in the smithy yard, Allison, calm and collected to all appearances but with heightened color and quickened heartbeat, reached into her bag for the Balmoral boots. Seemingly intent on changing her wet shoes, her attention was given—from the corner of an eye—to the two coaches, one leaving the yard, the other entering.

Hurryhurryhurry! she was pleading soundlessly to the public conveyance bearing Stephen away, and *Hide, Stephen, hide!*

Finding Stephen gone and determining he had fled by means of the stagecoach, would her father insist on pursuing him? It seemed likely to Allison, for Quincy would be filled with rage, intent on pouring it out upon the helpless and hapless male creature who had the effrontery to bring disgrace upon the name and house of Middleton. Frightened though she was, she determined to forestall any such action on her father's part by causing a delay by any means possible. Every minute would count as the public coach made its way northward, and so Allison dawdled, careless, unconcerned, or so it seemed.

Poor, weak Stephen—Allison couldn't find it in her heart to be angry with him and, admitting she was largely responsible for the present fiasco, even felt a little pity for him. But in some ways Stephen was better off than she was, Allison thought with a shiver as the heavy, ornate coach bucketed into the yard and the coachman pulled the horses to a walk and then a halt. Stephen was well away and safely out of the reach of retribution; Stephen, if he stayed with Mr. McCloud, would be set up with work, perhaps a career much better for him than becoming a shopkeeper like his father.

While she—

Better by far not to think what her fate might be. Perhaps bread and water for a season; perhaps—heavens!—a beating. Certainly disgrace.

But to cringe, to grovel, even to snivel, was not in Allison's makeup. Though her insides felt like pudding, her chin, her quaking chin, was up. Her expression, she hoped, was serene, perhaps even a little haughty. To the servants, certainly haughty. To her father, when he stepped from the carriage—

It was not Quincy who stepped from the carriage.

Allison was calmly removing her soaked slippers and putting on the despised boots when the coach pulled up alongside (if her father disapproved of the public display of her feet, one more infraction couldn't make much difference to the punishment awaiting her). Jenks, family coachman, hauled on the reins, and the hostler from the inn came hurrying. Although Allison refused to look up, giving her attention to her present occupation, she knew Buckle, sitting beside Jenks, was looking down at her.

Slowly she finished tying the laces, casually she raised her eyes. "Why, hello, Buckle," she said pleasantly. "Hello, Jenks."

Jenks, gruff Jenks—always gentle with Allison and Sarah, saddling their ponies, teaching them to ride—was expressionless, his attention focused on the horses' ears. Buckle had a grim look on his rather priggish face. He had been long-suffering with her across the years, perhaps at times even entertained by her exploits. His reaction now caused Allison's heart to squeeze—it was, obviously, a reflection of her family's disapproval. What she had done went beyond the unacceptable to the intolerable.

"Good day to you, Miss," Buckle said politely, his eyes moving on, searching the yard and the few people there, obviously looking for Stephen.

Finally, unable to delay the moment any longer, Allison lowered her gaze, with dread eyeing the door of the coach. It opened, and she held her breath. But the foot that was thrust out, reaching for the step, was a female foot, conservatively shod, a large, no-nonsense sort of appendage to a sturdy limb—Mrs. Buckle's foot, Mrs. Buckle's limb.

Mrs. Buckle. It was the worst possible scenario. Allison, prepared to face her father, get the harsh words over, the recriminations, the wrath, and then hearing and facing whatever punishment her father had in mind for her, would have to suffer the pangs of uncertainty all the way home. What's more, she would have to refrain from any discussion of what she had just been through, for one simply didn't talk about these things with the help. Other than polite conversation, it would be a silent trip. Yet with Mrs. Buckle's unspoken disapproval between them, the hours would be fraught with tension.

"Well, Miss," Mrs. Buckle said after she had picked her way over the ground to Allison's side, "this is a fine state of affairs, if I may say so."

Rather than contempt, such as servants were apt to show when "quality" or well-bred people slipped from their pedestals, there was sorrow, perhaps it was pity, in the housekeeper's eyes. It shook Allison more than a sneer might have done. Truly she had failed to count the cost of her impetuous escapade.

Like a small child, she whispered, "My father?"

"Is at home. Waiting. Get your things together, Miss Allison. As soon as the horses are changed, we'll head back."

Like a small child, Allison packed away the soggy shoes, stood, fastened her cloak more securely, and stepped meekly toward the coach. Mrs. Buckle picked up the bag—which she probably recognized as having come from the attic at Middleton Grange—

and followed. Jenks swung down, opened the boot, and stored the bag, still avoiding meeting Allison's eyes, turned, and mounted his seat again.

Trying to find comfort of a sort on the hard, tufted seat, with Mrs. Buckle seated across from her, stern and silent, Allison was startled when the door was flung open and the sharp face and gimlet eyes of Buckle appeared.

"Tell me, Miss—was there a ceremony?"

The cry that trembled on her lips was, "What business is it of yours!" But knowing Buckle was doing her father's business, she said quietly, "No."

"We supposed not," Buckle said, "knowing the residency rule. But in case there was—sometimes they do that, you know, to get the fee even though the ceremony isn't legal—I'd have gone in there—" Buckle looked toward the blacksmith's shop with tight, grim lips, and Allison knew he would have acted and acted firmly, perhaps harshly, on behalf of her father. Oh, the trouble her rashness had caused; even the poor blacksmith trembled on the brink of severe retribution, for Buckle would have no hesitation in setting the law on him if he had broken it.

"No," she said again, protecting the innocent blacksmith and raging again at her own ignorance in the matter of the three-week delay in Gretna Green marriages. She had indeed, as Sarah indicated, read too many novels. "Once upon a time" a Gretna Green marriage had been quick, sure, and binding. It was quick no longer; the authorities had seen to that.

The trip home would be no shorter, but it would be more comfortable. Allison was no longer crowded; it seemed a sort of dream that she had ever huddled in a corner of the stagecoach, hand in hand with Stephen Lusk.

She gave one final thought to Stephen Lusk. It was part relief that she had escaped being bound to him forever; it was part regret that the entire scheme was not worth it. She should have been dragged home despairing over the separation from her true love, and with a broken heart. As it was, she would be punished, and punished severely, for a thoughtless, foolhardy act. Allison grew up a little at that moment.

Mrs. Buckle had warm covers to tuck around Miss Allison; she had a basket of food—if it was to be bread and water only, it was not to begin yet—and Allison ate hungrily.

Mrs. Buckle produced a damp cloth, and Allison washed her hands and dabbed at her face.

Eventually her eyes grew heavy; her head nodded, bouncing in rhythm to the coach's movement. Mrs. Buckle slipped to the seat at her side, and Allison, as in days gone by, put her head in the comfortable lap, and slept.

If the innkeepers along the route recognized the quiet, unkempt Allison as the same proud, mettlesome girl who had come through a day or two ago, going the opposite direction, they gave no sign. They served the exhausted young woman and saw her on her way, well aware of the outcome of yet another Gretna Green wild-goose chase.

Nevertheless, when the coach rolled up the driveway of Middleton Grange, Allison put on a proud front. Sitting up, she straightened her clothes, made a useless attempt to bring order to the chaos of her hair (Mrs. Buckle had failed to produce a comb and seemed disinclined to fuss over her charge). Too late, Allison wished that she had asked Jenks to get into the boot and search out her slippers. She needed to walk like a lady, delicately, into the great entrance hall, nodding to whatever maid might be present at the moment, handing over her cloak, and *tap-tapping* her way, her skirts a-swish, her head up, into the drawing room where, at a glowing fire, her mother and father would be awaiting her. With an apologetic smile, she would pave the way for a merry account of her latest romp.

As it was, she clumped her heavy-footed way into the house but not into the great hall. And not into the warm drawing room. And not into the presence of her parents. And the jolly report of her high jinks never got past the wishful thinking stage.

Jenks pulled the vehicle around back; Buckle descended, cramped of limb and short on patience, and opened the door for

Allison's descent, followed by the housekeeper. Mrs. Buckle, now leading the way, entered the rear door, walked up the back stairs, and—without seeing a soul—opened the door to Allison's own room and ushered her into it. A cold room. Laying aside her wraps, Mrs. Buckle went about lighting a fire.

Slowly Allison undid the fasteners of her cloak and slid it off. Almost blankly she looked around. The mess she left had been cleaned up; the room seemed barren, strange, almost unfriendly. And there was no Fifi.

"Fifi—" she questioned, desperately looking for a welcome, needing to hold someone or something soft, loving, caring. It was not to be.

"In Miss Sarah's room," Mrs. Buckle explained briefly.

When the fire was blazing, the housekeeper—not too tidy herself, weary of face, stooped of form—hesitated for a moment, as though she would speak. Then, apparently thinking better of it, she picked up her heavy cloak, laid it over her arm, and turned toward the door.

Allison had the impulse to call after her, "Wait! Don't go!" But of course she did not. Protocol prevailed, and she stood silent and alone as Mrs. Buckle slipped through the door and shut it behind her.

Shut it, and turned the key in the lock.

10

When the last rig had departed, the last farewell salute given, Parker Jones opened the door to his small home, stepped inside, and shut the door behind him.

April, and no sign of spring. But it could come at any time now. Tomorrow could be the day of the chinook. There would be the soft wind, the change in the snow—a faint honeycombing of the vast whiteness, a dimpling as the snow grew wet and sank and settled. There would be the first beginnings of the runoff, the building of the countless sloughs in every hollow.

Next the sounds of honking overhead would bring the winter-weary settler to the door, to the window, to watch the first geese fly overhead, the graceful wedges pointing north. Of a morning, ducks would be found paddling in the sloughs, bobbing on the lakes, skimming the sparkling water with wide, scalloping wings.

There would be the splendid changing of air from the north to that of the south. Soon the blessed songbirds would follow, ushering in the season filled with sound, where all had been silence for so long. From sky and meadow, fence post and tree, it would lift, tone challenging tone, melody competing with melody—the music of the North.

There would be a little betting concerning just when the ice would go out on the Saskatchewan River, a river that, early on, had been recognized as the highway of the fur trade, a river vital to the expansion of the Territories. Known as a fickle waterway with its swamps, sandbars, rocks and rapids, and tawny waters—north and south branches splicing Saskatchewan—it was passionately appreciated by the people of the bush, as by the prairie dwellers. Last year it had "gone out" on May 6, and the sound had boomed across the community of Bliss, five miles away.

Once again Parker had to remind himself that there was no immediate need to hasten to his mother's side, a good thing, because as yet, the world seemed gripped in a frigid, iron grasp. It was as though winter's hand, frozen and stiff, would not, could not, loosen.

At the first sign of a thaw, the first drop of melt from the eaves, Parker would leave the bush.

He would not wait for the log raising. The timbers that had weathered all winter were water soaked, heavy to lift, making for a slow job. The board's plan to get them raised would be more delayed than they liked to think. Parker could not afford to wait that long. And anyway, his living arrangements would be torn up for some time; it might be a good time to be gone.

The supper that had so enticed him now seemed tasteless; his mind was elsewhere, wrestling with thoughts of winter's bondage, his mother's need, Molly's reaction . . .

Pushing the supper dishes aside, pouring himself a cup of tea, Parker drew a tablet toward him:

Dearest Mother,
How my heart aches to be with you. Having just received
your letter, I realize you and Samantha have been through a

*very hard time, and I haven't been there to be a comfort. It is
one price of being in the ministry and going far from home
that I hadn't been prepared for.*

    *It is my intention to come to you very shortly. I'm sure
Molly will understand. . . .*

Would she? Would Molly understand? Did anyone ever
understand the delay of dreams coming true?

Parker threw down the pen, put his face in his hands, and
groaned. A double grief was heavy to bear: not only the loss of
his father but the loss—in a way—of a wife. Who knew when
the marriage would take place now?

Molly had been patient during his personal battle against
uncertainties concerning his "call"; she was patient during the
delay until winter should be over and the parsonage put in liv-
able condition.

Parker thought now of a conversation they had had.

"I'll live there as it is," she had maintained stoutly. "After all,
my parents and many like them built structures not so different
when they first came west. In fact, I'm told I lived in one—"

"And that's one reason I can't move you back into one, Molly
love. After years of work and sacrifice, you've finally gotten into
a decent home. It wouldn't be fair—"

Molly, admittedly often short of patience, had made an impatient gesture. "Oh, Parker, those things don't count, not if we can
be together."

"I can't give you much, Molly," he had said, and he was infi-
nitely more patient, "but I won't move you into a shack. And
that's about what it is—crude, chinked, unpainted, small. Somehow, to me, it would put a shadow—maybe even a strain—on
our happiness right from the beginning. It would be like being
in a box together. In winter we wouldn't even have the yard to
stretch out into." And Molly knew he spoke the truth.

"A log house isn't going to be any palace, heaven knows," he
had concluded, "but it will be much better than a shack.

"Think what it would be like," he had continued, "to set up tubs and do a laundry in that small space. Think what it would be like to string lines of clothes around in there."

It wasn't just her own happiness Molly was thinking about. It troubled her, many a long winter evening, to think of Parker, alone and lonely, not a sound to break the heavy silence aside from his own hum or the crackle of the fire. More than one housebound settler, usually a woman, had gone stark, raving mad because of the isolation and the barrenness of days, trapped inside a small square of sod or of logs with nothing to do, no one to talk to for days, weeks, months at a time.

But Molly—though her dearest dream and fondest hope was to be the wife of Parker Jones—knew when she was defeated, and she gave in with good grace.

And now it appeared that she would be told the spring wedding was not to take place. Parker Jones envisioned staying at least six months with his mother and sister, getting things in order, settling them physically, financially, mentally for the absence of the men in their lives—their husband and father, their son and brother.

And the Bliss church? Would it hold the position open for him? Would it agree to a substitute? And could one be obtained that easily—some student, perhaps, who was willing to take the time out of his preparation for the ministry to get in a little hands-on experience?

No wonder the lonely silence was broken by the heavy sounds of Parker's groaning.

———

Picking up his pen, Parker finished his letter, assuring his mother of his presence very soon and that he would keep her informed of his plans.

He turned to the mundane tasks at hand, clearing away the remains of his supper. Having learned from experience and knowing full well that uncared-for dirty dishes would be there to mock him in the morning, he filled a dishpan with hot water from the stove's reservoir, rubbed a little Fels Naptha onto a dishrag, and proceeded with his household tasks, proficiently if not happily.

In the custom of the bush, he went to bed early; it saved coal oil. But before banking the fire for the night, before blowing out the lamp, he turned to his Bible. He found himself comforted by David's assurance of the Lord's deliverance: "Their soul is melted because of trouble. They reel to and fro, and stagger like a drunken man, and are at their wits' end. Then they cry unto the LORD in their trouble, and he bringeth them out of their distresses. He maketh the storm a calm, so that the waves thereof are still. Then are they glad because they be quiet; so he bringeth them unto their desired haven" (Ps. 107:26b–30). Desired haven—Parker dared hope for it even now.

Quiet in heart and spirit at last, he slept.

Mornings in the north, in winter, were times of desperation. Pity the husband and father, the man of the household, to whom was assigned the fire-building task.

Gritting his teeth, Parker slid from the cocoon of his quilts, thrust his feet into his shoes, and shivered his way to the stove.

Happy the dawning when a few live coals remained from the night's fire. This morning Parker wasn't so fortunate. First shaking down the grate and removing several scoops of ashes, he crumpled an old newspaper, placed it in position, covered it with fine chips and specially cut kindling, so called because it "kindled" or lit quickly, and set a match to it. Leaving the stove open for the moment, Parker huddled at its side, absorbing the first promise of warmth, feeding the fire with suitably sized wood until it was blazing brightly and popping cheerily.

The cold receded grudgingly, inch by inch. Soon the nail heads nearest the stove were free of frost; eventually the ice in the kettle thawed, the hot water began to steam, and a first washing of sooty hands was possible. Shaving would come later; baths were reserved for Saturday nights.

The day—when he started out later for the Morrison place— was sunny, bright with promise. Parker's boots slid and stumbled over the rut-frozen roads, but if the schoolchildren could navigate them day after day, in fair weather and foul, so could he. It was with relief, however, that he turned in at the gate and trudged the lane to the house. Smoke spiraled from the stovepipe, and Parker anticipated a hot cup of tea and perhaps an oatcake or scone, usually forthcoming from this Scottish family.

The door swung open while his gloved fist was still raised to knock, and Molly's fresh face and welcoming smile greeted him; her hand pulled him into the room. Her warm cheek was pressed to his cold one, and then she was unbuttoning his wraps, helping him out of them, hanging them up.

"Come to the fire," she urged and led him to the favored spot.

Mary, gentle Mary, Molly's mother, greeted him warmly, and soon Mam, beloved grandmother, came in to offer her cheek for a kiss. It was from Mam Molly got her abundant head of lively hair, though the one head was white now, and the other coal black; it was from Mam Molly got the bluest eyes imaginable, fading ever so little now in the lined face and sparkling with life and vigor in the other. Parker thought of his womanless estate and envied the life and warmth and beauty so abundantly displayed in the Morrison home. God willing, he would, one day soon, rob the house of its sweetest and best.

As he had anticipated, a hot cup of tea and a buttered scone were soon daintily served, along with a snowy serviette to cover his knee. Molly, lithe and lissome, restless with winter's restrictions, folded herself on a braided rug at Parker's feet, cup in hand, her eyes raised to his and filled with love and longing.

"What brings you tramping over here this time of the week?" she asked, knowing there had to be a reason in this weather.

"We need to talk, Molly," Parker said, handing her his cup and drawing a deep breath.

Mary was instantly alert. "Mam and I have things to do," she said with a twinkle, and the two—mother and grandmother—

left for one of the bedrooms that had been added to the original cabin, making a sprawling and not unattractive log home.

"What is it, Parker?" Molly asked, eyes shadowed with the dread that, once again, her longed-for wedding would not take place.

"First of all," Parker said, his voice a little unsteady, "it's my father. My mother's letter reached me yesterday, telling me that he . . . he died."

"Oh, Parker—" Molly raised herself to her knees, her arms going around the seated Parker. For a moment their tears mingled for the man he would never see again and she would never know.

"Sit down, Molly girl," Parker said finally, and she did so. Still her eyes were fixed anxiously upon him.

"It's like this," he said. "My mother needs me—it has to do with my father's affairs, selling the business, settling property rights, and so on. I've got to go, Molly."

"For how long, Parker?" Molly asked, just as directly.

"I think I should plan on several months. I'm going to suggest to the board that they contact a Bible school for a substitute; the church shouldn't be without a shepherd for that length of time."

"And us, Parker? You and me?"

"I have the solution, Molly. If you'll go along with it. You remember, last year, when I was in such a turmoil about my call and my future and thought I might go east and teach for a while? You prayed about that, remember? And you weren't agreeable to going with me; you said your place was here in Bliss—"

"For the time being, I said."

"What exactly did that mean, Molly?"

"It meant, you silly boy—" Molly's voice was rising with excitement, "that I didn't feel we . . . I . . . should go east and be a teacher's wife. It means I feel I have my own calling, and it's to be the wife of a pastor. Pastor Parker Jones, to be explicit."

"Then simply going out for a short time—that wouldn't be objectionable?"

"Parker," and once again she was on her knees in front of him, this time searching his face, his eyes, her voice tight with control as she asked, "are you suggesting, are you saying, we can be married, and *I can go with you?*"

The smile on his face was enough for her. With a small cry she flung herself into his arms. He gathered her to him as a drowning man reaches for a rope. And now the tears were those of exultation. There would be no more delays, no more uncertainties.

Mary and Mam were invited back eventually, and kisses and hugs were exchanged, with explanations made. They offered their condolences, then joined in the happy plans that were laid.

"I haven't thought of going until a thaw sets in," Parker said. "But that can't be far away—just weeks, maybe days."

"Just long enough to get everything ready," Molly added. "Oh, Parker, it can be a wedding trip!"

"At my mother's expense," Parker said a trifle ruefully, being as poor as a church mouse himself and the fact well known to his prospective bride.

"But you'll be such a help to her," Molly encouraged, taking his hand. "And I'll do what I can."

"Mother will love you, darling Molly," Parker assured her. "And my sister, too. What a wonderful opportunity for the girls in my life to get to know one another. My *other* girls," he corrected, with an apologetic grin at Mary and Mam.

And at that moment Parker Jones, in spite of flat purse and barren cupboard, worn shirt collars and no means of transportation save his own two feet, felt himself to be the richest of men.

11

Quincy Middleton, as a mill owner and part of the despised (in his thinking) merchant class—along with clergy, doctors, and bankers—supposed himself to have attained the rank of Third Class in British Society. No one had specifically qualified him as such, nor were there lists, to his knowledge, to which one's name was added when he attained a certain status or removed when he slipped from proper protocol and importance. No matter that the Map of English Society was drafted years ago; in people's minds, if not on their bookshelves, it existed.

Now, however, with these shenanigans of his older daughter, he felt he was in grave danger of slipping to the dreaded Fourth Class—along with lesser clergy, doctors, teachers, lawyers, shopkeepers, artists, and merchants of the lower class. (Quincy had nightmares from which he woke up perspiring over the dreadful possibility of such a demotion.)

People of moderate income were also in this bracket. Quincy's income remained large, though his workers were restless, grumbling concerning their need of better pay. But they hadn't a leg to stand on; Quincy had them where he wanted them. They lived in his houses, on his property, and if dismissed from the mill, they lost both wages—meager though they might be—and home.

No, Quincy had not slipped in the matter of his income, and he hoped that fact alone would suffice to maintain his place in the Third Class ranks.

"This evil," he was saying to his wife as he paced back and forth in the room that was designated as his study, his face red, his eyes snapping, "has got to be nipped in the bud. And quickly."

"Evil? Allison? Oh, Quincy! And anyway," Letitia, seated nearby, was twisting her handkerchief, "she's home again. It's over now—"

"Over? Over? People don't consider it over. They see a family brought low by their offspring. They see her actions as a horrible smirch, misconduct of the vilest sort. And it's destroying my reputation and the Middleton name!"

"Quincy," Letitia begged, "be reasonable! Your reputation has nothing to do with it. As for her own, perhaps, given time—"

"A canker, that's what it is," Quincy pressed on. "And it certainly does have something, everything to do with my reputation!"

"Canker?" Letitia repeated faintly and shuddered.

"Canker!" Quincy repeated, rolling the word around on his tongue like some sweetmeat. "Her behavior is like a canker, Letitia. A canker, for which there's no cure except it be excised! Cut out!"

"What are you saying, Quincy?" Letitia was alarmed—there was no operation to remove traits of character. And Allison was hotheaded, rash, independent. Only life itself would change the character of Allison Middleton.

"I'm saying," Quincy said, stopping before a window and staring out at the little kingdom he had built—wide green grounds around a beautiful house and, in the distance, the mill discharging heavy black smoke—"you can't put a plaster on something like this and expect it to get well. A *canker* is a gangrenous growth—"

Letitia was growing tired of the word and wished he'd move on. But Quincy wasn't finished.

"The only solution is to remove it."

His long-suffering wife sighed. "What do you propose?"

"You'll see soon enough."

Quincy stepped to the bell pull, gave it a hefty yank, and turned his heavy face toward the door, his finger tapping impatiently on the desk at his side, his cheeks flexing in cadence with the clenching of his teeth. Quincy, angry, was a fearsome sight to behold and a frightening power to encounter. Although his temper was not turned on her this time, Letitia was understandably nervous.

"Sit down, Quincy. Surely you don't have to pace around like a, like a wounded bull."

Her husband's high-colored face turned even redder. A wounded bull! Quincy desired, above all, to act and react as an aristocrat would. Letitia had, across the years, managed to curb his brutish side more or less by her criticisms, her suggestions, her mockery. Now, hearing her, Quincy bit his lip.

With massive control he turned to the chair behind the desk and sank into it. And though he would never admit it, Letitia was right—he immediately felt more dignified, more in charge than when raging aimlessly around the room. Like a judge behind the bench, he was ready to pronounce sentence.

"Yes, sir?" It was Buckle, standing prim and trim before the desk, having entered the room quietly, like the shadow he was.

"Bring Allison . . . Miss Allison, downstairs, please, Buckle."

"Yes, sir!"

He needn't sound so happy about it, Letitia thought with some annoyance. Quincy irate, Sarah sniveling, the servants titillated—it was a three-ring circus. Perhaps she, Letitia, should have insisted on seeing Allison, preparing her a little in advance for this moment. But the child had behaved shockingly; she should be made to suffer for it. And three days of seclusion on bread and water should have been sufficient punishment. But Quincy's wrath had not subsided one whit. Letitia was uneasy about Quincy's possible heavy-handed retribution.

It had been a long three days. Allison had grown increasingly impatient with her enforced incarceration. Once each day Mrs. Buckle had appeared to escort her to the bathing room, had shut her in, and apparently had stood outside the door until Allison was through with her ablutions. The inflexible presence in the hall had a dampening effect on the girl and kept her from dawdling over her bath, as she might have done otherwise. No, it was wash, dry, dress, and return to the prison of her room. Three times a day Becky scurried in with a tray of food, Mrs. Buckle once again standing guard outside the door.

Of Sarah there had been no sound. Perhaps her attempt to communicate with her sister had been observed and reported to their father. At any rate, there was no further contact, though once Allison had thought she heard a snuffling at the door.

"Fifi? Fifi?" she had called, lifting her head and listening.

Soft footfalls rapidly fading had been her answer.

Sitting by the window at times, dreaming of flight, Allison could see why she and Stephen had abandoned the idea of escape by means of the window—it was a long way down to the ground. Even Allison's intrepid courage faltered over the thought of descending, reaching freedom by such means, though she spent a few moments pondering the possibility of sheets tied together, making a rope of sorts. But she wasn't sure her knots would hold, and she could picture herself plummeting into the bushes below, to be ignominiously fished out and, once again, herded back to her room. And if she did make a safe descent, what then?

Allison's first spate of meekness, due perhaps to her weariness, was fast fading. If her father had called for her that first day or come to her room to see her, he might have found her tearfully begging for forgiveness, promising irreproachable behavior forevermore. As it was, with each passing hour she grew more restless, then peeved that she should be subjected to such humiliating treatment, then angry that it continued so unreasonably.

So when Buckle tapped on the door, was granted permission to enter, turned the key, and came in, Allison was already belligerent.

"Yes?" she demanded.

"Your father wants you downstairs, Miss."

So the moment of confrontation had come. Good! She was ready!

"I'll be ready in a moment, Buckle."

Still Buckle waited.

"You may leave, Buckle. I can find my way down, you may remember."

"Yes, Miss," Buckle said with a slight dip of the head. And he withdrew, to stand, she realized, just outside the door, still waiting.

It didn't help her attitude.

There was little to do to prepare herself; she was dressed—there had been nothing to do all day except see to her own needs, her toilette. Still, she fussed around a bit, banging this, rattling that, clattering her shoes back and forth across the room. In the end it availed nothing; Buckle still stood, and stood still, waiting for her.

At the last, as ready as she could be, she snatched up a shawl, a pretty thing of black cashmere with a five-knot silk fringe eight inches deep, and a favorite of hers. Its splendid richness gave her a dignity, she felt, which she badly needed. And besides, though her room was warm and her father's study would be warm, the passageways and corridors between were unheated and bitterly cold. The promised thaw had come but had not appreciably permeated the stone walls of Middleton Grange.

Passing Sarah's room, Allison ran her fingernails along the paneling, tapping gently. A muffled yap was the only response; if Sarah was in, she gave no indication of it.

It seemed good to be free. Young, vigorous, weary of being pent up, and still coltish in some respects, Allison could have kicked off her slippers, hiked up her skirts, and run along the stretching halls and down the wide stairs. Could have but did not. Buckle would have been scandalized; Allison giggled momentarily, thinking of the staid servant's predicament if she fled ahead of him, and the damage to his dignity if he was forced to chase after her, galloping along uncharacteristically and feeling severe humiliation.

Arriving at her father's door, Allison paused and tossed her shawl more gracefully around her shoulders, waiting for Buckle to step forward and open it. Once she was inside, Buckle closed the door and she stood before it, uncertain, for there was a grim atmosphere in the ordinarily comfortable room. It came, no doubt, from her father's expressionless face and her mother's bent head. Allison had to fight against the unreasonable sensation of being seven years old again and full of dread.

"Come here," her father said, and she half expected him to open the desk drawer and draw out a strap. A stinging blow across the palm had been his practice when dealing with childish disobedience. Allison had hated it not half so much as his coldness of manner.

Drawing in a deep breath, Allison stepped forward. "Good morning, Mama," she said politely, a faint quaver in her voice. "Good morning, Papa."

Letitia stirred but didn't respond or look up. Quincy's gaze, fixed on Allison's face, never wavered. Though there was a chair at the side of the desk, he did not motion her toward it.

This is ridiculous, Allison thought and asked, "May I sit, Papa?"

"There's no need," he said. "This won't take long."

Letitia spoke at last. One word. "Quincy—"

"Quiet!" was the one-word response, and Letitia subsided.

"Papa—" a one-word attempt.

"You'll be quiet, Miss," he ordered, and Allison, like her mother, subsided into silence. But after all, she thought, what was there to say? Squaring her shoulders, Allison determined to take her punishment calmly, even placidly. She was ready to get it over with and move on, back to her normal life. There was so much ahead to look forward to, not the least of all being the birthday ball that had been in her mind the last three days when she had had little else to occupy her thinking. Her ball gown would be of the handsomest silk moire, green, shot with silver—

"I needn't tell you that you've disgraced the family and the name of Middleton," her father began.

"I'm sorry, Papa—"

"Be quiet! If you think an apology of yours can wipe out the damage you've done, the pain you've inflicted, the shame—"

Allison closed her eyes as her father's wrath lashed out at her bitterly.

It won't take long, he had said. But once started, Quincy Middleton was a machine grinding out his grievances. Before he was half done, Allison found her knees trembling and kept her feet still with some trouble. This was dreadful! Never, in her moments of imagining this scene, had she supposed it would be this horrendous. Bowing her head, as Letitia continued to do, Allison let the fury fall around her like rain.

Finally, silence fell. Allison raised her head. Was there more?

There was; she could not have imagined what was to come.

Her father rose from his chair, walked to the window, and with his back to her and to his wife, said, "There's only one solution to disgrace such as yours. That is—expulsion."

Allison was puzzled. "Expulsion?" she repeated.

"Behavior such as you have demonstrated cannot be countenanced in a civilized country, in decent society—"

"Oh, Quincy!" Letitia's voice was strained.

He turned. "There are places for people like you. Scoundrels, scamps, second sons who get themselves in trouble. Remittance men. I'm sure you've heard of them."

"Well, yes, but—" What was her father saying?

"Shameful actions call for shameful measures. Yours call for nothing short of banishment."

What was her father saying!

"Pack your things, my girl. You're bound for Canada and the wild West."

The chinook!

Parker rose one morning to find a strange, silent change in the weather. Weary of winter, with a special reason for wanting spring, watching and eager for any sign of melting, he was quick to detect what seemed to be a faint settling of the snowbanks, banks compacted of snow piled on snow for more than eight months. When he opened the door and stepped outside, he was sure there was a softness to the breeze on his cheek. Before long he saw the first drop splash from the eaves and knew the fire in the stove had not yet warmed the roof enough to cause it.

Could it be the longed-for, the dreamed-of, the gentle chinook?

About April each year the people of the bush began that fervent watch, that eager longing for the magical moment—as though Mother Nature would wave a benign wand over the land—that would mean the beginning of the end of their snowbound existence. With warm breath she touched the land that had been ravaged by the icy hands and wanton will of one—Winter—who had had his capricious way long enough, shrieking out his fury at one time, casually dropping a curtain of near-impenetrable snow at another, obliterating their roads, vibrating their stovepipes, frosting their windowpanes, darkening their days at will.

The chinook. No one really understood the phenomenon, but Parker knew vaguely that it had its origin west of the Rockies. Moisture-laden winds from the Pacific Ocean struck the lofty barriers of the Rocky Mountains, precipitating snow and rain; but somehow, as the winds descended the eastern slopes, they became dryer and warmer until, reaching the prairie provinces, they ushered in a rapid thaw.

It was difficult to settle down to anything, Parker felt now. There was a leaping in his spirit, an expectation. But standing on his small porch and looking out at the softening snow, watching it glisten in the sunshine, he knew it was foolish to get out into it on foot, except for an emergency.

With reluctance he turned back to the house and his studies. Was it too soon for a sermon from that glorious passage—which he appreciated more fully since living in the northlands—about winter being past? "The time of the singing of birds is come," were the words that sang through his spirit.

Turning to the Song of Solomon, Parker's eyes settled on the first verse of the second chapter, beginning with the evocative "I am the rose of Sharon, and the lily of the valleys," proceeding through "his banner over me was love" in verse 4.

He lingered over verse 8: "The voice of my beloved! behold, he cometh leaping upon the mountains, skipping upon the hills."

About to become a bridegroom himself, Parker gleaned new meaning from the rich picture that he had always seen as Christ's love for His church.

The poignant and beautiful plea in verse 13, "Arise, my love, my fair one, and come away," expressed the longing of his own heart.

As never before, he felt the Lord's heartbeat through the sweetness and strength of verse 14: "Let me see thy countenance, let me hear thy voice; for sweet is thy voice, and thy countenance is comely."

He found his cheeks wet with tears; it had all been too much—the breaking of the weather, the anticipation of his marriage, the message of the Lord. Parker Jones, overcome with thanksgiving and filled with expectation, slipped from his chair to the floor, where he knelt and communed. Communed and praised.

A cheery "Helloooo" brought him out of his happy worship and up off his knees. He knew the sound; it was Molly, calling from the cutter.

Opening the door, he stepped out, saluting her with a welcoming smile.

"Can you come?" she called. "I'm going to Bliss. Get your coat and come with me, Parker."

They were already in the *community* of Bliss; she was going into the *hamlet* of Bliss, perhaps to the one general store, perhaps to the post office, most likely to both, since the post office was in a corner of the store. It was a very small hamlet, just the store and post office, a barbershop in the home of the local barber, the Stopping Place, a few cabins and houses, the massive grain elevator. And at the edge of town—the small white building that was school and church. Here children from all over the district gathered for learning; here the faithful congregated on Sunday for worship.

Small though it might be, the hamlet was the center of Bliss life, and the school/church was the center of Bliss.

Of course, even as Molly called to him to join her, Parker knew it wasn't quite so simple as snatching up a coat. Overshoes must be pulled on, not only for warmth but because of the wet condition of the snow, sure to ruin shoes. And Parker had one decent pair. Gloves must be located—probably from a warm spot under the stove where they had been drying. A hat or cap was essential. A scarf . . .

Then there was the delay while he put wood into the stove, closed the damper, pulled the coffeepot back where it wouldn't go dry during his absence. Finally, deeming everything shipshape,

Parker could turn to the door with a light heart. It suited him exactly to be getting out into the exhilaration of the chinook.

It was an exhilaration experienced by the entire district, he knew. Having shared their winter, he could understand and share their exultation in the promise of spring. He could imagine faces, reddened and chapped by winter's harshness, raised joyfully to the blue of the sky. Eyes, weary of squinting into glare, would be catching a glimpse of color again as woodpiles reappeared, as chicken coops rose, like the phoenix rising from ashes, out of oblivion into newness and life once again. Cheeks, frost-nipped, would crack into smiles when caressed by the pleasant wind.

A stanza of a poem learned in earlier days rose in his mind:

> There's a promise of spring in the air today;
> It starts with a chirp, and then
> It breaks on the land in a roundelay,
> All fury and sound, and the signs all say,
> It's the time of beginning again.

Yes, it was the perfect season for a sermon on the time of the singing of birds. He'd call it "The God of Another Chance."

Stepping out onto the porch, pulling the door shut behind him, Parker knew instinctively that the conditions were perfect for snowballs. He scooped a wet handful from the railing of the porch and pressed it in his gloved hands, turning it over and over speculatively, strongly tempted.

"Don't even think of it!" Molly warned from the cutter, breaking the spell.

With a joyous laugh Parker drew back his arm, gave a mighty heave, and sent the missile sailing straight and true to the outhouse, the only other building on the place. With a *splat* the snowball hit the weathered boards, clung momentarily, slid slowly to the ground.

"Marvelous control," Molly commented when he tramped out to the cutter. But whether she meant his aim or his decision was anyone's guess. Her grin was impish, and one supposed that, had she not had the horse to consider, she might have leaped out and engaged in a riotous free-for-all snowball fight for a few minutes.

"I've had a nagging aggravation with that outhouse," Parker explained. "It cants to the east."

"If you keep bombarding it like that, you just might straighten it. Or—topple it completely," Molly observed and pulled the blanket back invitingly. The sun might be bright and the temperature rising, but there was still a definite nip in the air.

Parker was kicking a foot against the side of the cutter, freeing it of the wet, clinging snow. Stepping that foot into the cutter, he kicked the other foot until it too was free of snow, then slid onto the seat and pulled the cover over his knees.

Only then did he turn and smile into the blue and blazing eyes of his true love for a long moment, his own face tender at last. Leaning slowly toward her, anticipating the moment, he kissed her rosy cheek, then her lips. Apparently they were not too cold to function properly, and the sweet contact lingered until the horse tossed its head restlessly, pulling at the reins in Molly's lax hand, catching her attention at last.

Molly's cheeks were pinker, her eyes brighter, her lips redder than ever—a colorful picture against a world leached and bleached of color and life.

"Here, you drive," she said, handing him the reins, and if her voice was ragged and her hands uncertain, it only served to enhance the moment.

As many a lover knew, cold bodies did not mean cold hearts; icy winds couldn't quench heated emotions. Though a geranium on a windowsill, cherished and pampered, rarely survived the season, love endured and blossomed, rarer and more fragrant, perhaps, because of the barren backdrop of winter.

Feeling like a king in a gilded chariot, Parker Jones turned the nag toward the road, a worn horse blanket over his knees, with no destination in mind save a backwoods handful of log buildings almost lost to the world in their remoteness and unimportance. But with the call of the Lord upon him in rich measure and the bride of His choice beside him, Parker did indeed feel himself to be a man of title: The Lord's Elect; Servant of the Most High God; Husband-to-be of Molly Morrison.

In his pocket, ready to be mailed, was the letter to the Bible school. It was the result of last night's board meeting.

<hr />

"Gentlemen," Parker Jones had said to his assembled board of four, "we are here today to do the Lord's business in a very special way. I speak concerning the need to obtain an interim pastor for our church."

"Has Molly agreed, then, to your being gone?" Brother Dinwoody asked rather anxiously. Parker's entire congregation had watched with interest, concern, sometimes despair, and prayers, the romance of their pastor and their own Molly Morrison. Though they had come to love and respect him, their loyalty was to their own: Molly should not be toyed with; Molly should not be disappointed; Molly should never be hurt. And yet, to a man, they understood Parker's present dilemma and concurred with his decision to go to his mother's assistance.

"Brethren," Parker said, and though his face glowed, he spoke humbly, "Molly has agreed to marry me and to accompany me out."

Angus, Molly's father, nodded confirmation.

"Well, then," Bly Condon said with relief, "we can be sure you'll come back. Or," he said sharply, thinking that once Parker got Molly out into the marvels of the world, she might never be satisfied again with the backwoods, "will you?"

"That's our pledge to you, brethren," Parker affirmed. "Aside from the Lord's intervention in some way that we can't see at this time, we'll be back. But we'll need about six months."

Angus didn't seem to be worried about the return of his child, so the other three determined to rest in the confidence that their much-loved pastor would indeed return to them, bringing Molly with him, of course.

"Well, then," Brother Dinwoody said, "I move we get the letter written and get this project underway."

"The sooner the better, I suppose," offered Herkimer and seconded the motion.

"Where shall we write—I mean to whom? Do we have a certain Bible school in mind? What do you say, Parker?"

"I suggest the Bible School of the Dominion."

"Never heard of it," Bly said doubtfully. "The Dominion?"

"A play on Dominion of Canada, of course," Parker explained. "Except in this instance it means the Dominion of Christ. It's a small school but has turned out some good men and women dedicated to serving the Lord in the Canadian Dominion."

"It's in the East, I suppose?" Everything that had to do with civilization, it seemed, was either in the East or on the West Coast where Vancouver Island was a bastion of all things English.

"Ontario," Parker said, "near London. Yes, it'll be quite a journey, but no farther than I came. And many of you. And to get a man with a spirit of adventure, a heart for the West, will be exciting, not only for us but for him."

"We need to be praying about the exact right fella."

Brother Dinwoody, as secretary of the board, balked at writing the letter. So as the four sat grouped around, Parker—with a little help and a lot of unnecessary suggestions—wrote, addressing himself to "The President of the Bible College of the Dominion, Dear Sir—"

"First tell him who you are," Brother Dinwoody, reluctant writer but ready instructor, advised. So Parker explained about the newly organized church at Bliss near Prince Albert in the Saskatchewan Territory and how he himself had been called as pastor—

"Better tell him about your father's death," Bly prodded as Parker paused. "Otherwise he'll think something is wrong here and may hesitate to send someone. A lamb among lions sort of thing."

"Six months," Herkimer prompted. "Tell him to send someone prepared to stay all summer and probably into the fall, maybe winter."

"Do you think that's wise, Herk?" Bly asked. "Could be off-putting to anyone having heard about our winters here."

"It might be well," Parker wrote, "for the ministering brother to be prepared to stay into the winter months . . ."

"Say we'll take good care of him."

"Tell him about the new parsonage."

"No, don't mention that! No man wants to get into a building project first thing. Especially if he doesn't know beans about logs."

"Well, you better explain about the cabin he'll have to live in. Otherwise they might send a married man."

The possibility sent the board into another spate of debate.

"The present parsonage," Parker wrote as delicately as he could and still be truthful, "is fine for a single man but would be of doubtful suitability for a man with a wife and family."

Finally, as the board sat modestly by, Parker stated, "The good people of Bliss will provide faithfully for the man you choose to send. He will find them devoted to serving the Lord and of kindly, godly natures. We believe the field is ripe unto harvest, and a rich ministry is possible."

"That should be a challenge," Angus said, nodding.

Parker read the letter over, made a few changes as directed or suggested, and rewrote the epistle, and Brother Dinwoody, with a flourish and without hesitation, signed it as secretary of the Bliss board.

No one knew how long it would take to be delivered or how long an answer might be in coming back to them. Weather always had to be considered; storms ruined schedules, bringing trains to a standstill, buckling tracks.

"If they overlook our request or haven't got anyone for us," Bly said grimly at the last, "we're in big trouble. There's certainly no one around here—"

"That's where you're wrong," Parker said warmly. "Any one of you could fill the pulpit if you had to. And you may have to. Be prepared, gentlemen."

"I move," Herkimer said with feeling, "we all go into intercession, deep intercession, immediately."

<hr />

"And what are we going to Bliss for?" Parker asked as they skidded along, the runners slipping on the wet snow.

Molly dimpled. "For the mail, Parker. Unless there's some delay I haven't counted on, my order should be in and ready to pick up."

"And it is—" Parker prompted, knowing, but wanting to hear it again.

"The material for my wedding dress!"

The announcement called for another kiss, another blinding revelation of the fact that it was really, finally, going to happen: Molly was about to become Mrs. Parker Jones.

"Tell me again," Parker insisted.

"It's to be navy blue in color, of high-grade Kersey. It will make a wonderful suit for traveling, Parker." And unspoken—it will wear for years and years.

"Wise, I'm sure," Parker said, confident his Molly could do no wrong.

Molly's decisions, even now, were shaped by the thought of her new status as preacher's wife—nothing too expensive or too stylish in design. Parker rebelled at the strictures Molly placed on herself, but she was adamant. "I might as well get used to the idea, Parker. Everyone will be studying me; some will criticize . . . are we spending their tithe money appropriately? Am I an example of the godly woman? And on and on."

Parker sighed and submitted to her wisdom. One thing he knew, Molly Morrison would be a beauty in whatever she chose to wear.

The package, in and waiting, was much larger than Parker had supposed; Molly was such a slender girl to need so much material.

"Remember," she said, her eyes starry, "it's going to have a four-yard sweep to the skirt. Do you think," she asked suddenly, a worried frown on her face, "that's worldly?"

Parker hastily reassured her on the matter.

"If styles change and skirts go slim, I can always cut it down," Molly said happily, seeing many years of wear ahead for the navy Kersey suit.

Molly did a little shopping for her mother, visiting with the few people who were in the store. Everyone commented on the weather; feeling was high in Bliss at the moment.

Parker handed his letter over to be mailed. A small act, but it served to convince him that, truly and at last, he would be marrying Molly.

"I know all about the four-yard sweep," Parker said on the trip home. "But still, why is the package so, so bulky?"

"This is the first time I've ever ordered everything necessary for a dress, Parker. This is no flour-sack costume! And it's not so simple, getting all the necessary materials together. The catalog lists everything needed and calls it a Finding Set."

"And what's in this Finding Set, may I ask?" Parker asked, casting a speculative eye on the package in her lap.

"It won't make sense to you," Molly said. Nevertheless, at Parker's urging, she continued, "Two yards of Selisia waist lining—"

"Selisia?"

"I said you wouldn't understand! Now do you want me to continue?"

"Please do," Parker said humbly.

"Four yards of cambric skirt lining; one and a half yards of canvas—"

"Canvas?" Parker asked faintly. Married life would reveal secrets he had never dreamed of.

"One spool of sewing silk," Molly continued, as though she hadn't been interrupted. "Two spools of buttonhole twist; one pair of dress shields; one set of sateen covered dress stays . . . and, let's see—"

"There's more?"

"Oh, yes, one yard of wigan; and I can tell by the look on your face you don't know what that is. Right?"

"Right," Parker answered cheerfully, certain he would soon be informed.

"Wigan is a stiff, plain-weave cotton fabric used for interlining."

Lining, interlining, binding—how complicated to be a modern woman!

"One card of hooks and eyes—the hump kind."

"Hump kind?"

"They have . . . um, a *hump* to them. They're not your flat eye, in other words. Easier to get the hook into."

Parker silently considered hump versus flat eyes.

"And that's all. Oh, wait—four yards of velveteen skirt binding."

Parker was speechless, more overwhelmed than anything.

"You find all that excessive, perhaps?" Molly asked, worried.

"Not at all, not at all," Parker reassured. "I was just thinking—how am I going to find my girl in all of that folderol? You *will* be in there somewhere, I presume."

Molly's laugh rang out across the bush—a happy promise.

The wilds of Canada—the back of beyond; remittance men—
the dregs of British society. Allison struggled to make sense
of it. Standing in a well-appointed room in a solid stone house
set in the English countryside, with every advantage known to
modern man her daily privilege, cosseted, gently reared, innocent of life beyond the four walls of Middleton Grange, she could
have no understanding of either threat mentioned by her father—
Canadian wilds or remittance men.

She may not have understood—but her mother did.

"Quincy!" she gasped. Not the best, the most involved, the
most caring of mothers, still she quailed at what her husband
had said. "You can't mean it!"

"Oh, I mean it," Quincy said firmly. And neither his wife nor
his daughter doubted it.

Letitia half rose from her chair, her face shocked, unbeliev-
ing. This ultimatum, even from Quincy, was beyond grasping.

"Sit, my dear," Quincy ordered, and Letitia sank back as
though collapsing.

Her mother's reaction, coming on top of her own ignorance of what her father had meant, shot a bolt of fear through Allison's heart. There was something dreadful, obviously, about the Canadian wilds, about remittance men. About her father's decision.

Quincy's attention swung to his daughter. Seeing what he interpreted as unconcern on her face but what was in reality the blankness of incomprehension and being dissatisfied with it, he took it upon himself to add fuel to the fire.

"Remittance men," he said. "In case you haven't heard the term, remittance men are a group of uncontrollable young men who are *an embarrassment to their families*—" Quincy's emphasis and his glare spoke of the intensity of his feelings.

"Papa—"

"An embarrassment, I say," Quincy continued bitterly. "For whatever reason—gambling, carousing, drinking, wasting the family fortune in some way and destroying the family name—"

"Papa—"

"Whatever the reason, the solution is the same: They are sent off to a far corner of the British Empire. Here they continue to receive a scheduled remittance or allowance from their families. If they choose to continue in their dissolute lifestyle, they hurt no one but themselves; the family is happily ignorant of their escapades. As we shall be of yours."

"Quincy—no!" Letitia said at last, gripping the arm of the chair and speaking beseechingly. "Not Canada. We shall never see her . . . rarely hear from her . . . not know how she's faring—"

"That's the general idea," Quincy said coldly. "There will be no more disgraceful actions to bring shame on the family. If that's the route she's chosen for herself, we simply won't know of it. Oh, never fear, I'll send financial support. But not enough," he added firmly, "to keep her in the style to which she has been accustomed. And which she was so willing to leave, may I add, to share the fortunes—misfortunes—of one Stephen Lusk. If that's the way you want to live, my girl," he said smoothly, speaking to Allison, "impoverished—"

"Impoverished!" squeaked Letitia. "But you said—"

"I said there would be an allowance," Quincy confirmed. "What do you think I am—a callous beast? But as I also said, it won't be lavish by any means. Why should I send my hard-earned money across the ocean to be frittered away in riotous living? If she chooses to support every Tom, Dick, and Harry, that's her decision. There will be no Papa to come running to for more; there will be no Grandmama sending gifts. There will be," he said, fixing his wife with a stern glance, "no Mother supplying secret funds."

Letitia knew he meant it; Allison was certain of it.

"When . . . how . . ." she managed into the silence that fell.

"I've been working on it. There are still some details to finalize, such as the ship's sailing date—"

Letitia's eyes glazed; she moaned.

Quincy's voice was a whiplash: "Give over, Letitia! Stop that foolish whimpering! We'll have no vapors, if you please!"

Regardless, Letitia's tears began to flow. Silently, as from an artesian well, unaccompanied by sniveling, sighing, wiping of eyes, or sound of any sort, they welled, ran over, streamed down the sagging cheeks, splashed onto the bosom of her gown.

Instantly Allison was at her mother's side, was kneeling at her knee. "Hush, Mama, hush, hush," she whispered.

With the situation more or less out of hand, certainly not what he wanted or even expected, Quincy rolled his eyes, put his fingertips together, leaned back in his comfortable chair, and waited grimly for the little drama to conclude.

"I'm sorry, Mama, I'm sorry!"

And at last, finally, Allison was sorry. The intensity of her father's anger had not been out of character, and though it stung, it affected her very little; like rain off an umbrella, she bent under the deluge of his words but hardly allowed them to touch her. But the anguish of her mother took her by complete surprise. That they were tears of self-accusation Allison never knew.

Letitia was reaping—in one desolate moment—the results of a lifetime of careless mothering. Her abandoned weeping—interpreted by her daughter as grief and despair over the harsh sentence—filled Allison with a regret over her rash actions that she had not experienced before. She had, in fact, enjoyed a certain glow of satisfaction over her daring escapade and coddled a smidgen of pleasure over her few hours of independence. But now, in response to her mother's supposed pain, Allison was guiltily regretful.

"Don't, Mama," she urged now, wishing with all her heart there was something she could do, say, to ease the pain. "Everything will be all right . . ."

And then her mother raised her soggy, somewhat bloated face and said drearily, "It's too late, you silly girl! How many times have I warned you against your impulsiveness, your heedless behavior! Now look what you've done!"

If a viper had risen up and struck at her, Allison couldn't have been more stunned. Recoiling as though from an injection of poison, Allison rose to her feet, slowly backed away, her eyes on her mother. Letitia had gone back to her soundless weeping.

With a colorless face Allison turned toward her father. "Be so kind," she said in little more than a whisper, "as to tell me what you have in mind . . . for me."

"Don't think I take any pleasure in this," Quincy said with calmness, apparently feeling some explanation was necessary. "I would much rather be planning your birthday ball; I would much prefer putting money into that. I would much rather think ahead, with anticipation and satisfaction, to your wedding. All that and more you have disqualified yourself for. Remember, if you are tempted to think hardly of me—the way of the transgressor is hard."

"My punishment, Papa. What exactly do you have in mind? The wilds of Canada, you said—"

"If you are going to behave like a savage, you might as well live among them. Like the remittance men, you will be shipped to that distant, wild, untamed frontier. However," he said, qualifying his assessment a little, "I understand the eastern provinces are more or less civilized."

Allison, ignorant of Canada east, west, north, or south, waited. "Yes?" she said quietly.

Quincy lifted a slip of paper from his desk. "You have a relative in Ontario," he said, tapping the paper. "A third or fourth cousin who would welcome a little extra income. According to her family she married some ne'er-do-well adventurer years ago; I'm getting in touch with her about the entire matter. As soon as a ship can be located and a berth arranged for, you will set sail."

"Before you hear from her?" Letitia asked, raising her head and looking at her husband with horrified eyes.

"That depends. If the sailing date comes before then, off she goes. Suitably chaperoned, of course. We have the address of this relative—"

"Who is it, Quincy? *Who is it?*"

Quincy's eyebrows raised, but he replied calmly enough, "Her name is Maybelle Dickey."

"I've never heard of her. Why haven't I ever heard of her?"

"As I said," Quincy continued, more than a little nettled now, "she is a *distant* relative."

"How distant? What's the family connection?"

Quincy tipped his head back, frowned, and figured it out. "Maybelle is the daughter of my Aunt Mildred's husband's cousin."

Frowning with concentration, Letitia tried to figure out the relationship. Finding it all too convoluted and too vague, she said, "That's *too* distant, Quincy. She's not really a relative by blood, just some in-law connection."

Quincy rose from his chair, tapping his fingers on the desk's polished surface, having given as much time as he wanted to, and more, to this tommyrot. "You'll have to leave it in my hands," he said impatiently. "I'll do what's best for the girl, you may be sure of that. She'll arrive on Canadian shores safely enough."

"But—alone, Quincy?" Letitia quavered. "Surely not alone!"

"Of course not alone, foolish woman!"

"You'll go with her? Or perhaps all of us—"

"Not at all; she'll go without her family. That's final!"

"Who then? Who will accompany her?"

"There are people who do this sort of thing ... chaperones."

Letitia could do nothing but shake her head and moan.

Allison drew a deep breath. Not understanding most of it, she understood some of it. Remittance men and their fate, or fame, were an unknown factor to her. Apparently her father compared her future to theirs. So be it.

Banishment. This was to be her personal fate. Banishment to a distant shore. Banishment from a land that was as old as history itself to a land only lately discovered, recently settled. She had no thought of escape; the ultimatum, like iron bands, coiled itself around her inflexibly. Other than death itself, nothing would stop her father's will and wishes.

But now, having heard the worst and finding it not only bearable but interesting, and being young and vigorous and, yes, adventurous, she couldn't help but feel a small flicker of excitement rising in her spirit.

Allison lowered her eyes lest her father see and suspect her reaction and be robbed of the satisfaction he was obviously feeling in regard to carrying out his parental duties.

Canada! New horizons! Challenges! Never in a million years would such an opportunity have presented itself to her under normal circumstances. Any mention of leaving the fair shores of England for the new, raw land of Canada would have met with instant refusal and a severe reprimand for even mentioning such foolishness.

Banishment, what her father meant as punishment. Much, much worse, she thought with a gust of pure relief, if she were to be kept locked away endlessly in her room, followed doggedly everywhere she went, her every move monitored, her decisions made for her, including an eventual marriage of convenience. Such a possibility, such prospects, were daunting indeed. Canada seemed, at the moment, like a way of escape. Her father, thinking to punish her for her escape to Gretna Green, was opening the door, thrusting her into the adventure of a lifetime. *And paying for it!*

"May I go now, Papa?" she asked politely, hiding her exultation.

"You may," he nodded. "It's probably too soon to begin packing, but you might like to consider what you will take and what you will leave behind. Remember, insofar as we can see now, this is a long-term assignment. Hopefully someday you may return to us, a dignified lady."

Allison's head was bowed in pseudo humility. Her passage to the door was accompanied by her mother's sudden wail.

Her mother's wail, and her father's pious summation of the entire matter: "Where no oxen are, the crib is clean."

14

If she had felt like skipping when she came downstairs, she felt like flying when she went back up. But already in big trouble and all on account of her unpredictable behavior, Allison's feet walked sedately enough—Buckle in faithful attendance—while her spirit soared.

With the click of the key in the lock behind her, decorum forsook her, however; propriety fled, pretensions collapsed, and Allison, holding her full skirts up and out of the way, kicked up her heels in a jig as full of fancy as of freedom and circled the room. Finally, collapsing on the bed, she gasped out her feelings in tears and laughter.

It was too unbelievable. The very thing she longed for, the chief desire of her life—freedom—was to be hers, and without any conniving or arranging on her part. Of course, she reminded herself guiltily, her unprincipled actions had brought it about. Even so, she couldn't find it in her heart to be sorry. Except for Mum . . . her mother's tears.

Thinking of them, Allison sobered. The excitement of the moment was shadowed by the remembrance of her mother's weeping. And then she recalled the heartless recriminations her mother had all but spat at her and rallied from her brief pang of compunction.

With nothing else to do, she settled herself for the time of waiting. Without some guidelines about Canada and what would be needed and suitable for that place and that climate, there was little she could do to prepare herself. But inertia, for Allison, didn't come naturally; often in the next days as she watched the approach of spring from her window, she felt cooped, restless. At times she paced the floor, devising ways to keep her mind engaged and her courage up. Imagining, planning, dreaming. Urging herself to be patient; what her father had ordained would come to pass.

Sarah was finally allowed to come to her sister's room. Allison recognized the tentative *taptap* immediately and had to admit that—at the thought of talking with another human being—her heart leaped at the sound she had once spurned as bothersome and interruptive. Mrs. Buckle's duties had brought her into the room from time to time to clean, to gather up laundry, to change the bed; Becky—with Buckle standing guard—brought trays of food three times a day. But Mrs. Buckle was grim and speechless, by nature and by design, and Becky, though her eyes rolled speakingly and her mouth grimaced soundlessly, was speechless by command.

"Come in," Allison caroled in response to her sister's knock, her welcome evident in her voice.

The key rattled in the lock, and Buckle held it open as Sarah stepped past him into the room; he then closed it and—both girls realized—waited just outside. It could put a damper on the visit.

Buckle might hear, but he couldn't see. And even his crusty heart might have been touched to see the girls bound across the room to each other, meeting in the center, embracing, weeping a little, rocking each other, all in a manner never experienced before. They had missed each other; they were aware of the approaching separation that would part them for years, perhaps forever.

"Come, Sister," Allison said at last, drawing back and taking Sarah's hand and leading her to a seat on the edge of the bed. It seemed a spot much more conducive to sharing, to whispering, than the chairs set in neat isolation on each side of the fireplace.

"Oh, Allie," Sarah said, weeping rather freely now, "I don't believe I can bear it—you going off so far from England. From home. Oh, Allie!"

"Come now," Allison said as cheerily as she could, "it's really not so bad."

"It's bad!" Sarah insisted. "Especially for you; partly for me."

Allison hesitated—how could she tell her sister that she was truly looking forward to the Grand Adventure, as she had termed it in her thinking.

"I'll be fine, Sarah. You mustn't worry about me."

"But, Allie—Indians! Think of the Indians! Indians scalp people! And your hair is so pretty—" Sarah's voice choked.

"Nonsense, Sister. I don't believe Canadian Indians ever did such things. But if they did, it was ages and ages ago. And anyway, you're talking about the West; I'll be in the East, in Ontario. Everyone knows someone who's been to Ontario, and I've always heard it's quite civilized, really."

"But so far away. Oh, Allie!"

Allison seemed unable to stem the tide of her sister's tears, until in desperation she confided, "But, Sarah, I quite like the idea. Now don't look so upset; that was meant to comfort you."

"You *like* the idea?"

"I do; truly I do."

"Is Stephen Lusk," Sarah asked, looking up darkly from the handkerchief she was holding to her wet eyes, "waiting for you over there?"

"Not at all! Stephen Lusk is a thing of the past. I've seen the last of Stephen Lusk, I'm sure, and probably heard the last of him."

Sarah's slender face filled with sympathy. "Ahhhh . . ."

"It's all right, Sarah! It's all right. Can't you see that this development—going to Canada—is much more exciting, much more to my liking?"

Sarah was on the verge of disapproval, of exchanging her sympathy for agitation. Obviously she was struggling with this shifting of passions.

"I'm sure it wasn't God's will for me to marry Stephen," Allison said piously, hoping to be rewarded by Sarah's acceptance of such a strong argument.

It was the wrong approach. Incensed now, recalling Allison's recent flagrant ignoring of scriptural admonition, Sarah demanded hotly, "What do you know about God's will, Allie? You're a big fraud, that's what you are! If you cared two pins about God's will, you would be a little more prayerful, a lot more careful about finding it."

"All right, all right," Allison soothed. "So I've got a little to learn about God's will—"

"A lot to learn!"

"All right—a lot. Maybe," she added coaxingly, "I'll learn all about it in the—"

"The wiles of Canada, Allie?"

"Not wiles, Sister. Wilds."

"Are you so sure?" Sarah said with wisdom far beyond her knowing.

———

Letitia came. Again Buckle stood guard.

"Why is Buckle stationed outside all the time?" Allison asked rebelliously. "It seems the silliest of precautions. Where do you think I might go if I got out of my room?"

Settling herself in a comfortable chair at the side of the fire, Letitia looked at her daughter—flushed, perturbed, the picture of imperious indignation—and spoke more sharply than she might have otherwise.

"You ran off once, and we certainly hadn't anticipated such an action on your part. Who's to say you wouldn't do it again?"

"Going to Canada—that won't be running off?"

"Under your father's direction. And of course this time we'll know where you are," Letitia pointed out. "And if you choose to associate with runagates, well—" Unspoken the thought that foolish actions on Allison's part would no longer bring embarrassment to her father and mother.

Allison was silent for a moment, the color coming and going in her face. Finally, quietly, almost humbly, she asked, "Mama, don't you care that I'll be so far away?"

"Of course I care," Letitia said. "I care that it's necessary; I care terribly. It gives me great pain." And Letitia bowed her beautifully coiffured head into her hands.

Although she didn't rush to bow at her mother's knee again, Allison repeated her apology to the best of her ability, wondering at the same time how meaningful it was if it was only half meant. And she *was* sorry, she realized, to have caused hurt, even shame—more thoughtless than intentional though it had been—but not sorry to be *going to Canada!*

Letitia dabbed tearless eyes, sighed, and changed the topic of conversation.

"I'm going to see that a trunk is brought down to you, and you can begin to sort through things, deciding what to take with you."

"Mama," Allison said, "I don't have any idea what to take. Are there any guidelines? I mean—will I be on a farm? In a city? Can I buy things there that I find I need?"

"I have no idea," Letitia said helplessly. "All I really know is that it gets cold, wherever you might be. Be sure to take heavy garments."

As a result of the conversation, a large trunk was deposited in a corner of Allison's room; she eyed it with a mix of dismay and enthusiasm. The first things to go in, down into a deep corner, were the Balmoral boots and petticoat.

But whether or not they would be necessary, she didn't know. Recalling the cold of Gretna Green, Scotland, Allison left the

Balmoral garments in the trunk and added the warmest gloves she could find.

⌐————⌐

Finally, her father came. It was the first time Allison had seen him since their encounter two weeks earlier in his study.

Startled at the unexpected sound of the key in the lock, Allison glanced up from the book she was reading, then stood as her father entered, her expression calm enough but her heart racing. Were there to be more recriminations? Was there a change in plans? Had—heaven forbid!—Stephen been located and drawn into the whole miserable affair once again?

Until now she had never considered what would happen if Stephen was tracked down, overcome, and dragged back to Midbury, and her father—full of righteous indignation—demanded that Stephen marry his daughter. It was an unsettling thought. Was it possible?

She was a little chagrined at the relief she felt when her father's first words put her uneasy conjectures about Stephen to rest.

"Plans are coming together very nicely," he said, gesturing her to sit, himself taking the other chair. "I've obtained passage on the *Griffin* for you and your custodian."

Custodian! Allison hated the word, hated the thought, dreaded the association.

"The sailing date is exactly ten days from now."

"Ten days, Papa?" It was actually going to happen.

"A week from Friday. So speed up your packing, my girl. Mrs. Buckle will assist you. I understand she has a relative in Canada and can give advice about the sort of things to take. She will also have the funds to purchase anything you may need."

"This . . . this custodian, Papa?"

"Miss—ah, here it is." Quincy fished a slip of paper from a pocket and read, "Theodora Figg."

"Have you met this Theodora Figg, Papa?"

"Buckle procured her services. I understand she does this sort of thing regularly—accompanying women or children, overseeing the sick or elderly, doing a little nursing if necessary, delivering her charges to their destination. Very capable, I'm sure. Highly recommended, of course.

"Once on the shores of Canada, she will transfer her obligations to . . . to . . ."

Quincy fished once again in a pocket, drew out another paper, and continued, "Maybelle Dickey. Mrs. Dickey will be there to meet and greet you—"

"You've heard from Mrs. Dickey?" Allison asked, surprised.

"Well, no, there's hardly been time. But if there is some slipup, Miss Figg will continue your oversight for as long as is necessary. Everything, I feel, is under control."

It sounded very tenuous to her, quite uncertain, rather alarming. But the adventurous spirit in Allison rose to the challenge; she wondered fleetingly, in that moment, if she were a pioneer at heart.

Not much more was said. Quincy, businesslike as usual, said what he had to say, then turned to leave. At the door, his back to her, he never saw Allison's hand, tentatively outstretched, never saw the pleading in her eyes.

"Papa?"

"Yes?" he asked and turned. Asked too crisply, turned too late; the hand was down, the eyes shadowed.

"Nothing. It was . . . nothing."

Mrs. Buckle came. Mrs. Buckle came and lit into the task at hand as though she were a tornado in skirts.

"There'll be no need for this," she'd say, tossing aside a favorite gown. "Too extravagant . . . too indecorous . . . too elegant . . . ostentatious."

Allison hadn't known her wardrobe was so useless, so contemptible, so preposterous, and she watched with dismay as Mrs. Buckle, with a sniff, disdained most of it and filled the trunk with warm petticoats, flannel nightgowns, warm vests, boots, ulster coat, pea jacket, twelve handkerchiefs, twenty-four pairs of stockings, six pairs of gloves, a "housewife" with buttons, needles, and thread. "There won't be anyone at your beck and call to sew and mend and replace buttons," Mrs. Buckle said firmly, adding a pair of scissors and a darning ball.

"I'm putting in soap for rinsing out your clothes," she went on, fitting in a bulky packet. "This chaperone of yours won't do your laundry, I'm sure of that. As for ironing—" Even Mrs. Buckle's confidence wavered at the thought of ironing.

"Shoe polish," she said, proceeding doggedly. "Curling iron—you won't need it. You'll have to do your own hair, of course. I'll put in some hair nets—"

Somehow the Adventure no longer seemed quite as Grand as it had in Allison's dreams.

15

Brother Dinwoody, church secretary, stopped by the parsonage with the letter from the Bible School of the Dominion. His feet, in tall rubber boots, splashed through the remains of winter's snow, a rich slush; his head, in its shapeless hat, was lifted into the bluest sky imaginable. He was surrounded by the freshest fragrance—of life reawakening, earth reappearing, buds swelling. Phlegmatic man though he was, Brother Dinwoody was stirred in heart.

As he waited on the stoop, his jaunty whistle vied with several issuing from the bush that pressed close on all sides (they really would have to cut that back if the parsonage was to have a garden). His cheery grin greeted his pastor when Parker Jones opened the door; it would have taken a frozen man to resist the blandishments of spring in the Canadian bush.

"I thought it was a robin out here on the porch," Parker said, smiling.

"An old crow, more like," Adonijah Dinwoody responded with uncharacteristic jocularity.

If he keeps this up, Parker thought, *we'll have to call him a name more frivolous than* Brother *Dinwoody. Ijah, maybe?*

"Come on in, Brother," is what he said, however, and his board secretary obligingly did so. No matter that he tramped water all over the floor; it was nothing but rough boards and would benefit from a little scrubbing when it was mopped up. Besides, any day now the building of the new parsonage was to begin.

"We have a response here to our letter in regard to a supply pastor," Brother Dinwoody said, and he took a rather crumpled envelope from his pocket.

Parker showed his guest to a chair, took the proffered letter, opened it, and read it silently, assuming Brother Dinwoody had read it previously.

"It's good news," he commented. "At least they're working on our request."

"We wrote at the right time," Brother Dinwoody nodded, "just when school is about to let out for summer. He—the fella who wrote—hopes to have someone lined up by that time. This letter was just a courtesy, I guess you'd have to say, lettin' us know they had received ours, and advisin' us that they are workin' on it and will give us the final word later on."

"Yes, that was thoughtful of them," Parker said absently, thinking ahead, realizing the arrival of the interim preacher would be several weeks away at best.

Molly was ready for the wedding: dress completed and waiting, other mysterious sewing finished, plans made for the day of the ceremony. And, heaven knew, he, Parker Jones, longtime bachelor, was ready. Ready and eager, and feeling a keen sense of disappointment that there might yet be a delay of several weeks before he could claim the delectable Molly Morrison as his bride.

"I think Molly and I won't wait," he said now firmly, and he saw Brother Dinwoody wilt and lose some of his carefree satisfaction with the day and the weather. Obviously visions of having to preach rose in his mind.

"We'll go ahead with the wedding if Molly is willing, and I think she will be. This means, of course, that we'll be away from here before the new man arrives. You may remember, Brother, I exhorted you and the other board members to be prepared to fill the pulpit if it became necessary. Well, it looks like it's going to be necessary. Have you given that some thought?"

Though the day was far from warm, Brother Dinwoody seemed to break out in a sweat. "Isn't there some other way, some other solution?" he asked feebly.

"Short of a miracle—no," Parker said. "But I know you can do it. If each of you takes a turn, that'll take care of a month of Sundays. You can come up with a sermon in that length of time; I know you can."

Brother Dinwoody seemed far less certain than his pastor. Gloomy-eyed, he pocketed the letter that had spelled the end to his carefree days. His good-bye was far more muted than his hello had been; there was no rollicking whistle; even his hat seemed to have forsaken its rakish angle and sat on his head in a manner most subdued.

Parker followed the dejected man to his buggy and stood alongside for a moment. "If you think you need extra time to prepare, Brother," he said kindly, "speak up for the fourth Sunday before the others beat you to it."

Brother Dinwoody's chest heaved with a burden he'd not had when he arrived. Then, he'd been full of the joy of life, anticipating the bush's glorious spring with nothing more alarming to trouble him than a broken plowshare, a gimpy horse, and a calf due too soon.

The board met and voted—after considerable discussion—to accept Parker Jones's suggestion that they themselves fill the pulpit, freeing him to go ahead and get married and leave for the East before the Bible school man arrived.

Last-minute plans for the wedding, long in the works, were finalized. Everything was ready except the actual setting of the date, which the couple now announced. The entire district was agog with expectation. For this would not be a home wedding with only the family in attendance, as was the custom, but a "church" wedding. That is, it would be held in the schoolhouse, and the full congregation, the entire district of Bliss, would be included.

⸺

Brother Dinwoody was too slow in expressing his wishes—or too wishy-washy—concerning his choice of speaking dates; Bly Condon obviously had the same thought, and before Brother Dinwoody could say "fourth Sunday," Bly had the date snatched up for himself. Brother Dinwoody's despair accelerated; how could he bring anything meaningful to the people of Bliss when he himself was so mired in the slough of despond?

Angus Morrison would take the first Sunday, Herkimer Pinkard the second; Brother Dinwoody found himself slated for the third Sunday. Maybe, he thought with faint faith, if he prayed fervently enough, the new preacher would arrive before his turn came up.

Even then Parker Jones was saying, "If the new man doesn't arrive by then, you can start the slate over again."

⸺

Two weeks later, on a glorious Sunday morning, the school-house was packed long before Parker Jones took his place behind the makeshift pulpit to deliver the day's sermon; the wedding ceremony would follow.

It was an unusual arrangement—Sunday sermon, followed by a wedding. Saturday would have been a better day, particularly for the groom with his pulpit responsibilities. But spring work was underway, and Parker and Molly would not ask their hard-working neighbors to set it aside for them. Since most of them obeyed the biblical injunction to labor six days, their attendance at church on the seventh was a matter of course, barring illness or tragedy.

They were present and in place on this day, eager for the most special occasion of the year, easily rivaling the Christmas concert in importance and excitement—the marriage of their pastor and their own Molly Morrison.

The hymnbooks—*Hymns of Praise Number One,* with shape notes, bound with jute manila—were distributed. Sister Dinwoody at the organ was at her best. Her generous hips, wider by far than the crimson mohair organ stool on which she sat, pumped energetically, bringing up the pressure in the bellows; her work-worn fingers set the stop knobs just so and pounded out the melody on the yellowing celluloid keys. The hymn of choice made a fitting opening for the occasion: "O Happy Day!"

And though the small congregation couldn't rightly fill the quota mentioned in "Hark! Ten Thousand Harps and Voices," their enthusiasm—when they reached the chorus of "Alleluia! Alleluia! Alleluia! Amen!"—swelled and lifted through the building, out the open door, and across the bush in glorious, if ragged, testimony.

Parker Jones, shined and pressed, did his best to preach. But it seemed he would never be done smiling; it was not a day for rebuking or chastising. It was a time of expectation, of assurance, assurance first of all that Christ would return one day and, secondly, that he, Parker Jones, though leaving them temporarily, would return to them.

"Philippians, chapter one, verses 25 and 26," he announced as he began, Bible in hand, and there was a rustling of fragile leaves as the faithful turned to the proper place: "I know," he read, "that I shall abide and continue with you all for your furtherance and joy of faith; that your rejoicing may be more abundant in Jesus Christ for me by my coming to you again."

Heads lifted, eyes shone, a few mouths smiled; Parker Jones had taken the words of the apostle Paul and applied them to their present situation. The Philippians' consolation was theirs. The Philippians' admonition was theirs—Pastor Jones concluded with a portion of the twenty-seventh verse: "Whether I come and see you, or else be absent, I may hear of your affairs, that ye stand fast in one spirit, with one mind striving together for the faith of the gospel."

Amen and amen.

So consoled, so admonished, they were bound to stand fast until their shepherd should return to them.

A brief closing prayer followed the short exhortation, and then, rather than the usual dismissal and turning toward the door and home, an expectant silence fell.

"It's our privilege, mine and Molly's," Parker Jones said simply, laying his Bible aside, "to share with you our exchange of vows. Brother Temple—if you will kindly step forward . . ."

From the back of the room, Rev. Temple, an itinerant preacher who was known to many of them, worked his way through the desks. Reaching the front, he embraced Parker Jones, shook his hand, and turned to face the congregation, a smile on his cadaverous face. With little or no physical beauty, Rev. Temple exuded the simple love of the Lord. Everyone knew his devotion, his dedication, his sacrifice, and they gave him their attention now.

Parker gave the bemused Sister Dinwoody a quick glance, and with a start and a blush, she turned to the organ. As prearranged, she played, as soulfully and meaningfully as she could, "Savior, Like a Shepherd Lead Us." The second time through, the tempo became quicker, the sound more vigorous; it was a sign to the breathless audience. As one person they turned and followed the direction of Parker Jones's eyes.

Through the door, walking alone, stepped Molly—head lifted regally, slim shoulders straight, face flushed prettily, her vibrant hair intertwined neatly with ribbons. Lightly she came, brightly, gladly, through the aisle that opened for her.

No petal-strewn path or flower-decked arbor was ever trodden by a bride more proudly than Molly Morrison walked the oiled schoolhouse floor; no cathedral held guests nobler than the pioneers crowding into Bliss's scarred desks; no bride looked into faces more supportive than those that turned to Molly now.

There were no flowers; there were none to be had. Though vases of budding boughs had been placed strategically at the front of the room, the earth had not produced one crocus as yet, no brave early violet to pin to the bride's shoulder. But the sweet fragrance of lily of the valley perfume accompanied her, and in her hand Molly carried a small Bible.

Straight and true she went—brave in her navy Kersey with its jabot of frothy white—to the waiting Parker Jones. His face was alight, as though he had seen or was even now seeing a vision. With never a falter Molly walked through the crowd and into arms that came out automatically to receive her.

It was so unexpected, the embrace, so spontaneous, that the crowd, awed and silent until now, broke into applause. Only then did Molly turn and Parker raise his head—as though waking from a dream and astonished to discover they had an audience— to smile at their audience, then step apart and turn to face the minister.

Afterward Molly was to say she heard only the familiar "Dearly beloved" and nothing more—although she was assured she gave her pledge at the proper time—until Rev. Temple directed the new husband, "Salute your bride," and Parker, in front of a deeply moved, even tearful congregation, kissed her as his wife, Mrs. Parker Jones.

There was no recessional; there was no way a path could be made through the packed building. Rather, friends and family crowded around, with hugs and handshakes, pats and kisses being the order of the day.

It was not a day for dispersing; it was a time for fellowship, for reminiscing. It was a time of eating together. No home was large enough, no hall available. Though it was not yet really warm, it was sunny. The snow was gone, the earth was drying; it was possible to set up trestle tables in the school yard.

Every household in the district, and several from surrounding districts—well-wishers who had come for the wedding— produced boxes containing every taste treat imaginable. It was a celebration. Who would want to go home to a cold dinner eaten alone when special food was available for the taking, with conversation flowing richly?

Winter's hardships were still sharp in the memory; spring's promises were not yet fulfilled. This day, with its food and fellowship, was a time of transition, a laying aside of the old, a laying hold of the new.

Parker and Molly, as was right and proper, took time to go from table to table, group to group, even family to family, expressing appreciation for each guest's presence, assuring one and all of their return. But it was obvious they were biding their time, and they turned gladly toward Molly's brother, Cameron, nodding their willingness to be on their way when he looked at them inquiringly. Cameron was to take them to Prince Albert where they would spend the night at the Maple Leaf Hotel. The next day they would take the train to points east and Parker's childhood home.

In the wagon, packed and ready, was the baggage they would take with them.

"Good-bye, Mum, Da," Molly murmured in the arms of Mary and Angus. "Thank you for everything."

In her grandmother's arms Molly was speechless; love had its silent language. The hardy little Scotswoman had promised to be around to dance at Molly's wedding, and though the church's influence might mean self-disciplined feet, hearts were free to dance all they wanted, as often as they wanted, as wildly as they would. If Mam's blue eyes meant anything, her heart was doing a merry jig.

But in all the farewells, there were no tears. It was a radiant Molly who started on her life journey, her wife journey, having so recently promised, "Whither thou goest, I will go; and where thou lodgest, I will lodge: thy people shall be my people, and thy God my God: where thou diest, will I die, and there will I be buried: the LORD do so to me, and more also, if ought but death part thee and me" (Ruth 1:16–17).

Sitting on the high seat of the wagon between Cameron and Parker, Molly turned for one final wave to the watching, waving, cheering crowd.

"You'll miss out on the shivaree," Cameron said, feigning sympathy, clucking to the horse and starting the wagon on its way.

"Thank goodness!" Molly and Parker chorused with fervency.

16

Theodora Figg, her little finger curled elegantly, lifted a teacup to lips that, Allison suspected, were enhanced with a touch of artificial coloring. And she felt sure her mother viewed their guest with less than complete approval, for Letitia's head was lifted in a regal manner, as it was prone to be in the presence of lesser individuals, and her nostrils were pinched, as they were prone to be when something didn't entirely please her or come up to her standards.

As for her father, who applauded himself always for being a keen judge of character, he was quite clearly bemused, caught up in the obvious attractions of his daughter's "custodian," blind to any hint of Theodora Figg's unsuitability. Letitia watched him, her face tight, quite clearly thinking, *Silly male!*

"I advise a special kind of luggage trunk," Miss Figg said in her somewhat nasal voice and with an accent that was affected, as she continued with the litany of things to be done for the voyage, items to be taken, items to be struck from the list Letitia had prepared. "It's known as a steamer and is specially designed to fit into the fifteen-inch space between the berth and the floor of the luxury- and saloon-class cabins. If you don't have such a piece of equipment, I'd advise you to purchase it."

What Theodora Figg didn't mention was that the presence of such a trunk was a telltale sign that a young man using it and coming into any western Canada community was probably a remittance man. Nor did she mention that the luxury- and saloon-class cabins would be overflowing with these young scalawags, the offscourings of British society. Had Letitia known, she would have swooned; Quincy himself might have balked at the arrangements he had made for his wayward daughter.

"You did reserve the best, did you not?" Miss Figg cocked her eye rather sharply toward Quincy, who hastened to assure her that he had paid for the finest accommodations offered by the *Griffin*.

"Fine," she said, sinking back with relief. "Some parents do otherwise, having a need to economize, I suppose, although I'm sure you don't fall into that category. I cannot abide traveling steerage. It's a trip that's uncomfortable enough, I assure you, under the best of circumstances."

Theodora Figg wanted it known that she was expending great effort, making concessions, to accommodate the Middleton family's need. "More than uncomfortable," she continued. "A veritable trial to the nerves."

Allison had no trouble believing her, having read J. Ewing Ritchie's *To Canada with Emigrants*. "Nothing can be drearier than a trip to Canada," he reported. "Now and then a whale comes up to blow hard, and that is all; the foghorn blows dismally every few minutes . . . the icebergs are monotonous—when you've seen one, that is enough. . . . In the saloon, we are a sad, dull party; even in the smoking-room, one can scarcely get up a decent laugh. I pity the poor emigrants in the steerage."

"Now," Theodora said, setting aside her cup and dabbing her lips daintily with her serviette, "about the young lady's funds—"

"All arranged for," Quincy said, coming to himself with a start as his flow of thoughts concerning the woman—whatever they were—were interrupted. "I've looked into this matter carefully and am advised that letters of credit can be redeemed in all parts of Canada—"

"Your banking house?" Theodora asked shrewdly.

"Brown, Shipley & Company."

"The best," murmured a sagacious custodian. "Such letters are a fundamental requirement for anyone going to North America.

"It is also recommended," she continued, "that the traveler carry along with her a goodly sum of Bank of England notes; these are salable in large towns at full value. But in case a person finds herself to be in the smaller outback towns of the West— not that this is pertinent to Miss Allison—it is advisable to carry small denominations of Canadian circular notes. This will avoid problems with exchanging Bank of England currency."

"Ah, yes—"

These small bills, Allison knew from her perusal of *The Englishman's Guide-Book to the United States and Canada,* could be cashed on sight without the necessity of providing references or identification.

"Your knowledge is to be commended," Quincy said admiringly, while Letitia's nostrils pinched until they were white. "And your counsel is much appreciated, I assure you. It's good, indeed, to have someone with such a grasp of the situation to take charge of our daughter and her affairs. We shall feel secure, I'm sure, in the fact that she is in capable hands."

Miss Figg smiled and dipped her head in a brief acknowledgment of the compliment. "No doubt my previous clients have assured you—"

"We're having a little trouble," Letitia inserted, "contacting any of them. The Bridgeman family, for instance—"

"Oh," Theodora said, surprise in her voice, "are they abroad again? It's that time of year, I suppose."

But it wasn't; it was too early to go gallivanting abroad; much of Europe was still frozen, the haunts of the rich and famous shut down for the winter.

It was not, however, too early for a ship to the colonies. Such ships began plying the oceans the first of April and continued through the first of November, departing weekly. It was from the port of Liverpool that most remittance men sailed, and so would Allison, heading for North America, putting ashore at Quebec City some two weeks later.

These were the glory days of steamships; steamships reduced the time and torments associated with sailing vessels. Though these vessels still operated, Allison would not be submitted to such an ordeal, largely because Miss Figg, who was to accompany her, had made it clear she would refuse the assignment unless it was by steamship.

"And Lord and Lady Paxton?" Letitia pursued. "Are they abroad also?"

"No doubt they haven't come to London yet; did you contact their country estate address?"

"You gave us the London address—"

"There's hardly been time to hear from them," Theodora said peaceably. "Mr. Middleton first contacted me less than three weeks ago. We can delay our departure if you wish, until you have time to hear from the Paxtons and the Bridgemans . . ." Her voice trailed off.

"Not at all! Not at all!" Quincy spoke quickly, placatingly, and gave his wife a shriveling glance. "I have contacted Mr. . . . Mr. . . ."

"Kryzewski. Johann Kryzewski," Theodora supplied. "Yes, Mr. Kryzewski knows me well and my work."

"But who *is* he?" Letitia asked bluntly, only to be glared down again by her husband. Flushing, she subsided.

A few more things were discussed, the hour of meeting was set, last-minute instructions made, and Theodora Figg rose—a woman in her early thirties, curvaceous because she was tightly corseted, dressed with an indefinable air of too much, too cheap, too redolent—to speak her gracious good-byes and take her departure.

"I don't feel good about that woman," Letitia said with a sigh as soon as Buckle had accompanied Theodora out of the room.

"She's the only possibility that presented itself," Quincy stated firmly, once again himself since the woman was gone. "And anyway, what could happen? Buckle will see them aboard the ship, and Maybelle will meet them when they arrive. All Allison has to do is behave herself on board ship, follow instructions, and that's it."

"You *hope* Maybelle will meet them," Letitia reminded him. "You haven't heard from her, either."

Quincy grunted and directed Allison back to her room; her parents were still quibbling when Buckle closed the door on them.

———

Allison's final moments with her sister were the most painful she was to endure. Sarah's tears flowed freely.

"Oh, Allie," was about all she could manage, and this she kept repeating in broken tones.

What was there to say? Of what use were words? Nothing would change their father's decree. What had been, was; what was to be, would be. No comments were necessary.

But they both understood it was the end of life as they had known it. Sarah, shy and reclusive, would be more alone than ever; Allison would never again experience undemanding love such as her little sister had given.

Locked in each other's arms, wordless for the most part, it was Buckle's approach that allowed them to regain a semblance of normality. Allison wiped her eyes and attempted to speak briskly: "Take good care of Fifi for me. When you come to Canada, she can come with you."

Sarah shook her head in despair, refusing to be cajoled.

Her small face twisted with misery, Sarah thrust into her sister's hand a small purse—Grandmama's contributions to her across the years. It was to be a gift more meaningful than they could have imagined.

⸻

Standing in the great hall, coated and wrapped, her baggage being carted out to the coach by Buckle, Allison spoke her good-byes to her parents. If her face was white and her eyes large, luminous with unshed tears, her parents were unaffected.

Her father reached a large, white hand and patted her shoulder. "You have Maybelle Dickey's name and address," he said. "You have your letters of credit. You have Miss Figg to see that all goes as planned."

"Yes, Papa," Allison said, as one frozen in time and place.

"And may this . . ." he began judiciously but, to do him credit, hesitated without adding the useless and pointless and hurtful words *teach you a lesson.*

Her mother, to do her credit, did not pretend grief she did not feel. She planted a cool kiss on her daughter's brow, as though she were leaving for the season in London. "Be a good girl," she said, as though sending off her child to an overnight stay with a friend.

With blind eyes Allison turned and walked woodenly through the door of Middleton Grange, down the steps to the coach where Buckle held open the door for her and Jenks held the reins. Stepping inside and taking a seat beside Mrs. Buckle, she left behind everything she knew and faced everything she didn't.

Eventually she loosed her grip on the farewell gift her mother had handed to her at the last minute and which she hadn't looked at until now: a generous supply of Cockle's Antibilious Pills.

O nce aboard ship, Theodora dropped the respectful form of address, forsaking the "Miss" for simply Allison. Allison, who wouldn't have thought a thing about it in most circumstances, found herself strangely nonplussed. Since she deemed *Figg* to be a most unseemly name, one that she had trouble uttering without a snicker—a childish reaction that she avoided—she followed her chaperone's example, promptly dropped the "Miss," and called Theodora by her given name. Anyone hearing the two of them would have supposed they were friends traveling together. This, too, Allison found unsettling. She had never considered herself a snob, thinking she had little to be uppity about, but she was sorely tempted where Theodora Figg was concerned.

Though she controlled her baser instincts sternly, Allison was enough her mother's daughter to leave the housekeeping chores to the hired help. And the longer she knew her, the more she considered Theodora Figg hired help. Certainly she was hired, though her help, as the trip progressed, was to become more and more in question. Allison had no idea of the amount paid for her services, but knowing Theodora a little and having noted her father's fatuous reaction to her charms, she was sure he had opened his purse generously, perhaps lavishly.

When the steamer trunk had been fitted snugly into its allotted place, Allison escaped the small compartment, leaving Theodora frowning over arrangements, and made for the deck. Though there were busy goings-to-and-fro behind her, the rail was comparatively empty of people. No doubt other passengers aside from herself had made an attempt to peer through the drifting fog bank, found it hopeless, despaired of waving farewell to family and friends on shore, and abandoned the idea in favor of warmer quarters.

It was April at its worst; the fog hung heavy and gray, curling about the small, distant figures on the wharf until they seemed disembodied, unreal, nothing but voiceless actors in a pantomime. Occasionally a shouted word emerged from the gray, shifting curtain; occasionally an unseen boat sounded a warning out of the murky shroud. Waves lapped dismally against the side of the ship; debris slapped against the hull, resembling soiled and tattered petticoats hemming a billowing skirt.

Allison drew her shawl around her shoulders and leaned against the rail, searching, in spite of herself, for some familiar form on the dock. There was none; the family coach was long gone. Jenks had held the horses steady while Buckle assisted Allison and Mrs. Buckle from the coach, and while Mrs. Buckle walked to the designated area and met Miss Figg, Buckle had unloaded the steamer trunk. If the housekeeper had expected Allison to follow her, she was mistaken and no doubt chagrined, when she looked back, to find Allison waiting by the coach. Frowning, Mrs. Buckle led Theodora Figg, into whose hands she was placing her charge, back to the coach. Although Allison couldn't read the expression on the chaperone's face, she had a feeling her reaction was much the same as Mrs. Buckle's—annoyance.

If either woman had expected a meek and sorry girl, humbled by the situation, they were in for a surprise. Allison, more the lady than at any time in her hoydenish life, nodded to Theodora, bade Mrs. Buckle a brief good-bye, managed a smile for the gloomy Jenks, and walked toward the tender that would take her out to the ship. Theodora Figg, with a startled look on her face—after all, she was supposed to be the one in charge—hastened to keep up.

Allison's one glimpse back had been a revelation. Buckle, having seen to the disposition of the baggage, turned toward her and gave her what appeared to be a brief, crisp salute. Then, stepping up into the coach beside his wife, he shut the door, leaving Allison with the curious sensation of having received an ovation. But why would Buckle, the quintessential servant, applaud her escape to freedom? Allison would always suspect that, at the last moment, he had given her a glimpse of his dissatisfaction with his own status, before, wordless, he turned sternly back to it. Jenks clucked to the horses, and the conveyance lumbered off, out of Allison's life as quickly as it dropped out of sight.

❧━━━━❧

Not even a memory lingered on the dock.

Every tie was broken, every contact gone. A bell tolled somewhere, a knell that spoke of loneliness and dreariness. Standing on the ship, separated from the shores of England and home, with everything familiar swallowed up in the fog as though it had never been, Allison bowed her head on the railing and struggled with her emotions.

Could such a journey—so coldly begun, so blindly, so futile as to purpose—end happily?

❧━━━━❧

Allison was jarred from her reverie when an elbow bumped hers, someone pressed to the rail at her side, and a voice said hollowly, "It's impossible to locate anyone in this weather."

Turning, she saw a young woman not much older than herself. The newcomer's attention was fixed on the shore, her eyes searching, searching. Like Allison she had a shawl—not as lavish or as lovely as her own—clutched around her shoulders and pulled casually over her head. Even so, Allison could see that the face was slender, the eyes deep set, shadowed with sadness at the moment, wet with a dampness that was not of the fog.

"Yes," Allison agreed, and she never understood why she added, "but I'm not looking for anyone, so it doesn't matter, I guess."

"Well, then," the stranger said, still straining to see, "you said your good-byes earlier, at home. But my family, God bless 'em, insisted on being here to see me off. And now I can't see 'em!"

"That's too bad," Allison said with sincerity.

"I give up," the young woman said at last, with a sigh. "Obviously they've given up too and are gone. I suppose," she said thoughtfully, "the sensible thing now is to do what Paul did—"

"Paul?" Allison prompted when the stranger paused as though hesitant to say more.

"The apostle Paul. He said something about forgetting those things which are behind and reaching forth unto those things which are before."

Another Sarah!

"And did you," Allison asked, "have a governess, as I did, who meted out Scripture quotations as a means of discipline or for practice in recitation?"

"No, indeed," the young woman said with a small laugh. "There was no governess in my life, I assure you. No, I learned that verse and others because I needed them."

Needed them? Allison didn't ask for an explanation.

It was too absurd, really, having a conversation at the railing of a ship, with a stranger, about—of all things—Scripture. Perhaps, in a normal moment, it would not have happened, but on this day it was just one more unreal experience.

Still, there was truth in what the girl had said; it was apropos, to be sure. Allison allowed herself to think of it fleetingly: In essence she was saying the past is over and done. Move on; forget it. The future is ahead, offering new opportunities, another chance at happiness and fulfillment. Paul or no Paul, Scripture or not, the concept was a good one and worthy of consideration.

With a sigh, the girl turned her back on the distant dock and the hope of waving one final time to her loved ones. "It's just as well, I suppose," she said. "I need to get used to the idea that they are no longer part of my life. I made my choice, knowing it would cost me my family. It's one of the prices we pay for going so far away. We might as well be going to the moon, as far as seeing them again is concerned. But I'm not sorry for my decision!" The girl's voice had no hesitation in it, no hint of second thoughts.

Though Allison was reluctant to pry, she was intrigued. "Ah, mmm," she said cautiously, "it was that important to you, then?"

The deep-set eyes turned to Allison with a fervor that might have lit the eyes of Joan of Arc.

A pioneer! The girl was consumed with the passion of the pioneer. Allison was sure of it. "Well, then," she said, "you are heading for the Canadian prairies, perhaps, to take up land?"

The girl looked surprised. "That may well be," she said. "But that's not my reason—"

"So why," Allison found herself asking, "are you going? What is so compelling as to take you halfway around the world, leaving your family—"

"That's an easy question to answer. I'm going to Canada to be married." The words sang, the young woman's eyes shone, the mouth couldn't help but smile.

Remembering her own abortive attempt at marrying, Allison was tempted to feel a belated pang of regret. But then she recalled Stephen's too-willing acceptance of her investment in his future and arrangement for his escape and was filled with a profound thankfulness that she had found him out in time. Allison Middleton could never settle for a weak man.

"I think we should get acquainted," the young woman at her side was saying. "My name is Georgina Barlow—"

"And I'm Allison Middleton—"

"Georgie for short—"

"Allie—"

With a burst of laughter, the two young women sealed a friendship that was to mean more than they could have known.

<hr>

David Abraham had felt the pull of the land. Free land! It was a magnet drawing men from all parts of the older world to the Canadian Northwest, and David Abraham, a day laborer mired in a meaningless job and destined to slave at it for the rest of his life, had broken away. Though it meant leaving the girl of his choice behind, he had dared take the chance in order to make a new life for both of them.

"It was three years ago," Georgina said, recounting the story, and Allison thought she could see in the girl's eyes the painful price that had been paid.

And now it was to pay off.

"David has been working in Ontario, saving his money," she explained, "but is ready to take up homesteading at last. One shouldn't go West without a certain amount of money, you know, or the entire experience may be a failure. It's a gamble anyway, with many terrible stories of defeat. But David and I are young and strong, and—" Georgina's voice lifted, "we'll be together."

Allison realized how quickly, how easily, she and Stephen had forsaken their plans and each other, and recognized that love, true love, had not been experienced by either of them. How blessed to have that sort of love, the kind of commitment that endured. The "until death do us part" kind of commitment.

"David will come to Quebec City to meet me, of course," Georgina said. "He will quit his job at that time and have things in readiness for us to head for the Territories where we'll file for our quarter-section of free land. We'll be married right away and head off together."

Off—into the unknown. Into drudgery, into sacrifice, into backbreaking labor harder than they had ever known. Into challenges they could not imagine, deprivations of the meanest sort, and discouragements to daunt the hardiest soul. And do it willingly, happily, even eagerly.

Allison felt humbled before such dedication, such commitment. Consequently, her answer to Georgina's inquiry into her own plans began as a mumbled sketch.

"I'm going to, that is, hoping to . . . Oh, fiddledeedee, Georgina! I might as well start off by being honest with you. You see . . ."

What followed was an outline of home, hopes, plans, failure, and repercussions—the whole story in a nutshell. "I can see now what a childish thing it was I tried to do and how foolish. It was a romantic venture, I suppose, certainly not love. I don't know what love is, at least not love such as you and David have for each other. And I'm not a bit sure of what lies ahead for me.

"This Maybelle Dickey, for instance, who is meeting me and into whose care I'm to be placed—I've never met her. In fact, my parents have never met her." For the first time, Allison admitted a sense of desperation, even fear, regarding the unknown future.

"So you don't know where you'll be, or what you'll be doing," Georgina said thoughtfully, quite neatly summing up the entire situation.

"That's it, I guess," Allison acquiesced, wondering where her bravado of earlier in the day had gone. And gone so quickly. And so totally. She was, she realized, a frightened girl . . . child—for she felt terribly young, terribly ignorant, dreadfully alone.

"Georgina!" It was a voice calling for their attention.

Suddenly it dawned on the young women that the ship was moving, had been underway for a while and they had not realized it.

"That's one of the girls I'm traveling with," Georgina explained, and she waved at the woman, indicating she'd heard and would come in a moment. "I suppose it has something to do with arrangements. You are billeted first-class, I imagine—"

Allison nodded.

"I'm in steerage and happy to have that. But," Georgina said, stepping away as she spoke, "I don't know how often we'll get to see each other—"

"Often, I hope," Allison said feelingly.

"Perhaps there are rules about the different classes mixing. We may have different times scheduled when we can come on deck. Our meals will be . . . well, let's just say they won't be at the captain's table." A glint of humor lit the deep-set eyes, the thickly lashed eyes, the kind eyes. "You haven't said—are you traveling alone, Allie?"

"I haven't gotten around to mentioning . . . Miss Figg."

Georgina's eyes were shrewd. "A traveling companion?"

"I suppose she'd agree to that. Just how companionable we are—well—"

"You needn't feel like you are alone," Georgina said. "I have a friend I can recommend, and He'll be with you, stay with you—"

"He?"

"You can talk to Him, and He'll listen to you—"

"He?" Allison repeated skeptically.

"Jesus, of course," Georgina said, smiling, and with the air of introducing a familiar friend. "Just thought I'd mention it. Ta ta for now, Allie."

18

Although it was Sunday and not a proper day to meet and transact business, it only made good sense during a hectic summer. And it was, after all, the Lord's business.

Mary Morrison greeted Bly Condon, Herkimer Pinkard, and Adonijah Dinwoody as they arrived, holding open the screen door, inviting them to join Angus and partake of the lemonade she had prepared for them after their dusty excursion in the middle of a hot afternoon. Where she had obtained the lemons was a mystery; the ice, of course, came from the icehouse, having been stored there the previous winter. If occasionally a leaf or some unrecognized object appeared as the ice melted, the drinkers wisely refrained from speculation and downed the cool and refreshing drink, grateful for it.

Having forgone their usual nap for the meeting, they sank wearily into their chairs, happy for the only rest they would enjoy this Lord's Day.

No one had an evening to give to board meetings or anything else, aside from dire necessity. Beginning their day at four in the morning and having completed a normal day's work by noon, they returned to their fields and barns to put in another eight hours before caving in for the night. Their wives and children spent few if any idle minutes as well.

Angus, before the others arrived, had searched for a Scripture that would be fitting for the occasion of this day's meeting, deciding against David's "The king's business required haste" in favor of Jesus' words "Wist ye not that I must be about my Father's business?" The work-worn men, hearing it, nodded affirmation and were relieved of any niggling worry they might have harbored concerning the breaking of the Sabbath, and they bent shaggy but humble heads to ask for divine guidance on their deliberations.

"Welcome, gentlemen," Angus said, and the meeting was officially brought to order.

It was obvious that Brother Dinwoody, who had stood in the pulpit and delivered his heart that morning in the sermon of the day, was experiencing some tension. Sitting on the edge of his chair, playing with his drink, looking expectantly around the circle, he was awaiting the reactions of his fellow board members. A desperate light in his eye revealed his poorly hidden anxiety.

"Congratulations on the sermon," Bly Condon said at last, opening the subject and expressing nothing. Perhaps he was remembering that it would be his turn next Sunday.

Herkimer said thoughtfully, "I never heard that particular Scripture interpreted in quite that way before," and neatly passed the problem on. "How about you, Angus?"

"Er," Angus hesitated, then proceeded with caution while Brother Dinwoody waited. "It was a new thought to me, too."

Brother Dinwoody, dissatisfied, said, "I thought some people looked at me a little strangely afterwards. In fact, it seemed people avoided meeting my eyes, sorta looking through me and past me."

"Especially the women, I'll be bound," Herkimer said with a guffaw, unable to restrain himself any longer.

Brother Dinwoody frowned. "Angus?" he pursued.

"It's a touchy thing, I suppose, to lift portions of Scripture out of context—"

"But it needed to be said!" Brother Dinwoody defended.

"What, exactly, needed to be said?" Angus asked, though he suspected.

"Haven't you noticed the trend among women of late?" His wife, he meant.

"What trend is that, Brother?"

"Putting their hair up on *top* of their heads!"

"I don't see—" Bly Condon began, mystified.

"Distracting! Worldly! What's wrong with a bun on the back of the head?"

The three listening board members obviously struggled with mixed feelings—hilarity over the foolishness of Brother Dinwoody's opinion and dismay over the public airing of it. In spite of themselves, their weathered faces creased before their grins could be controlled.

Adonijah Dinwoody, his dignity injured, breathed righteous indignation.

⸻

The plan for the board members to take turns preaching Sunday by Sunday until the new man arrived had started out well with Angus and Herkimer taking the first two Sundays, and they had all been lulled into a false sense of satisfaction concerning the arrangement. But this morning, from the pulpit, Brother Dinwoody, the most reasonable of men under most circumstances, had taken the opportunity to flail out at his wife in particular and all women in general.

One day the previous week, Vesta Dinwoody, a dumpling of a woman trying to cool her heated neck, had casually pinned her hair on top of her head, had found she rather liked it that way, and had continued the practice. Accustomed to the rigid bun on the back of her neck, Adonijah, for some reason, had found himself aggravated by the change—perhaps it was the heat, perhaps he was overtired. He had simply frowned at first, then, when she ignored his disapproving glances, he fussed a little. Still Vesta went her own blithe way, and Adonijah, more and more churned up about it, demanded, then commanded, that she return to the modest hairstyle of previous days, calling the new arrangement worldly, even scandalous.

Vesta had laughed. She laughed! In fact, she had laughed merrily. She had laughed and ignored what her husband considered his better, wiser judgment.

Adonijah Dinwoody—wishing he'd never started the controversy but driven, somehow, to insist on having his way—found himself helpless to do anything about his wife's dereliction from her known duty to obey her husband and brooded all week.

Having been married for twenty-five years and both being of easygoing natures, Vesta and Adonijah had gotten along together very well until now, amicably solving any problems. This was the first time he had tried to exert his masculine prerogative, and he had failed. Stung, Adonijah grew moodier as the week progressed.

Vesta put her hair on top of her head in the morning and left it there all day, with only an occasional swipe of her hand to catch up any recalcitrant curls that, surprisingly, appeared in the short hairs on the back of her neck. Rather than enjoying them, Adonijah found himself glowering at these marks of Vesta's independence.

"For goodness' sake, Ijah," Vesta had eventually been driven to say, "quit grumbling about such a small matter. Go out into the highways and byways and reform the drunkards and gamblers and leave women to their few simple pleasures."

There was nothing left to Adonijah but silent indignation.

Quite thoroughly silenced at home, defeated on his own turf and resenting it, the poor, foolish man had used the pulpit as an opportunity to expound on the subject. No matter if his wife, listening in surprise and dismay, spluttered and fumed silently; no matter if—as soon as they got into the buggy headed for home— she took her turn at preaching.

Brother Dinwoody had taken as his text the twenty-fourth chapter of Matthew. His topic was the abomination of desolation, a controversial topic at the best of times and one better left in the hands of biblical scholars.

Undaunted, he had plowed through the list of coming tribulations, culminating in verses sixteen and seventeen with the instructions regarding fleeing to the mountains for refuge during those dreadful days. "Let him which is on the housetop not come down to take any thing out of his house." It was a simple enough verse with a clear enough message: Let no one on the roof of his house go down to take anything out of the house.

But Brother Dinwoody, wholly untrained and untaught and with a bone to pick with his spouse, had isolated the words "top not come down," giving them a meaning never intended, a twisted meaning. Perhaps in his ignorance he really believed "top not" meant "topknot"; perhaps he misquoted it purposely to use it against his wife.

"Topknot, come down," he thundered with appropriate thumps on the pulpit, and numerous topknots had quivered—whether from the wearer's laughter or indignation was not clear.

"It was the most flagrant misuse of Scripture I've ever seen," Angus had declared to Mary as they made their way homeward, leaving bedlam of a sort behind them. "I don't know if we'll survive until our pastoral replacement arrives. We can't have any more fiascoes like this one."

"He's taken his turn," Mary soothed, "and won't need to do it again for four weeks. Surely by then the new man will be here."

Angus sighed, the responsibility of the church heavy on his shoulders.

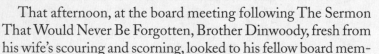

That afternoon, at the board meeting following The Sermon That Would Never Be Forgotten, Brother Dinwoody, fresh from his wife's scouring and scorning, looked to his fellow board members for some crumb of support.

"The proof of the pudding," Herkimer offered finally as the men sat contemplating Brother Dinwoody's unorthodox sermon, "is in the eating. If topknots come down all over the district, we'll assume you were a sower whose words fell on good ground. On the other hand . . ." he mused. Herkimer had heard the preacher of the day castigated by the usually long-suffering congregation.

"I declare!" more than one had said with some heat.

"What next!" "For heaven's sake!" "Saints above!" These comments and others had accompanied the shuffling feet out the door.

"Poor Sister Dinwoody," a few had murmured.

"Poor Brother Dinwoody!" most had concluded.

"Well," Angus said, clearing his throat and getting the wandering attention of his board members, "I think no damage, no permanent damage, was done." And that, apparently, was the only solace he could come up with.

And with that, the strange case of Brother Dinwoody's pulpit ministry came to a conclusion, in the church if not at home.

More than a little surprised at the ruckus he had raised and struggling between satisfaction and embarrassment, Brother Dinwoody's thoughts turned to the vagrant curls—the cause of it all—that had sprung up damply on the nape of Vesta's neck, and he fought against developing a liking for topknots.

Anyway, he thought with mixed feelings, he had concluded his pulpit assignment. In spite of the repercussions, he had quite enjoyed the renown.

"Let us move on," Angus said finally and turned to two letters laid out before him on the table.

"This first one is to me and my family," he explained, "and I won't read it aloud but just report that Parker and Molly arrived at their destination safely, have settled in, and Parker is finding much to do to help his mother and sister."

"Does he mention when he'll come home?" Bly asked hopefully, all the while knowing it could not possibly happen before next Sunday and his pulpit assignment.

"No. I think he'll stick by his plans as outlined to us when they left. It'll be several months, I'm sure, maybe even taking us into winter."

Bly Condon groaned inwardly but brightened; nothing, nothing could be worse than Brother Dinwoody's pulpit performance.

"That's fine," Herkimer said. "It'll give us time to complete the parsonage."

The discussion switched to the building, its progress, its problems. It would be a fine substantial home when completed, of that they were confident and to that they were committed.

"Now, Angus," someone said, glancing at his pocket watch, "do you have some word for us from the Bible School of the Dominion?"

"Aye." Angus read the brief epistle assuring the church at Bliss that a man had been selected and would be on his way shortly.

"His name," Angus supplied, "is Ben Brown."

"How old?" someone asked.

"They dinna say. Young, I would assume, since he's been a student at the Bible school for a couple of years."

Brother Dinwoody stroked his chin thoughtfully. Chances were the youthful preacher would not be a fount of knowledge where the Bible was concerned; end-time prophecy would surely be beyond him. There was, Adonijah thought with relief, only the faintest of chances that this Ben Brown, greenhorn, might ever speak on the twenty-fourth chapter of Matthew and the housetop.

The board meeting was adjourned, and the weary men turned their rigs homeward for evening chores, a short night's sleep, and another week of struggle to wrest their livelihood from land that, some years, seemed to frustrate their efforts at every turn, and grudgingly at all times granted its bounty.

Contemplating a cold supper that would certainly be coolly served, Adonijah Dinwoody's suspicion—that he might yet favor topknots—became a positive fact, a sure thing.

Quite anticipating the happy results, he clucked to his horse and hurried home.

19

With the British Isles lost behind her in the fog and the Dominion of Canada hidden somewhere in the fog ahead, Allison had the sensation of being a leaf cast on the sea of life, a speck in a mighty universe, disconnected. For a few days she floated free, unanchored, her beginnings gone and her future uncertain.

Perhaps the feeling was shared by others, and celebrated, for in the ship's salon a general air of bonhomie existed. These sportive passengers—Allison noted as she stood in the doorway, hesitant to enter and perhaps break up the party—were men.

They were young, they were well dressed, they were spend-thrifts. They were the sons of the aristocracy. The graceless sons.

Since medieval times Britain had operated under primogen-iture inheritance laws: The eldest son inherited the real property of the family estate. Second sons, though living like young princes and attending the best schools, had no preparation for any worth-while contribution to life and no guarantee of a means of liveli-hood. While it was unfair, it was a reality, and it caused upheaval in many families for centuries.

British schools had an obsession with teaching classical languages and literature such as the works of Cicero and Virgil, and the very students who needed preparation for life were poorly taught in practical matters. They excelled at games—rugby, cricket, tennis. They were dedicated rowers in colorful regattas and were able competitors in track and field.

Their code included being loyal to their own kind, but they were not always thoughtful of anyone else; in fact, they were prone to bully less fortunate individuals. Elite, in a class by themselves, they enjoyed the moment, carousing much, studying little. Schoolmasters were tolerant of their escapades as befitting sons of the upper class, demanding little in the way of discipline and getting no more than they expected. In short, many of them were hellions, troublemakers living aimless, useless lives.

Eventually these libertines were turned out into a world as unready for them as they were ill prepared for it. As charming rakes, they were in demand as weekend houseguests, excelling at riding, playing games, drinking, gambling. But as for the serious task of doing something worthwhile, benefiting society, they were totally unfit.

Some settled eventually into a career in the army, while others chose to become clergymen, hoping to obtain a well-to-do parish where they could have a good living and mix with a congregation of similar class stature; England's spiritual life was in the hands of clergymen who chose the calling for purely practical reasons rather than in response to a higher call.

Most, however, led purposeless lives, their time and attention given over to cavorting and carousing. Besides being an embarrassment to their families, they were a drain on the family revenues.

One solution that had come into favor among aristocratic families was to send a superfluous son to a far corner of the empire; it was a simple solution that brought sighs of relief to worried parents. Once a young man was on a distant shore, a small payment from home each month would support him until he was able to do something useful, perhaps buy land or establish himself in business.

The transition from the old life to the new was luxurious, however, as these men traveled to their destination "saloon" or first-class. Taking approximately two weeks by steamship, they ate well the entire time, slept well, bathed and shaved each morning, and spent the day with other chaps equally unregimented, playing cards, smoking expensive cigars, and drinking.

It was into this melee that Theodora ushered her charge.

"Heavens!" Allison murmured, standing in the salon doorway, bombarded with sights and sounds never before encountered.

"Go ahead, Allison," Theodora said impatiently at her elbow. "The salon is provided for the pleasure of all of us, not just these rogues."

While Allison hesitated, a good-looking youth leaped to his feet, raised his glass in a salute to her, and made his way to her side.

"Bertram Wallingford at your service, ma'am, better known as Binky," he said with a courtly bow.

Allison was taken aback and wordless for the moment.

"Come join us," Binky Wallingford invited cordially; then he added in a merry tone, "We're harmless, I assure you."

"Look now," he said, watching Theodora as she moved past them into the salon, "your companion is not hesitant. And I offer a comfortable seat and good company. Are you waiting for a better offer?" His pink face, young and unlined, was smiling, his eyes twinkling with great good humor. Allison found herself smiling back in spite of herself.

"I don't like to intrude on a private party."

Binky Wallingford laughed heartily. "It's not private, and it's not a party. It's a way of life, my dear Miss—"

"Middleton," Allison found herself responding, lured by the open countenance and teasing ways.

Taking her elbow, Binky Wallingford directed Allison toward a table that was even then scrambling to make room for one more. Besides herself, there was one other female, an owl-eyed, stiff-necked young woman who looked sadly out of place. No doubt she, too, had been accosted by Binky Wallingford or his associates and escorted, willy-nilly, into the maelstrom of males lounging at the table. Her name was lost in the hubbub of welcome that came from right and left as names were called out, glasses raised, a toast offered.

Drinks were generously ordered, and Allison hastily made a choice of shrub—water slightly soured by fruit juice; she was to drink more of the innocuous shrub than she had imagined possible before the voyage was over.

With Binky on her right and a cheery, cheeky young man on her left answering to the name of Freddy, Allison had little need to do or say anything, being surrounded by constant chatter and spontaneous laughter. Whether the carefree mood would last the entire trip or whether seasickness would deplete the jolly group, time would tell.

For a moment she searched the crowd for Theodora, but her attention was claimed again by the antics of those around her.

"Here's to the far-flung reaches of the empire," someone toasted, and everyone drank to that.

"Long live the queen!" another offered, and glasses were raised again.

Theodora had proceeded into the room as though she had a destination in mind, a purpose, and Allison located her eventually in a cozy tête-à-tête with a man of dark visage and considerable facial hair and who was rather fussily overdressed. Theodora's manner seemed not to be that of a stranger meeting a stranger; she and the man, with heads close together, talked intimately, animatedly. Puzzled, Allison wondered if he could be Johann Kryzewski, the man her father had mentioned vaguely as being his contact in locating Theodora as a suitable traveling companion. If so, what was he doing on board the *Griffin?* Johann Kryzewski—the name and the man and Theodora's attachment to him raised a faint uneasiness in Allison.

Binky Wallingford, the soul of hospitality, ordered more shrub for Allison and something more invigorating for himself, then introduced her to Gilbert "Gilly" Greenborn, and the merriment continued.

And so it was, that day and every day. Amused at first, Allison soon found herself bored, restless, impatient with the empty, meaningless hours spent in the company of England's finest and best.

Here, in the noise and distraction, there arose in her mind a portion of Scripture she had memorized as a child, a couple of lines isolated from the Book of Jude that seemed, suddenly, to have an application: "Clouds they are without water, carried about of winds; trees whose fruit withereth, without fruit . . ."

She shivered.

"More shrub!" Binky, the most attentive of hosts, called out.

———

"Remittance men," Theodora said later that day in answer to Allison's query.

Remittance men! So these were the scalawags her father had spoken of. The famous—or infamous—remittance men. Fun-loving, happy-go-lucky, hail-fellow-well-met. Purposeless, aimless, useless. Thinking of them, Allison had a strange, hollow feeling.

"Yes, remittance men," Theodora repeated. "And you, my dear Allison, may very well qualify for history's first remittance girl."

———

It was a daunting thought, a sobering thought. It was a bitter thought. Allison made her way again to the ship's railing to watch the tumbling seas and the vacant horizon and wonder what life was all about.

Clouds without water . . . trees with withered fruit. Empty horizons. Purposeless landfall. No call . . . no beckon—

But there was a call. And there was a beckon.

"Allison!" She heard the call and, turning, saw the beckon.

It was her new acquaintance, Georgina Barlow, calling from behind a roped-off area, beckoning.

157

Allison made her swift way toward the girl. It was reassuring, somehow, to touch again the one person she knew with a sure voice, a sturdy confidence, a hope, and a known future. "Georgie! It's good to see you. How are things going down below?"

"As well as can be expected, I suppose," Georgina answered, greeting Allison with an open smile. "Fortunately we're not traveling under sail, or the time would be much longer and the conditions much more grim. I can stand anything for two weeks. And three days have already slipped away, thank goodness. Are you all right? Standing there at the rail, you looked—"

"Bored?"

Georgina hesitated. "No, not bored—"

"What then?" Allison asked, knowing. Knowing very well what had been on her mind and how she must have looked to a keen observer.

"Troubled," Georgina supplied. "You looked unhappy, sad. Troubled."

"Oh, Georgie," Allison said abruptly and honestly. "Theodora says I'm . . . I'm a remittance girl."

"I see," Georgina said slowly, leaning on the dividing rope, reaching a quick hand of sympathy toward this troubled young person.

"Do you know about remittance men, Georgie?"

"Well, of course I do," Georgina said. "But you don't need to align yourself with them."

"I'm like them, Georgie. I've come to the conclusion I'm truly like them," Allison said. "No purpose, no goal, getting money to enable me to live as I always have, only living somewhere other than home. I don't like the comparison, Georgie; I don't! Those men in there—I see what aimless creatures they are. And I see where I'm like them in some ways, and, Georgie, I don't want to be. I want life to mean more!"

"Have you prayed about any of this?" Georgina asked gently. Perhaps it was that unexpected yet expected solace Allison was seeking. At any rate, it was the one solution Georgina had to offer, and it was what she gave.

"No," Allison said. "I haven't. Would it really make a difference?"

"Allison!" The peremptory call made both girls start.

It was Theodora, tardily checking on her charge.

Allison looked mutinous. "Listen to her! You'd think she'd been sticking close as a burr all this time, wouldn't you? You'd think she really cared. Truth is, I've gone my own way, and she's gone hers—"

"You better go and see what's on her mind," Georgina said. "But I don't know if I'll get to see you again, to talk to you. Allison—"

"Yes, Georgie?" Allison was reaching across the rope as a drowning person reaches for a rescuing hand.

"Allison! What would your father have to say!" It was Theodora.

"My father!" Allison gritted. "A thousand miles away and not caring a whit! But I suppose he warned her that I might try and run away, or something like that. What were you about to say, Georgie?"

"I'm going to be praying, Allison; I'm going to be praying for you. Everything will be all right; you'll see."

With a last touch of fingertips, the girls parted. Allison, in spite of the insistent strident voice calling, watched Georgie Barlow disappear below with a new, faint thread of hope that she hadn't known or felt before.

There were no words to describe the excitement that pervaded the air. Passengers crowded the rails, waiting for the gangplank to be lowered and disembarking to begin. On the dock, equally excited, stood another mass of people. Eyes, from ship and from shore, searched for a familiar face. Occasionally an arm was raised in a vigorous wave. More often than not silence prevailed, though here and there mouths could be seen moving, offering up murmurs that seemed to be prayerlike in fervency. For many it was a time of reuniting with family members, loved ones left behind when they emigrated.

Anxiety was heavy on the faces of some who waited; they knew what it was to be disappointed, to search among the passengers of a newly arrived ship and find no familiar face, to conclude once again that the distant one had failed to make the proper connections. Would this ship, this time, bring the expected loved one?

Not yet having stepped foot on the new land, Allison felt she could sense the raw energy of it. Looking out over the crowd below, she could see it was unique, not a British group by any means. Though some people represented England and Victorian propriety, many were obviously of foreign extraction. Clothing was rough, and babushkas were much in evidence. Though this was Quebec City, buckskin and good English tweed rubbed elbows, Scandinavian lilt blended with Scottish burr.

Aboard ship, there was no separation of the classes now; regulations were overlooked in the excitement of the moment as steerage joined saloon, as the holds were emptied and bleach-faced travelers from below joined those who had made the crossing in comfort, even luxury. Class was forgotten or perhaps ignored. Were they not in Canada, the land of the free?

Allison searched for a glimpse of Georgina Barlow, wondering which sturdy male on the dock was also watching for her, straining for a glimpse of that well-loved figure not seen for three years. Together at last, they would make their way to the Territories and a new beginning.

At Allison's shoulder stood Theodora, and at Theodora's shoulder, the man Allison had come to the realization was Johann Kryzewski. Though the mysterious man had been in the background during the voyage, Allison had caught sight of the dark, slick figure numerous times and always in the company of Theodora Figg. Now he had forsaken circumspection and caution and pressed forward to a place at Theodora's side, bold at last. Allison did her best to ignore him; soon, she consoled herself, she would be in the company of Maybelle Dickey, and Johann Kryzewski and his inamorata—if that's indeed what Theodora was—could go their devious ways.

But Maybelle Dickey was not here in Quebec City; she lived in Toronto, and it would mean a train trip to make connections. Allison wondered if the tenacious Kryzewski would cling stubbornly to them as she and Theodora continued inland.

I don't suppose I can complain, Allison thought briefly. *The voyage wasn't too bad; I'm here safely, and that's what Theodora was hired to accomplish. Papa would be so pleased—*

Allison stiffened; a strong whiff of Bay Rum revealed that a man—in fact, Johann Kryzewski—had moved up behind her, so close that she could feel his breath stirring the hair on the nape of her neck. Pushed against the railing, she could only endure.

What a crush! Fortunately, at that moment there seemed to be a forward surge. The objectionable pressure at Allison's back disappeared, the man caught away, she supposed, in the crowd.

"At last!" someone muttered and took a few steps.

"Here we go!" others exulted, and it was echoed throughout the passengers.

Inch by inch they pressed ahead; Allison was happy when, turning her head slightly, she could no longer catch sight of Johann Kryszewski; neither could she see Theodora. No matter; they had discussed this very thing and had determined to meet at the baggage distribution area if they became separated.

Allison's last glimpse from the ship, before she disembarked, was the dockside reunion of Georgina Barlow and David Abraham. Though she could not hear the sound, the shout of the man reached Georgina's ears; she turned at the familiar voice, and, it seemed to Allison, her spontaneous cry of joy joined the myriad calls, cries, shouts, and cheers with which the air was punctuated. Locating each other at last, held in a grip as tight as human arms can manage, the lovers met, and the scene brought a mist to the eyes of the watching Allison. *Happy ending,* she thought, and she realized that, for them, it was actually just the beginning.

The young couple hadn't seen her, but before Allison turned her attention elsewhere, she honored their future together with a small salute, at the same time recognizing a hollow feeling at the realization that she would never see Georgie again, never meet David.

And so she stepped onto Canadian soil—rather, a dock made of Canadian timber—turning toward her own future with eagerness and expectation. Slowly she made her way to the edge of the throng of greeting, weeping, rejoicing people. Others, alone and with no one to meet them, stared around soberly, uncertain and unsure.

"Allie!" How startling, here in this shifting mass of humanity, to hear her name called. It was not the vulgar tone of Theodora Figg, that much Allison knew. Turning, she came face-to-face with Georgina Barlow, at her elbow a large, beaming young man.

"Georgie! I had given up ever seeing you again!" And Allie found herself wrapped in the arms of her short-time friend, each of them regretting that life would now separate them, and by thousands of miles.

"I just had to see you, Allie, to say good-bye before we take off."

Even in the midst of the most confusion she would see for years, perhaps for the rest of her secluded life, Georgina had thought of her shipboard acquaintance. With David in her arms, she had found room for Allison.

"This is David . . . Davie," Georgina was saying, her eyes like stars. "Davie, this is the friend I was telling you about—Allison Middleton."

The two—Allison and David—met warmly, only to part immediately.

For David was eager to be on his way; the marriage ceremony awaited and a long, long trek. "Come, love," he said eventually, his eyes shining, and Georgina turned without reluctance to follow. The girls clung together in one final embrace.

"Allison," Georgina said at the last moment, calling over her shoulder before she disappeared in the crowd, "write to me!"

"But where?" Allison had the presence of mind to call after her. "Where will you be?"

"Davie says," Georgina's voice grew thin, almost lost in the hubbub, and Allison strained to hear, "he says . . . Saskatchewan . . . Prince Albert. We'll be in Bliss."

Allison promised silently, knowing Georgina was beyond the sound of her voice, "I'll write . . . oh, I will!"

There, Allison told herself mournfully, all sight of Georgina gone, *goes a true friend. Or she would be, given half a chance.* Georgina had shown sincere interest in her, had cared. Georgina had prayed.

Would anyone pray for her now?

With a sigh Allison swallowed the lump in her throat and turned her thoughts to present matters, such as locating Theodora. Not finding her immediately, she turned her attention to locating the baggage area. There, she asked that her steamer trunk be moved out and set aside for her, sat down on it, and waited.

She was enthralled with the amazing diversity of the people around her, not only in their manner of speech but dress. "Anything goes" seemed to be the accepted mode. Being an onlooker, Allison was touched by the winds of change that blew across this great, raw land, recognizing the necessity for it, the naturalness of it. Out with the old, in with the new, would be an exhilarating step for Allison. Now, if this Maybelle Dickey, when she located her, would be forward looking—

Maybelle Dickey was still miles away. Where then was Theodora, who had the address of this Dickey person, who had made train arrangements, who had the money? There had been plenty of time for Theodora to have shown up, as prearranged.

Three children, thin, possibly underfed, dressed in strange woolen garments, sat solemn-eyed on some bags nearby. A babushka-covered woman sought privacy to nurse a fussing baby by turning her back and opening a garment much in need of laundering. A boy strolled past pushing a small cart stacked with apples, reminding Allison that she had eaten very little breakfast and nothing since and was hungry, famished, in fact.

"Young man!" she called impulsively, and the boy turned toward her.

"Over here, young man," Allison said, beckoning. Would Canadian apples taste better than English apples? She would soon know. Grinning toothily, the child approached, singing out, "Epples! Sveet epples, five cents!"

Allison groped in the depths of her handbag for a coin, grateful she had exchanged all English funds for Canadian while aboard ship. What fun they had had, she and Binky, Freddy, Gilly, and the others, acquainting themselves with nickels, dimes, quarters, and so on. The "boys" had played games of chance, and though Allison had not joined in, she had become familiar with the new, strange money as it passed from hand to hand or lay in piles on the table.

"A nickel, right?" she said now, producing the coin triumphantly. The young peddler grinned, took the money, picked up an apple from a dwindling supply, swiped it on the arm of his coat, and handed it to Allison with a flourish.

"Velcome to Canada," the urchin said with a rather courtly bow, which delighted Allison and made her laugh. Their laughter mingled as the apple salesman went his way crying his wares.

Theodora—where was she? Allison stood by her trunk, munching on the apple, but her attention was given to searching the dock, now comparatively free of people, for a glimpse of her companion.

Just when impatience changed to fretfulness and then to alarm she didn't know; it crept upon her like a fog and was recognized with reluctance.

It couldn't be! It simply couldn't be! It couldn't be that Theodora would desert her, leave her alone, penniless, friendless.

But it could be. It certainly could be. Somehow it didn't seem at all out of character where the careless Theodora was concerned. Part of Allison accepted Theodora's perfidy wholeheartedly, unsurprised. If there was any surprise, it was to wonder why she hadn't suspected something of this sort long ago.

When the truth settled in, the suspicion accepted as fact, the fear began, sweeping over Allison in waves. Never in her life had she been alone in public; women, young women particularly, were escorted everywhere they went. Consequently, she had never done any thinking for herself along lines of being independent.

When she looked around, saw the departing people, noting the absorption of everyone with their own affairs, panic swelled in Allison's heart. Sitting down again on the steamer trunk, she tried to still the tumult in her bosom, tried to think rationally.

She would need to get herself off this dock. But how? Where would she go? Frantically, desperately, she jumped to her feet and called to a lone man hurrying past. "Sir . . . Sir . . ."

The face that turned toward her was cruel, it was crafty, it was sly. Or so she, not a practiced discerner of character, assumed.

The man's dark eyebrows raised questioningly.

Hot blood flooded Allison's face—would he think her a loose woman making an overture?

"It's nothing," she managed. "I'm sorry, it's nothing," and the man, with a shrug, moved away.

Limply she collapsed on the steamer trunk.

"Oh, God! Help me!" If ever a cry of desperation ascended to the throne, this was it.

Always someone had been there to care for her, to supply her every need; no wonder she hadn't prayed. Now, with no earthly resource available, she turned to God as surely as a homing pigeon seeks its cote.

And didn't she have good reason to do so? A passage of Scripture—an invitation—learned in childhood, suddenly had meaning: "Call upon me in the day of trouble: I will deliver thee" (Ps. 50:15).

So once again Allison, alone and helpless, called. "Oh, God! Help me!"

She opened her eyes to see the young apple peddler trundling past, his wares depleted. Without thought, without planning, her voice raised in a spontaneous call.

"Oh, apple boy! Young man!"

The youngster, no more than twelve years of age, paused and looked her way. Recognizing her, a quick grin lit his face. In response to her beckon, he approached.

"Epples all gone," he said proudly.

"I see; that's wonderful, I'm sure. I'm wondering if you can assist me. May I employ you to take my steamer trunk to the depot?"

"Employ . . . steamer trunk . . . depot?" the lad repeated, blinking.

"Yes. You see, my . . . my transportation has deserted me." Noting the eyebrows of the lad had knotted in puzzlement, Allison forsook formal conversation.

"Listen," she said simply. "I need to get to the train station. Can you take me? I'll pay, of course."

Suddenly she realized she wasn't a bit sure she could pay him or had the train fare to get to Toronto. Muttering for him to wait a minute, she dug into her bag, locating a few coins in the bottom of it. Then, with a catch in her throat and a sob of pure relief, her hand encountered Sarah's small purse, handed to her at the time of farewell. Sarah's love gift, the money Grandmama had given her over the years and which she had never spent. It was a lifeline, pure and simple.

Allison had only a moment to wonder: Had her heavenly Father—knowing she would call upon Him in her extremity in faraway Canada—prepared the answer *before she called?* It was an awesome thought and one she would pursue more thoroughly at her leisure. The small possibility of it was enough to square her shoulders, lift her head, and put a note of confidence in her voice as she spoke again.

"Now . . . young man—"

"Mik," he said simply.

"Now, Mik, if you'll give a hand here, we'll get this onto the cart."

Regardless of a few interested bystanders, Allison helped heave the trunk up and onto the cart, where it seemed in imminent danger of tumbling off but did not, due to the fact that, as they creaked away, she walked alongside, her hand holding it steady while the boy Mik did the pushing. She felt quite like a pioneer trekking across the vast expanse of the prairie.

Mik, sturdier than he appeared, seemed to know the city well and, without hesitation and only resting three times—mostly, Allison felt, for her benefit—went directly to the train station. Here, at Allison's request, an employee helped lift down the trunk, and she turned toward Mik to smile, thank him warmly, and hand him a bill that caused his eyes to brighten with delight and perhaps amazement.

Realizing she'd have to watch her money more carefully in the future, Allison gladly paid the generous sum, said good-bye, and turned to the ticket office, ready for whatever came next. She'd been in Canada less than a day and had already been treated miserably and treated kindly. And was to be treated well again.

As she painstakingly counted out the money for a ticket to Toronto, a familiar voice spoke in her ear.

"I say, it's Miss Middleton, isn't it?"

Feeling more relief than she would have dreamed possible, Allison turned to face Binky Wallingford, her shipboard acquaintance.

21

O h, Binky!" Allison cried, half weeping, half laughing, so great was her relief. Even Binky Wallingford, useless creature that he was, seemed a haven in a terrible storm.

"There now," he comforted, recognizing some sort of emergency and rising gallantly to it. "Is something wrong, old girl?"

"Oh, Binky," Allison managed again, and she could not control her trembling. Until this moment she hadn't known how frightened she was. "It's more dreadful than you can imagine!"

"Come, come," Binky said kindly, and he led her to a nearby bench. "Tell Bink about it."

Allison searched out a handkerchief, wiped her eyes, and blew her nose. Finally, with a measure of control, she asked, "Where are the others? Or are you alone?"

Binky glanced around.

"They're around here someplace. Off getting a cup of Canadian coffee, I expect. Trying to get used to it. Have you noticed how dreadful the tea is here in this backwoods of civilization?"

Slowly, under the casual conversation, Allison calmed down. Binky, though patting her hand, watched with expectant face and questioning eyes.

"It's Theodora," Allison said finally, tragically. "She's gone . . . disappeared. She's forsaken me, Binky!"

"You mean—she's left you in the lurch? Are you sure? It can't possibly be. Can it?"

"It can't be, but it is! I waited and waited for her, until nearly everyone else had gone, and it was clear to be seen she wasn't there and wasn't going to show up. She's gone, vanished, and that Johann Kryzewski with her, I assume. Or her with him. They slipped away in the crowd; her baggage was gone, too. Binky— she purposely deserted me!"

"But that's wizard!" Binky said brightly, approvingly.

"Wizard? Not really," Allison objected, uncertain of what he meant but recognizing his stamp of approval on the entire matter. "I can't see what could possibly be . . . wizard—"

"Well, old girl," Binky said, "it sounds like a good thing to me; not bad by any means. I believe I'd thank my lucky stars, if I were you. You'll be much happier without Theodora the Dragon draggin' around your neck."

"But, Binky," Allison said, and her desperation threatened to surface again, "she's got all my money!"

"Your money?" Binky was taken aback this time. "She's got your money?" This was a tragedy of major proportions. How could one manage without money? How could one survive? And how could one possibly be jolly, when even with plenty of change in one's pocket, jollity had to be worked at, at times?

"My . . . my remittance money," Allison muttered, never having made the confession, the explanation, before.

Her companion's thought processes showed quite clearly as his usually genial face slowly changed, from the approval he was feeling, to thoughtfulness, to understanding, and back to approval.

Binky Wallingford, family scamp that he was and sent away because of it, understood Allison's situation perfectly after just a few moments of groping through her words. His surprise that

170

this adorable acquaintance could possibly be a troublemaker slowed him down a bit in grasping the true state of affairs. But the light dawned, and Binky felt he was face-to-face with a kindred spirit.

Because of Binky's own escapades and his inability to pass even one of the exams for which he sat, his father had shipped him off, a scapegrace. He had quickly fallen in with other young men in the same category, remittance men one and all; they understood each other, they had a certain camaraderie. Yes, he caught on to Allison's brief explanation quickly, without the need for her to say more. Perhaps a lot of things fell in place for him at that time—why a young woman, gently raised, of obvious good breeding, would be sent off to Canada, and with someone who seemed, to Binky's critical eye, entirely inappropriate. Yes, Binky grasped Allison's halting explanation.

Miss Middleton—Allison—was one of them!

"By Jove," he said admiringly, "who'd have thought it. A remittance, er, person."

"It . . . it wasn't all that bad, what I did," Allison defended, but she was not a bit sure she convinced the captivated Binky.

"That's what we all think," he assured her and was no comfort at all. "Well, welcome to the club! Now then," he said, getting serious, or as serious as Binky Wallingford ever allowed himself to get, "this Figg individual has all the money, you say? How did that happen?"

"I'm not quite eighteen," Allison admitted, "though I will be in a couple of weeks, and my father considers me ineffective, silly, ignorant, and helpless, I suppose. Theodora Figg carried everything—the funds to get by on until contact with home could be resumed, the letters of credit, the address of the person I'm going to live with in Toronto—"

"Person?" Binky asked, puzzled.

"A lady—"

Not certain whether or not the "person" was a lady or another such as Theodora Figg, Allison corrected her description: "A woman. A woman I've never met."

Binky whistled. "You don't know where you're going, you don't know the person you'll be living with, and you have no money. Adzooks!"

"Actually," she continued with as much dignity as she could muster, "I have some money. I can certainly get myself to Toronto.

"But when I get there—how will I locate this person, this Maybelle Dickey? Theodora has all the correspondence, all the instructions. And did Maybelle Dickey get my father's letter? You see, he didn't wait long enough to get an answer back."

"An unknown destination in an unfamiliar city." Binky was shaking his head at the thought, and the problems conjured up. "And a stranger to meet you."

"She's a relative of a relative, I suppose you'd say," Allison explained and felt no better for it.

"What a confounded position to be in!" Binky said sympathetically. Then, brightening, he added, "I say! Why don't you come with us? With me and the other chaps to British Columbia? We'll just zip—well, probably not zip—trundle by train on through the prairies and the mountains and the backwoods until we reach civilization and our own kind again."

"It seems quite civilized here," Allison interjected. "At least they've come a long, long way. And I quite like the freshness of the place, the newness."

What she called fresh and new, others would think of as dust and dirt, raw and makeshift. The finished and the unfinished produced a mix that the land had yet to adjust to, as well as the people involved, for they, too, often seemed raw and crude. Having come a little way, there was much to do, a distance to go.

"Here in eastern Canada," Binky explained, "or so the guidebooks say, it's all been tamed into farmlands. Very pastoral, really. Terribly bucolic, if you like that sort of thing. And it's tamed so much that there's small opportunity for adventure, or for business opportunities for that matter, which some chaps need if they mean to survive. So you see, most remittance men head directly to the Canadian West."

172

There it was again—the lure of the West. Even social outcasts found it irresistible, loading steamer trunks and boxes of supplies onto the Canadian Pacific Railway as soon as they were unloaded from the ship and rolling westward.

"On the other side of the continent, in British Columbia," Binky continued, "remittance men are able to live in communities already established by British people. It'll be like home—tea in the afternoon; games of squash; congenial interaction with people who speak and understand our language." All of them had commented on the hodgepodge of languages swirling like chaff through the immigrants.

So that's what Binky had meant by "our own kind," Allison thought. He'd come all this way simply to settle into another British environment.

"I'm surprised you haven't heard of them," Binky said blithely. "Windermere in East Kootenay, Nelson in West Kootenay. Isn't that name just a scream? Kootenay!"

"I find it rather . . . appealing," Allison murmured, while Binky talked on.

"We know about these communities, you understand, because they are touted all over Britain. Beautiful places, we are told, paradises where British people can live the lifestyle to which they are accustomed, the aristocratic way of life, so to speak."

Something in Allison rebelled. Something in her resisted the very thought of recreating the lifestyle to which she had been accustomed. She might as well have remained in England! In the Kootenay communities she would find the same stifling Victorian conformities she had struggled against back home, and they had no appeal for her.

With glad cries of welcome, Freddy and Gilly fell upon them, and when told by Binky of Allison's difficulties, repeated his invitation to join them until Allison was bombarded by goodwill and the generous offer of comradeship.

"Wait, wait!" she managed, laughing in spite of herself. "Give me time to think."

With the three young men posed around her, Allison gave serious thought to the situation. After a few minutes Binky took out his pocket watch, looked at it, and said, "Well? What have you decided?"

Not one whit less confused than she had been, Allison could only sigh and throw up her hands. "I don't know what to do," she admitted.

"Choose one of the British communities," the fellows at her side encouraged. "You'll be welcomed and made to feel at home."

"And you'll be chaperoned by us—at your service!" Three well-groomed heads bowed gracefully.

But did she want to feel "at home"? And wouldn't thoughtfulness dictate that she not move on without at least contacting Maybelle Dickey? To leave her in the lurch without explanation would be as bad as what Theodora had done.

"I need to get myself to Toronto first of all," she decided. "This Maybelle Dickey may be the answer to everything."

Binky and company had to be satisfied with that, though they sighed and shook their heads, expressing their disapproval and disappointment. A remittance person, be it man or woman, could still command a good life if proper plans were laid. For once in their short lives they were in a place to make their own decisions, and unanimously, it was to go on to Kootenay's British communities.

Shrugging, they made preparations to board the train; there would be no dawdling in Quebec City. They hastened to leave the unknown for the known, the unfamiliar for the familiar. Prepared for adventure, they settled for routine.

Allison was astonished at the amount of luggage Binky and his friends had brought with them.

"We have to be prepared for every contingency," they explained solemnly, checking on the stack awaiting loading. Allison could see tennis rackets, cricket bats, fishing rods, guns, boxes of games, a chest of medical supplies, an easel and paint boxes, a croquet set, a couple of musical instruments—a violin and tuba—and, pointed out with pride by Freddy, a full tea service of fine china and silver.

In their trunks, they reported, was a veritable repertoire of outfits. First of all, of course, was the formal dinner wear, a necessity wherever one went. Then the supply included polo uniforms, croquet party clothing, hunting wear, and even, in Freddy's case, a cowboy costume.

It made Allison's own steamer trunk seem pathetically inadequate to face whatever this land might offer or threaten.

Thus it was that eventually Allison, Binky, Freddy, and Gilly, plus additional "boys" of the remittance variety, found themselves gazing out the windows of a passenger coach chugging relentlessly out of Quebec City and headed west.

Allison had allowed herself to be talked into first-class accommodations, though she flinched at the inroads on her funds. She hoped that Maybelle Dickey would be well fixed, able to extend the financial help she would need until she could write her father, explain the situation, and receive a remittance from home.

The day offered the usual round of drinks, much laughter and good-natured chaffing, an occasional stroll through lounges, corridors, and stately dining rooms set with flowers and crystal and attended by thoughtful stewards. Just a car or two away, second-class passengers, bunched together like a hive of bees, made tea and cooked sausages on the communal stove, changed wet and smelly nappies, consoled their sick and elderly, and did it all with a conglomeration of languages that fell on the ear of the listener like water over Niagara.

But in first-class, civility reigned. Cocooned in the familiar, perhaps they shrank from the reality of what they were facing and the road to reach it.

Talking, strolling, eating, and drinking, their attention was rarely given to the countryside. One young man, glancing out, said uneasily, "I say, it's deucedly overrun with trees!"

Allison, more attentive, was stirred and awed by what she saw. Trees were everywhere, as far as the eye could see, the greenery laced with silver birches and all untouched by the woodcutter's axe. She lost count of the lakes, some of them still frozen, dotted with islands. Silently, overhead, passed great phalanxes of geese, drawn by some inner compulsion to the untouched waters of the north. Miles and hours passed without sign of houses or people. They stopped occasionally but saw no stations.

The train was a small caterpillar creeping its way through a vast primeval forest.

P ale in spite of the summer sun's relentless battering, shaking in spite of good strong muscles developed from the homestead's unending workload, Blystone Condon took his place behind the "sacred desk," knowing it was simply hand-hewn black poplar and he the frailest of clay.

It was his Sunday to fill the pulpit.

In spite of earnest, even desperate, prayer, the interim preacher had not made his appearance between last Sunday and this one, Bly Condon's appointed day to bring the message.

As full of words as a cloud is of rain when face-to-face personally with any one of the people seated before him, it was another thing to see them in a group, dressed in their Sunday best, their eyes turned on him expectantly. The sight caused Bly's sturdy knees to knock and his mouth to go dry.

Knowing he was sure to blunder badly, Bly wished he hadn't been so critical last Sunday of Brother Dinwoody's sermon, poor as it was. And Brother Dinwoody, in his corner, could be excused if he had a rather defensive look on his face that seemed to say, "All right, Mister, let's see how well *you* do."

Angus Morrison had opened the service; the singing had been spirited, the prayer satisfactory. The offering plates had been passed—all blurred insofar as Bly Condon was concerned. With his Bible clutched between his knees, he had been engaged in one final, desperate prayer, and it wasn't for words of wisdom and grace, for power to preach the Word unflinchingly, or for high and lofty thoughts to share. It was for deliverance, for some miracle that would keep him from the pulpit.

But God, Bly recalled, had not delivered the beleaguered Daniel from the lions' den; he had chosen, rather, to bring him through the ordeal. This truth should have been encouraging, could have seen him through. But Bly, certainly no Daniel, pled for deliverance, for bodily translation to some distant place far from the congregation gathered to hear him preach.

Angus had announced a brief meeting of the church board to follow the service. "We are still in the process of getting the interim pastor here," he explained to the patient congregation, and they nodded. "I encourage you men to set aside a few hours here and there to put in some work on the parsonage. As you know, the logs are up, the roof on, the floor in, and we are putting in the door and windows and working on the chinking. Here our women can help . . .

"And now, Brother Condon will bring the message of the morning."

Bly Condon sat like a rock imbedded in a school desk. Doom had struck. It was the fateful hour, and he had not been translated; neither had the Lord returned to catch his bride away, for which Bly, in his desperation, also had prayed.

His wife nudged him in the ribs and hissed, "Up, Bly! Get up!"

Bly stumbled to his feet and tottered to the front of the room, to wonder eventually how he got there—the memory of those few steps was forever blanked out.

The only Scripture that seemed real at the moment was Job's plaint: "The thing which I greatly feared is come upon me, and that which I was afraid of is come unto me" (3:25). Bly groaned in spirit.

But then his glazed eyes noted the lifted faces of his friends and neighbors. Without exception they were kindly, supportive, expectant (Bly wisely kept his gaze from the corner where Brother Dinwoody sat).

Of course! One and all, they were waiting for the Word of God to be disseminated to them. Sheep they were, awaiting what the faithful shepherd would give them for the day. And humbly he saw that no matter how faltering, how halting, how inadequate these lips of his might be, the Word of God would minister to them. For did not the Bible say, "The words that I speak unto you, they are spirit, and they are life" (John 6:63b)?

Strengthen these weak hands, O Lord, Bly prayed silently, touched by the need and inspired by the supply, *and confirm these feeble knees,* and dared to believe it had been done.

Yea, verily!

Bly had forgotten the scribbled notes he had pored over so painstakingly all week and laid aside whatever dim plans he had made. Lifting his voice, he said, "The Word itself will minister to us. This is going to be your service. We'll call it an old-fashioned people's meeting. Everyone who wishes to do so will have an opportunity to share a favorite Scripture, perhaps tell us why it means so much in their life."

It took the congregation only a moment to make the adjustment; it took a little longer to have the courage to stand before the others and witness to God's grace.

Slowly, creakily, old Brother Polchek rose and recounted how God had brought him and his numerous children and grandchildren from the old country. They had dared step out and make the change on the strength of Acts 7:3: "Get thee out of thy country, and from thy kindred, and come into the land which I shall show thee."

"Dis iss God's country," he declared earnestly, his rheumy eyes aglow. "For da Polcheks, dis iss God's country." And only his wife Olga's tug on his coattail stemmed the words of gratitude that threatened to flood forth and take up the entire hour.

Brother Polchek wasn't alone. Following his testimony it was as if a dam had broken, and the water spilled out as, one after another, the good people of Bliss stood and with smiles and tears gave God simple praise.

Each story was the same, yet different. One after another they recounted the dangers involved in their trek to the new land, the fears overcome, the grace experienced. And without exception the audience listened, enthralled, hearing their own story once again in someone else's words.

It wasn't until the Drop Octagonal, the schoolhouse clock, tolled the hour of twelve that Bly Condon, as caught up in the heartfelt stories as any of them, reluctantly announced that the time had run out.

"The LORD hath done great things for us; whereof we are glad" (Ps. 126:3), he read in closing to hearty amens. Offering up a simple prayer, he dismissed the service.

And when enthusiastic comments came his way, or compliments, or praise for the morning's events, it was with true humility Bly shook his head, confessing his helplessness and God's help.

But, "Lord," he whispered fervently, doubtful it could ever happen again, "let that man get here before another four weeks roll around!"

No one was happier than Bly Condon with the results of the short business meeting that followed the morning service (unless it was Brother Dinwoody, who was still smarting under his wife's unabated fury and still bearing with her continued wearing of her hair atop her head, a style he suspected she herself was weary of but too stubborn to change).

180

"It's a letter from Ben Brown," Angus, as chairman of the board, reported.

"Let's hear it." Herkimer, a bachelor, was never in a hurry to get home.

Gentlemen,

Thank you for your patience as I've made preparations here to be gone for a few months, disposing of certain possessions, renting my small apartment to a friend until my return to finish my studies.

I look forward to being with you, feeling God is in your invitation and in my decision.

My train will arrive in Prince Albert on the 15th. You are familiar, I know, with the unreliability of the railway and if I should arrive off schedule and find no one there to meet me, I'll understand and find transportation out to Bliss, as you suggested.

Sincerely,
Ben Brown

Two would-be preachers, at least, sighed with relief, lighter of heart than they had been for weeks, and vowed they'd never again criticize a man of the cloth as long as they lived.

Weary to the bone, soiled and in need of bathing, half nauseated, Allison opened her eyes to another day trapped in the train.

She was berthed in a section serving four people. When the beds were made up, Allison, horrified at the arrangement, refused to consider climbing into a bunk, even fully dressed; her bunk mates were Binky, Freddy, and Gilly. So she had stepped into the corridor until the young men were in bed, cheerily calling out the all clear, then had returned to sit, stiff as a poker, cold and uncomfortable, the entire night.

In the ladies' room in the morning, doing her best to wash herself and bring order out of the chaos of her clothes, Allison could only imagine what it was like in tourist- and second-class accommodations. If this was roughing it, that must be barbarism.

Her clothes were locked away in her steamer trunk; her portmanteau held only basic items, not articles of clothing. Allison would have felt highly embarrassed at the condition of her toilette if she'd been the only one; everyone was in the same state of disrepair. Even so, she was chagrined, dismayed, perturbed. No one, nothing, had prepared her for this sort of life.

The discomfort helped her make up her mind: She would, under no condition, consider going on with Binky and the "boys." Grateful to them, still she didn't relish putting up with their lifestyle any longer than was necessary to get to Toronto. There she would attach herself to—submit herself to?—Maybelle Dickey, at least for the present. It would give her time and opportunity to see what this new land might have to offer an immigrant of the female variety. Brushing elbows already with freedoms she never knew were possible, she found herself longing to explore, to step out, to dare. But she knew not what, or where, or how. It was a daunting thought . . .

A loud banging on the door startled Allison out of her reverie. Hastily gathering up her scanty personal items, she made way for a wan lady with a handkerchief pressed to her lips who pushed past with more vigor than one would have imagined in a woman so pallid and prim.

When the train pulled into Toronto, huffing and puffing to a standstill at last, Allison would not be cajoled into going farther, though Binky and company did their best to persuade her to reconsider.

"Thank you, thank you so much," she said with some depth of emotion, for truly the young men had been a port in a dreadful storm. But the train trip had given her time to think, to get her bearings, to pray—hesitantly, it's true, not confident of her rights. *Does the Good Shepherd hear the bleatings of a lamb outside the fold?* she had asked herself.

Binky and the others would be going on—on to Winnipeg, on to Calgary, on to Kootenay. The very thought of the trip made Allison feel faint. No, thank you, she would stay in Toronto.

Still, it was with tears in her eyes she stood on the platform, her luggage at her feet, waving at the three young men outlined in the train window. Their farewell hugs had been warm and generous; Binky's final call repeated their invitation one more time.

"If you change your mind," he shouted, "come on. You know where to find us—"

"Yes . . . Kootenay . . ."

—————

Toronto was Quebec City all over again. As there had been no Theodora Figg in Quebec City, there was no Maybelle Dickey in Toronto.

But this time there was no Binky. Binky had been dismissed, had thrown a good-bye kiss, had waved farewell from an open train window. Binky had disappeared down a train track until all that remained to Allison's vision was a faint trail of smoke lifting into the blue of the sky. Soon that too was gone.

It was then Allison turned to search the platform, the waiting room, the people coming and going. In the first place, she had no idea what this Maybelle Dickey looked like, how old she was, what she might be wearing—a flower in the lapel would have helped, a discreet sign bearing either her own name or Allison's would have been an excellent idea. She might have left word at the ticket counter—Allison inquired so often the agent eventually shook his head when he saw her approaching.

Not knowing what else to do, Allison found herself intercepting any woman who showed signs of pausing, lingering, looking around. "Are you, would you possibly be, Maybelle Dickey?"

At first she was hesitant, apologetic, mannerly. But as the hours passed and darkness threatened and the negative answers accumulated, she grew quite desperate, finding herself prone to grasp some woman by the arm, or step in front of her as she was about to pass by. Her voice sounded shrill to her own ears: *"Maybelle Dickey?"*

At one point a crowd of immigrants gathered on the platform to meet an arriving train, a heaving, shoving, jabbering host of people bent on boarding, having waited days and fearful of waiting more. Allison could only back off, circling the throng, continuing her search as she could, finding herself rejected impatiently by those whose thoughts were turned elsewhere. Many of them couldn't understand her and shook their heads and pressed on toward the quickly packed train.

Finally, worn-out, hungry, sick at heart, Allison sank onto a seat in the waiting room and let the panic surface: strange surroundings, no friendly or sympathetic face, very little money, alone. And cold. As the day waned the cold set in; the northern winter was not yet a thing of the past but lingered, blustering intermittently, reluctant to give up its grip on the land.

Large boots, solidly planted, plunked themselves before her downcast eyes. Slowly Allison looked up, past the boots to the uniform—it was the policeman she had seen patrolling the area from time to time and watching her suspiciously.

"Now then, young lady," he said brusquely. "Want to tell me what in the world you think you're doing?"

The law! It was the last straw. Allison's face crumpled; tears welled and spilled.

"Here, here," the large man said. "This'll never do. I think you may be searching for someone. You have all the earmarks of being forsaken. Am I right?"

Allison nodded miserably. But even this contact with another human being was an encouragement, and she spoke up, explaining her predicament. "Do you know a Maybelle Dickey?" she asked at the close of her account.

Of course the policeman did not; the city was large and growing rapidly, with vast numbers of immigrants arriving almost daily, moving on, being replaced by others.

"I don't know her, never heard of her, wouldn't know how to find her," the man said, not unkindly, slapping a nightstick against his sturdy leg in a manner Allison found nerve-wracking. "But," he continued firmly, "you can't stay here forever looking for her. You'll have to move on; you don't want to be labeled a transient. Get yourself a room is my suggestion. After a night's sleep you can consider your options—going back home being the sensible one for a young lady alone."

England? That was out of the question. Perhaps her face looked as hopeless as she felt; at any rate, the policeman said, "I can direct you to a nearby hotel, Miss, and see that your baggage is taken there. That'll get you out of the cold, at least. Agreed?"

Allison could only nod helplessly; what other option did she have? Perhaps tomorrow . . . perhaps Maybelle Dickey had her dates mixed. Perhaps the ship's arrival had been off schedule—Allison wished she had paid more attention to details rather than leaving everything to Theodora—and Maybelle Dickey had given her up. Perhaps Maybelle Dickey, like Theodora, was faithless, unconcerned, a deserter. Perhaps, and this seemed most likely to Allison, Maybelle Dickey had never received her father's letter; perhaps she didn't even live in Toronto now, if she ever had. Allison felt a stab of bitterness toward her father. It was squelched as being useless, serving no purpose whatsoever, wasted emotion.

The room in the simple hotel was barren, impersonal, not a place one would want to linger. It had a fireplace, however, and was warm, and the dining room was adequate. Paying for her room, ordering a bowl of soup, Allison's heart quailed to see her funds dwindling. Tomorrow must yield some solution!

But it did not. Allison, in desperation, went from establishment to establishment, speaking the name of Maybelle Dickey so often it became a shibboleth. Almost she expected to hear criers running up and down the streets calling the name of Maybelle Dickey until it echoed the length and breadth of the city.

Her effort was useless before it began. Leaving the area around the railway station and making her way to the mercantile district, she was stunned at the length and breadth of King Street, a glittering thoroughfare of fashion and commerce with magnificent emporiums and elegant shops and thronged with people. And none of them Maybelle Dickey, insofar as anyone knew. Allison, a country girl in the main, rarely having been out of Midbury, was acutely aware of the swirl of the city about her and felt like a fly on the windowpane of the world, infinitesimal, unimportant, dispensable.

She stumbled back to the hotel both angry and frightened. Helpless. Hopeless.

That night, sitting on the side of the bed, she emptied out her remaining money and counted it. After some figuring, she decided she could pay her hotel room and eat for approximately thirty days or take the train to Kootenay. But what would she do when she arrived? Who would pay her way then? The knowing, too-eager look in Gilly Greenborn's eyes, until now ignored, had to be recognized as rapacious; Gilly would offer succor, Gilly would extend largesse—but at what price? It was not to be considered. And if she chose to stay here, what would she do when her current funds ran out? She could never hear from her father in thirty days, perhaps not twice thirty days.

Suddenly home and shelter loomed large and important and then faded to far, far away and unreachable. There was no hope from that quarter. She could not go back; they would not come to her. She recalled her father's stiff and condemning farewell; her mother's good-bye had been accusing, careless. Home and shelter, mother and father, love and nurture, were nothing but memories; the reality was a small, remote room in a strange city.

At that moment of complete aloneness, Allison was flooded by hopelessness; her unflagging spirit collapsed in despair.

With a sigh that was surrender, a sob that was a prayer, she fell back onto the bed, her meager worldly goods scattered around her, and looked beyond the barren walls, beyond Gilly Greenborn, beyond Maybelle Dickey, beyond Theodora Figg, even beyond her father, mother, and sister. Looked to the One who, through it all, had never forsaken her, the One whose voice she had heard but had silenced, whose presence she had sensed but had rebuffed. In her prosperity, with her youthful strength, because of her wit and will, she had ignored the presence, turned a deaf ear to the voice.

She heard it now: *When my father and my mother forsake me, then the Lord will take me up*.

With a small cry Allison was off the bed and digging into her trunk, looking for the Bible she knew was there. The passage had rung a familiar bell, and with a little searching she found it; with tears she read it—David's twenty-seventh psalm. Here was another such as she, needing shelter, needing deliverance: "In the time of trouble he shall hide me in his pavilion . . . leave me not, neither forsake me . . . lead me in a plain path . . . I had fainted, unless I had believed to see the goodness of the LORD."

There, secreted away in a small corner of a second-rate hotel, in a burgeoning, bustling city in a vast, mostly unexplored country, the Father found His child. There, on a sagging bed, deserted and alone, the child crept into her Father's arms. And found acceptance, found love that would never let her go, found rest.

And in the creeping and in the finding she confessed her foolishness, her waywardness, her rebellion, her selfish independence, her sin. How sincerely she regretted them; how gladly she abandoned them.

Finally, with the very peace of God settled in her heart and stamped upon her face, Allison drifted off to sleep.

She awoke to the realization—clear and bright in the gathering gloom of the room—that she would buy a ticket for, turn her attention to, follow her heart to . . . Bliss.

24

It was a new day, new in more ways than one; new in ways that counted.

"And now, Father, lead me through this day," Allison prayed before ever rising from bed, and she was conscious of her heavenly Parent's love, of His presence, warmly reminded of His promise never to leave her nor forsake her.

Never forsake her! The realization brought quick tears to her eyes and a glow to her heart, and for a moment she took time to revel in the wonder of it all: once an outcast, thrust from home and fireside and family, disgraced, guilty, now welcomed, forgiven, warmly embraced, *approved.* It was enough to fill her heart with happiness and her day with sunshine.

Her decision of the previous evening—to make her way to Bliss in the territory called Saskatchewan—held steady, as though it were right and proper.

It was, in fact, the only thing to do. To align herself with the remittance men in British Columbia was out of the question; there wasn't time or money available to continue her search for

Maybelle Dickey; there was no way of going back, back to Quebec City, to the ship, to England.

The thought of locating Georgina Barlow, probably Georgina Abraham by now, was a slim but substantial lifeline. If this plan was of her heavenly Father, it would work out; somehow it would work out. But there was much to be done.

Rising, bathing, packing took but a short time. At the desk following a quick breakfast, Allison arranged to have her trunk transferred to the railway station. Following her baggage, she approached the ticket office.

The man in the ticket window recognized her immediately, her frantic inquiries of yesterday fresh in his mind.

"No, she hasn't showed up. And no one has asked about you," he said rather curtly, perhaps torn between duty and sympathy. He heard so many strange tales, answered so many questions, was asked to solve so many problems, that he might be excused for his reluctance to get involved one more time.

But his tautness melted before her smiling face; his defensiveness faded before the small dimple at the corner of her mouth. It was a total turnaround. Had this young woman been playing games with him? Or was it that she . . . could it be . . . was it possible that under yesterday's heavy strain, she had *snapped?* For if he had ever seen anyone distraught, it was this young woman, yesterday.

"I understand," she was saying now serenely. "I've given her up—the person I was searching for. And now, sir, I'd like to purchase a ticket for Bliss."

The man had faced some ridiculous, some dreary, some desperate situations in the course of his workday, but this topped them all—a ticket for Bliss. She *had* snapped! Either that or she *was* playing games with him. In either instance the ticket seller was of no mind to cooperate.

"Bliss, eh?" he said with exaggerated interest, his sympathy dissipated. "We'd all like to find it, I'm sure. And if we could sell tickets to it, we'd have a trainful in a minute. Would you care to settle for a ticket to ecstasy? Or paradise?

190

"Now, lady," he concluded, having had enough of this foolishness, "if you'll just move on; I've got serious customers here."

Allison said with a twinkle, "You don't understand. Bliss—it's a place, a real place in . . . well, somewhere in the Territories. Saskatchewan, I think."

"Saskatchewan, you think," the man said, becoming peevish. "Well, I can tell you it isn't on the list of stops for the Canadian Pacific, that's for sure. Maybe you're thinking of the Heavenly Express, ma'am. Now, if you please—"

And he dismissed her, moving his gaze past her to the man behind her in line peering over her shoulder, listening with interest.

"Help the lady," the listener said. "I'll wait."

With a sigh, the ticket seller turned back to Allison. "Bliss, you say?"

"Bliss," Allison supplied. "I have it on good authority—there is a place called Bliss. Would you, could you please ask? Ask someone back there—" and she indicated others working beyond the man serving her. "Perhaps someone will have heard of it."

"For Pete's sake!" the man muttered, adding other, less acceptable words under his breath as he walked rather stiffly to a desk in the rear. There a brief conversation took place, and the ticket man, rather subdued, returned to report, "There is a hamlet by that name in northern Saskatchewan. In the bush country, actually. But no train goes there. The nearest station is Prince Albert—the end of the line. Is that where you want to go?"

He sounded skeptical, not sure why anyone would choose to go to the "end of line" by choice. A hopping-off place, that's what Prince Albert was.

"That'll be it," Allison said, though not entirely certain. Still, the little arrow inside her heart pointed in that direction; the peace persisted.

The ticket seller raised his eyebrows when Allison—a young woman of obvious good breeding, whose clothing was expensive and whose manner reflected the delicate things of life—requested a one-way, second-class ticket.

"You can have tourist-class for just a little more," he suggested, to be kindly but firmly refused.

Allison walked away, pocketing her ticket, leaving the man shaking his head, racking up one more unbelievable story to tell around the boardinghouse table that night at supper. "Bliss!" he would say. "Can you believe it? Bliss, in the bush? Someone with a belief in fairy tales must have named it."

This journey would not be like the previous one; there would be no amenities in second-class. Allison understood this, but the state of her finances had demanded the lower-priced fare. She stepped out onto a platform bright with the morning sun and already crowded with people.

There was nothing to do but wait; the stationmaster could make no promises regarding the schedule. Allison was intrigued when a train chugged into the station with a large white canvas sign stretched the full length of one car: Solid Trainload of Settlers for Alberta, it read, and a great mass of humanity, having boarded in Colorado, poured out, stumbled out, more than ready for a break before resuming the journey. How weary they looked, how battered. How harassed the adults, how rambunctious the children. And how grimly, soon enough, they climbed back aboard, enduring what had to be endured until their goal should be reached. They would grind across Manitoba, then Saskatchewan, finally reaching Alberta and, for them, the end of the rainbow.

The sight awed the watching Allison. She caught a glimpse of the lure of free land and the tenacity of men to have it for themselves.

When at last a train was announced for Saskatchewan and points north, Allison hastened to board, locating the second-class car without any trouble—she followed the bulk of the crowd, the unwashed, the weary, the bedraggled, the single-minded crowd. Standing helplessly in the aisle as this mass of humanity surged around her, Allison was eventually invited to join a young couple and their three children. Gerhardt and Sylvie Barchev had quickly dumped their belongings and plunked their children into a section designed to hold four people. But noting the number of passengers, some standing with little hope of finding space, they wisely gathered their gear together, put their children on their laps, and offered a seat to Allison. With gratitude she sank into it.

Families of six to ten members were attempting to accommodate themselves in the small sections. Overhead was a tray-shaped affair used for baggage, closed up for the day. At night the baggage would be removed and stowed under the seats; the trays would be pulled down and became beds into which two adults or numerous children could climb; the seats below made two additional beds.

The car was greatly overcrowded at first, although Allison was to discover it would become roomier the farther they went, as family after family disembarked, some at sidings where no station existed and no one awaited their arrival. They and their meager belongings were set out alongside the track and the train pulled away, leaving them alone with only stretching prairie as far as the eye could see. Others on the train, heading for the same fate, watched in silence.

Before that, however, came the boarding, locating seats, getting seated, and the hubbub was great. While mothers attempted to settle their families and arrange their goods, children bounced up and down, screeching, crying for attention, eager to run the crowded aisles and finding it hard going because of the mass of bodies.

"It was good of you to make room for me," Allison said with appreciation once she was seated, with her portmanteau shoved precariously into place overhead. "I don't know where I would have found a spot otherwise. I . . . I didn't realize it would be quite like this."

Sylvie Barchev smiled wanly and admitted, in her broken English, "We would have had to make room for another adult, I'm sure, for we've come all the way from the east coast by train and have seen how people have to shove together. We found right away we were smart to make the selection ourselves rather than have someone force their presence on us."

Sylvie's gaze swung to the next section where an elderly couple and their daughter had found part of their space taken over by a rough-appearing man, unkempt, whiskery, large. Poor man, his looks were against him. Actually, he settled himself with a sigh, closed his eyes, and caused no trouble aside from the fact that his feet were large and always in the way, and—obviously long without a bath—his odor permeated the space like heavy fog.

It was only one smell among many; soon the foul air in the car was almost more than a person could bear—not only body odors but soiled babies, garlicky cooking, and eventually the smell of sickness. But to open a window allowed for soot and smoke, with many complaints on that account.

The daughter of the elderly couple was obviously ill. Seriously so. At first she leaned her head back, pale and perspiring. Soon her face became flushed, her eyes too bright, clearly feverish. The man in the corner of the seat, with no alternate seating available to him, did his best to keep out of the way, sleeping much of the time, looking on uneasily at other times. The old mother wrung her hands, helpless to do anything to help her daughter.

It was then Allison noticed him for the first time—the man who was to make a difference in the entire atmosphere of the car, who was to spread cheer wherever he went. And he went everywhere. No baby too croupy but what he took it in his arms and walked the aisle, giving the distracted mother a chance to rest, to sleep. No child too wild but what he calmed it. Groups of restless children were enticed into quiet games. Cups of water were brought from the cistern to the aged and infirm, cups of tea were provided for those needing solace and comfort.

In spite of herself Allison found her eyes following the tall young man with fascination. Who was he? Was he an employee of the railway? This she doubted—he certainly wasn't the usual conductor. For one thing, his "uniform" was a dark suit, far from stylish, in fact rather shabby, as though having seen much use. For another, she had never seen a railway employee dry the tears of a youngster who was upset for some reason or other.

The Barchev children, before the day settled into night, became restless, hungry, whining for something to eat. The prepared food from a basket had been doled out earlier in the day, and now Sylvie made the decision to use the stove at the end of the car to heat a meal of sorts. The crowd there had thinned a little; perhaps she could find a spot to set a pot into which she was emptying a can of beans. These, with some bread from her basket, would feed the family for the night.

Sylvie looked hesitatingly toward Allison.

"I plan to buy what I need," Allison said quickly. "There will be peddlers up and down the aisle soon, I'm sure."

Sylvie seemed relieved; the can of beans was small. "I'll have to leave the baby with you, Gerhardt, and Tina, too," she said. "Gus can come with me."

Gus hopped happily from the seat to the aisle, jigging impatiently, happy for this variation in the long, boring hours. Gerhardt took the baby, but Tina, only two years old, frightened at the unaccustomed sounds and sights, screamed at her mother's retreating back, struggling in her father's restraining hand, trying to follow her mother and brother.

"No, Tina! Sit down! Wait—Mama will be back soon," the father entreated, his face growing red with effort and frustration as Tina's screams and struggles increased and the baby, startled, set up a cry.

Ignorant when it came to children and their needs, Allison hesitated, watching the little drama with sympathy. Tina would never come to her, a stranger, but the baby—

While she hesitated, slow about offering to take the bawling babe from the father's arms, a tall, dark-suited form bent over the seat, gently disengaged the infant from Gerhardt's grip, lifted it over the heads of those in the seat, and cradled it on his broad shoulder, a shoulder showing signs of a previous child's spit.

"Let me help," he said, and who, being in trouble, could refuse? And where could he go but up and down the aisle, in plain sight of all? The baby was obviously safe, the parent greatly relieved. Gerhardt turned his attention to Tina and soon had her calmed.

Their savior was the young man Allison had watched all day. She watched again as he strolled slowly along, tottering at times as the train swayed, the baby on his shoulder perfectly happy. At the end of the car, he turned and strolled, perhaps staggered, back. This he continued to do as Sylvie, hot kettle in one hand and holding Gus with the other, came from the stove and sank into her seat, to locate spoons and feed her family. Then the baby was brought, peaceful and contented, back to its mother's arms.

"Thank you, oh, thank you," Sylvie said gratefully.

The young man, looking nothing like a nursemaid, said, "You're welcome," and added with a smile, "I need the exercise."

Allison, sitting not two feet from the face that bent over her, saw the smile up close. Saw the square jaw, the firm mouth. Saw the warmth in the eyes that were turned briefly on her, blue— deeply blue—eyes.

This was no wishy-washy, namby-pamby male. Masculinity breathed from every part of him, showed in every movement. But it was a masculinity tempered with gentleness, concern, thoughtfulness. *Iron clothed in velvet*, she thought. Silly—but there it was, her impression of him.

Beans. The simplest of fare. Allison watched the little family eat and, not having eaten adequately all day, found her mouth watering. How foolish not to have thought of bringing food along. The Barchevs cleaned out the pot with apologetic faces, but there was little enough for the two adults and two children; the baby, quiet now, nestled asleep.

The diner! Surely her presence would be acceptable. Hastily Allison straightened her clothes and her hair, spit on a corner of her handkerchief, and swiped at her face. Then, rising on unsteady feet, she made her way down the jolting carriage, through another and yet another, not so crowded, less smelly, finally coming to the dining car.

She had taken its opulence for granted. Designed for the wealthy, it reflected the luxury of the day. Holding her head high and her shoulders back, Allison commanded the attention and service afforded those who qualified, and she obviously qualified. Sinking into a richly padded chair, she ordered tea and—to the superciliously raised eyebrows of the waiter—toast.

Sipping the invigorating brew, feeling herself revive, Allison was startled to note the helpful man of the second-class car making his way down the aisle. As he passed her, his gaze dropped to her lifted face, and again he smiled, obviously recognizing her.

For a moment Allison's attention was distracted from her teacup; at that moment a vicious jolt of the train caused her arm to jerk and the tea to spill. She gasped as the hot liquid splashed over her hand.

The man in the aisle, thrown off balance momentarily, regained his footing, steadied himself, and lifted the cup from Allison's trembling hand. Setting it down he picked up a serviette, giving it to her for the purpose of dabbing at her hand, her clothing, the tablecloth.

"Are you burned badly?" he asked, concern showing in his voice. "Perhaps we should ask for some help; there may be balm available, or some such remedy."

"I think I'm all right," Allison managed, examining her wrist and hand. The skin was red but not seriously burned. "The tea usually isn't hot enough to suit me," she said shakily, "and in this instance I guess that was a good thing.

"I'm going to have the teapot refilled," she said, noting the waiter hurrying toward her. Appreciative of the stranger's help, she added, "Why don't you sit still long enough to have a cup? After all," she said, to justify her boldness, "I feel I know you, having watched you all day as you helped this one and that one with one thing and another."

The man hesitated, then, with a nod, sat down. "A cup of tea would be refreshing. It's a madhouse back there, isn't it?"

"Bring an extra cup, please," Allison requested, and the waiter hurried off, stepping like a dancer in a lively jig in time with the sashaying of the car.

"Heavens! What can be the trouble?" Allison wondered, swaying in her seat.

"I believe it's because the track shifted through the winter's freeze. The ground tends to swell; I suppose the rails may warp. It seems to be particularly bad along here. It's so open, you see, no trees, no protection. I can only imagine what winters are like. Fierce, I expect."

"Did you wish to order?" Allison asked belatedly, lamely. She realized she had been bemused by the man whose presence seemed to work some sort of spell on her so that she wasn't herself at all.

"Thank you for reminding me. I'm here to see if I can get a bowl of soup . . . if they'll accommodate me in that way. It's for the woman in the section next to yours—"

"Feverish. Sick. Do you mean," Allison asked slowly, "you are looking after her?"

"Someone needs to," the man said with a shrug. "Obviously her elderly parents are overwhelmed—"

"Why?" Allison asked abruptly. "Why do you do it? Are you a doctor?"

"No, indeed. I suppose it's because I see a need and get satisfaction out of filling it. And," he added with a grin that made his face boyish under a thatch of sandy hair much in need of straightening at the moment, "I might as well keep on the move. You see, I haven't got a seat."

"No?" Allison was incredulous. For hours this young man had been on his feet, with no break.

"Actually," he admitted, "I had one, but there were people standing. My mother," he said with another grin, "taught me never to sit if ladies had to stand."

The grins gave him away. The sober suit branded him a serious man, perhaps a businessman, but the grin—it was that of a mischievous lad.

The tea arrived, and Allison had just begun to relax when her companion set aside his cup, stood, asked again if she was sure she was all right, and explained that he really should be seeing about soup or some other nourishment for the sick woman.

As he made his way down the swaying car and returned with a bowl balanced in one hand, Allison found herself disappointed that the conversation had been so brief. Passing her, he shifted his gaze only momentarily from the bowl and its sloshing contents to give her, once again, his wry grin.

Turning her head, she watched, impolitely she was sure, as he made his way with grace and as much dignity as possible through the car, past various encumbrances including unsteady passengers, to exit the car.

She saw him no more that day; perhaps he had found a seat after all. But the woman in the next section seemed to perk up a bit after her nutritious meal and, when night came, managed to climb into the tray-bed, along with her aged mother. It was a painful, precarious procedure, reenacted up and down the length of the car.

In their section, Allison and Sylvie and the baby occupied the seats for the night, curling up, sleeping fitfully, while Gerhardt and the two older children made the climb overhead.

The makeshift sleeping arrangements were the cause of much grunting and groaning, shifting and complaining from time to time all through the night. Two children, somewhere, fell out of the overhead trays, to fill the night air with shrieks and howls. Babies wailed, women plodded to the stove or the cistern. Somewhere, muffled by its mother's efforts to silence it, a child coughed the night hours away. In spite of it all, people slept. Worn by the day's stressful inactivity and wearied by the anticipation of another such day ahead, they slept.

The morning brought great stirrings, much shifting of supplies, and dogged preparations for another meal. Allison, no doubt inspired by the selfless service of the unnamed man of the day before, offered to hold the baby while Sylvie took her turn at the stove, preparing sausages to go with the drying bread from

199

her basket. Nothing would do but that Allison must share the simple meal, which she did with gratitude, for no peddler had made an appearance, and no stops of any account had been made.

She was caught unawares when, without warning, her heart lurched. A lurch caused not by the rough tossing of the car but by catching sight of yesterday's man, once again making an appearance, walking down the aisle. For a moment she thought he was heading directly to her; to her thudding heart was added a quickened breath.

"Good morning!" he called cheerily, going past her to the ailing woman in the next section. Allison was disappointed.

"How are you this morning?" he asked her neighbors, and he spent a few moments listening, a few more moments encouraging. Then he proceeded along the car, being greeted by numerous voices as he went, stopping occasionally to make an inquiry, to touch a hand, to ruffle a child's head. Everywhere he was greeted with smiles, albeit some wan and all weary.

He had made a difference. In one day he had made a difference. Into Allison's mind flashed a thought of the remittance men and their self-absorption along with the guilty realization that she was, after all, such a one—a remittance girl. Or so she had been labeled, first by Theodora, then by Binky and his friends. Now it all seemed so useless, so selfish, so *wrong*.

Later, coming from the small, crowded, odorous room allotted to women and their needs, she came face-to-face with him again. And could do no less than smile, even as others had been doing. With little to smile about, she could only smile into the face that some, less observant, would casually call handsome but that she knew was much, much more.

There, swaying in the aisle, surrounded by confusion, they paused a moment while he inquired about her burn. Allison assured him it was fine.

"You're traveling alone, aren't you?" he said. "I don't believe you are part of the little family in your section. Will you be meeting someone? I mean—is there someone special waiting for you up the line somewhere?"

"Friends," Allison explained. "I'm meeting friends." Strange, but she had a feeling that, given time and opportunity, this man, this stranger, would be a kindred spirit, perhaps knowing the Lord, for surely his actions indicated this.

"I don't know your name," she said, turning to go to her seat and feeling that a rare treasure, a once-in-a-lifetime acquaintance, was slipping away from her. "I watched you all day, I had tea with you, and I don't even know your name."

"You may not believe it," he said with another of his wry grins, "but my mother actually named me Ebenezer—"

Allison had only a moment to glimpse the startled face of the young man Ebenezer as the train's brakes shrieked and the train did its best to grind to a halt, a moment while everyone was frozen in position. And then—as the train jerked to a stop—all fury broke loose. People were tossed into the air, into the aisle, on top of one another . . . screaming.

Overhead, the trays disgorged their contents like a volcano spewing forth its lava. Tumbling, falling, bouncing—a wooden case fell with particular force onto Allison's head. Fainting, falling, she heard her voice, like a distant whisper: *Ebenezer . . .*

I t was the church board's final meeting before the arrival of Ben Brown.

He couldn't rightly be called Reverend because he wasn't ordained, having been a student until now. Perhaps, being young, he would feel the necessity of a formal title—like "Pastor," certainly "Mr."—to give him a sense of his position in the community. Perhaps, being young, he would settle for the casual "Ben." "Brother Brown" was what most people would call him.

"Tomorrow," Angus reminded the board unnecessarily now, "is the day of his arrival."

No one had forgotten; they had the date marked on their calendars—it was liberation day for them. It was a day setting them free of the onerous task of preaching. But to admit this was another matter.

"Well, pshaw," Brother Dinwoody said offhandedly, "I'll have to put away the message I was working on. It was coming along well, too—"

"What is this one about, Brother?" Herkimer asked, gravely innocent. "Now that you've brought down the topknots of the district."

Brother Dinwoody spluttered but refused to be baited. Rather, with a fine and unusual dignity and a rare flash of wisdom, he counterattacked, "I'm thinking about 'Be ye kind one to another.'"

"Good choice," Angus interjected quickly, calming the troubled waters.

Brother Dinwoody, poor man, would never live down his one and only sermon. Although his wife seemed to have forgiven him and allowed him back into her good graces, she seemed devoted to the new hairdo. It was like a burr under a saddle blanket to her husband, who was thus constantly reminded of his inglorious attempt at preaching, an attempt that had given him the exact opposite results of those he had hoped for.

"Perhaps this Ben Brown fella will be sick some Sunday and need a fill-in," Herkimer, the rascal, who loved to tease, offered. "If I was you, Brother, I'd go ahead and get the sermon ready."

"Brethren," Angus broke in, "we are here to see if there are any last-minute details to be taken care of before the new man's arrival."

"The parsonage is finished—"

"But did the linoleum get laid?"

"Yep. Linoleum laid, firewood stacked—"

"But is there an axe?"

"In the shed."

"Food?"

"The ladies are set to stock the cupboards in the morning—fresh milk, bread, butter, and so on."

And thus it went, until someone asked, "Who's going to meet the train? You, Angus?"

"I thought I would," Angus said.

"Aren't you too busy for that?" Bly Condon asked.

And Brother Dinwoody saw his chance. "We're all too busy," he interjected firmly. "All us men, anyway. But," this is where he got devious, "how about one of the women doing it? They could easily take the day to go to P.A. to meet the train. Say!"—an amazing solution seemed to present itself—"I'll bet Eliza would do it!"

Eliza Dinwoody, Brother Dinwoody's oldest daughter, was turning seventeen, a marriageable age. She was a pretty girl, and the young swains of the district were gathering around like mosquitoes to an exposed ankle. Brother Dinwoody, desperate at the invasion, was of a mind to solve the problem himself. And who better, more trustworthy, than a man of God?

Angus, Bly, Herkimer—all turned reproachful eyes on Brother Dinwoody. After all, their gazes said, this is the Lord's work and serious business.

Brother Dinwoody, with a sigh, gave in and gave up, and proceedings went on as though they had not heard his solution. Eliza Dinwoody indeed! A minx if there ever was one, as they all knew. She'd find a husband, they were convinced, without the help of anyone, her father in particular.

But it showed how certain members of the district, fathers included, were scheming, planning, working—a new, single man was a challenge. The supply of bachelors far exceeded the demand, and unmarried females could afford to be choosy. It was rather like the bees' courtship, some thought: A vast number of suitors for the queen bee's attention were disdained, rejected, refused, and her favors were granted to one and one only, but the one of her choice. The women of the Territories—widows and singles alike—often had numerous proposals before making up their mind, before settling on the one of their choice.

"I need some parts for the mower," Angus said now, "and so I don't mind taking the time off. It may take most of the day, for who knows whether the train will be on time or not. Probably not."

"You'll be lucky just to have it come in on the right day, if you ask me," Bly said, knowing well how undependable the train could be and usually was. But they all remembered the days not too long ago before the railroad reached them and the isolation they had felt. The train track was a slim thread of contact with another world. Schedules were kept much better in summer than in winter, when sometimes for days, even weeks, trains couldn't get through. Still, even in summer anything could happen—a log across the tracks, collision with wild animals, torn-up tracks, surprising snowstorms.

"What's the word from Parker and Molly?" someone asked, having discussed Ben Brown "until the cows come home," as Herkimer put it, weary of the subject and having "milked" (Haha-haha—Herkimer again) it to death. Angus reported that things were going well for his daughter and her new husband; they had settled in with Parker's mother and sister and were getting certain things accomplished.

"Parker is having opportunities to preach from time to time," he said, "and that pleases him."

"When you write," Brother Dinwoody said with a mix of anxiety and pride, "do you report on the services here . . . the, uh, the sermons, for instance?"

"I do," Angus replied. "Or Mary does. Between us we keep them informed of how things are going."

"Does Parker, uh, ever ask for sermon notes?" Brother Dinwoody continued with an innocent face. The further removed he was from the cataclysmic day of his preaching, the more time pulled a blanket over the sorry aspects and magnified the good, such as a picture of himself standing boldly before a congregation, expounding the Word of God. A high and holy calling, and he had attained to it—once. He was convinced now that there were certain redeeming features to the discourse; perhaps Parker Jones would benefit from them. And Molly—Molly's hair was often left free; the modest bun, suggested delicately, was certainly appropriate for a minister's wife. His sermon might yet bear fruit.

"Not yet," Angus replied with a straight face, "but you must remember mail takes a long time going and coming. I'd hang on to those notes, if I were you."

Mollified, Brother Dinwoody headed for home. *It's funny,* he thought, *how things have a way of turning out all right, if you just*

wait. He suspected he could feel another sermon coming on. Perhaps something about "let us not be weary in well doing, for in due season we shall reap." One thing he knew for certain— there'd be no more mention of women's hairstyles.

⁘———⦿

As it turned out, Angus was not the only member of the welcoming committee. Several families of the Bliss congregation were represented the following day, few men among them, it's true.

When at last the train, much overdue, chuffed its way into Prince Albert, scattering cinders far and wide, shrieking its welcome to the skies, shooting steam in great gusts, the crowd on the platform—many of them having come just to marvel at this amazing example of modern inventions—included a dozen or more Bliss people, eagerly waiting, anticipating; they had been a long time without a pastor. Ben Brown might look like a gargoyle and waddle like a duck, but they would be happy to see him.

As it was, framed in the door of the car, awaiting his turn to step down, was a fine-looking, clean-cut, upstanding young man. Sturdy of build, one had the impression that he may have outgrown his clothes all his life. Nevertheless, his suit fit him fairly well, though it was considerably wrinkled. His shirt collar was rumpled, his narrow tie awry. His hair, obviously just wet, had been slicked into place. And not a mother in the group but what had her heart go out to him and longed to launder his clothes, iron his shirt, feed him.

His eyes—curiously taking in everything, from the wide, stretching sky to the raw settlement rapidly becoming a full-fledged town—settled on the eager faces lifted toward him, and his square face broke into a smile. Recognizing that they were there to greet him (the rapt gazes were fixed on him), he lifted a hand in greeting.

Stepping from train to Saskatchewan turf, Ben Brown could only dream what Bliss might hold in store for him.

26

She awoke to the sound of drumming; it was not a sound typical of the train car.

Allison was having difficulty opening her eyes; her eyelids seemed too heavy to lift, as if they were inclined to remain shut forever.

"Shhhhh—stop that! Put your spoon away! You'll bother the pretty lady!" The tone was hushed but urgent. It was cross, a harassed mother-voice. "Don't you see she's asleep?"

"Why don't she wake up?" a child asked fretfully, giving one final *whap* with his spoon before the sound subsided.

"I'm awake!" Allison said, and she thought she shrieked but uttered nothing aloud.

"Now sit up and eat your supper," the mother-voice continued, and there was the scraping of a chair, the tinkle of tableware, the bustle of movement. The smell of fresh-baked bread.

The smell of fresh bread? Allison was puzzled. Fresh bread—it was a fragrance not smelled aboard ship nor on the train ride.

And what had happened to the movement of the train—the swaying, the jolting?

Allison struggled to sit up only to fall back with a groan. Her head! What had happened to her head? Gropingly she raised a hand, encountering wrappings.

A further fumbling disclosed the reason for her sightlessness—the bandages not only circled her head but covered her eyes.

Panic rose in Allison's heart. Was she blind? And why? Where was she?

Ebenezer . . .

That name—why was it wrung from her subconscious?

Obviously her movements had been noted. There was the swish of clothing, the tap of a foot, and a gentle hand took hers and laid it down on the coverlet.

"She's restless," a voice above her said, and another, farther away, suggested, "Perhaps she's waking up. Try speaking to her, Mother."

The gentle hands took both of Allison's; the gentle voice asked, "My dear, can you hear me?"

Allison licked dry lips.

"I do believe she's coming 'round."

"Try lifting the bandages. I notice they've slipped down over her eyes. The poor dear can't see a thing; now hush, Petie, and eat."

Gentle hands worked at the wrapping, lifting the edges, folding them back.

Allison's eyes opened to look directly into a kindly, aging face.

"Where am I?" she whispered. There was nothing trainlike about her surroundings. Bare boards stretched overhead, and the smell of tar paper vied with the bread fragrance.

The face bent above her was not a face she knew—the face of a stranger worn with years of living, compassionate with years of kindliness, concerned.

"You're in my home, dearie. It's nothing but a tar-paper shack, I'm afraid, but it gives us shelter, and now you, too."

"What . . . what happened?" Allison asked in a dazed tone, raising a hand again to the curious wrappings on her head—a bandage, insofar as she could determine.

Ebenezer . . .

The name, coming from she knew not where, slipped away into the shadows of her mind.

"I'll tell you all about it; but right now, perhaps you should rest—"

"Where is the train?" Allison insisted and struggled to sit up. "Where is . . ." Who was she asking about?

An arm went around her shoulders, lifting, shifting, arranging a pillow at her back.

"There now, is that better?" the woman asked. "Just be still for a bit, my dear.

"You've had quite an injury. As soon as we know you're not going to faint again, we can talk, if you wish. Dora," she raised her voice, "pour a cup of that tea, if you will, and bring it over here."

Dora brought the tea. The angel of mercy—with lined face, wise eyes, gray hair—held it carefully to Allison's mouth, allowing a sip or two. "There now," she said again. "That should be what the doctor ordered. Trouble is, there's no doctor within a hundred miles, maybe more. And that's why you're here, my dear; it was the only solution. Do you remember receiving the injury to your head?"

Allison shook that member, or tried to, shut her eyes momentarily, and waited until the pain subsided.

"Of course you have a massive headache," the tea-offering lady said. "I had to . . . well, I had to sew the gash—"

Allison put her hand to her head again. "Maybe you better start at the beginning," she said. "I need to hear what happened. The last I remember, I was on the train, talking . . ." Her voice trailed off, uncertain.

"You haven't asked who you are," the woman said with a small smile, "so I trust that means you remember. We determined, from your belongings, that you are Allison Middleton, apparently come from England."

"Midbury," Allison said, "and heading for Prince Albert—a long, long trip." A strange trip, an unbelievable journey that had brought her to a strange bed in a tar-paper shack in the middle of nowhere.

No one, no one in the whole world, knew where she was. Perhaps no one cared.

In the midst of desolation, bright and clear came the consolation she needed, the reassurance: "He calleth his own sheep by name, and leadeth them out. And when he putteth forth his own sheep, he goeth before them" (John 10:3b–4a).

Quick tears beaded Allison's eyelashes. She blessed, and not for the first time, the governess who had insisted on memorization in the classroom and had chosen the Bible as a convenient source.

She wasn't lost from the care of the Shepherd.

"I'm Ella Dabney, mother of Dora and grandmother of little Petie over there," the woman at the side of the bed said, dabbing at the tears in Allison's eyes, not thinking them strange after what the young woman had been through.

What *had* she been through? Allison was not to know for another minute or two as Ella digressed to explain that her husband, as well as her son-in-law, Dora's husband, were out on the homestead, breaking sod, planting a crop.

"Potatoes," Ella explained, "are the best first planting and can be dropped into the ground as soon as it's turned over. Though we haven't been here long, we should get some sort of crop this first season.

"Now then—as to what happened. Is it possible you don't remember?"

"I remember being on the train . . . talking—" Again Allison's memory faltered.

"The blow knocked all memory of the accident out of your head," Ella said.

"Accident," Allison repeated, trying to remember.

"It may all come back to you at some later date. It happens that way at times. At any rate, somewhere back down the line a man showed up beside the train, sort of popped up from nowhere, I was told—perhaps he had been sleeping, waiting; trains are so often way off schedule. He was waving a flag, wanting the train to stop for him. The engineer put on the brakes quickly, too quickly, I guess, or else they froze up. Anyway, the train stopped far more abruptly than it should have. People were tossed around, bags and boxes fell, and that's how you got injured. The sharp corners of a big box fell on your head."

"Heavens!" Allison said faintly.

"Scalp wounds tend to bleed heavily. You were unconscious and blood-soaked, and the railroad personnel couldn't determine just how seriously you were hurt. And they didn't know what to do about it. I understand there wasn't even room to lay you down decently. The decision was made to stop at the next place and see if someone could help.

"That's how you came to be with us. We—Joe and I and Jerry and Dora—when we arrived, made the decision to live alongside the tracks rather than go off to the other end of the homestead. We felt we wouldn't feel so isolated, somehow. And the noise of the train doesn't bother us one bit. We step outside and wave, and just the sight of another face, even though it goes by so quickly, lifts our spirits. And who knows, perhaps a town will spring up here someday.

"Anyway, the train stopped here, and as soon as they found out we were willing to take you in and do what we could for you, they carried you off the train, with your possessions—"

"My trunk?" Allison asked.

"Yes, it's here—over there in the corner. A woman came off with you . . . said you'd been sitting with her and her family; she was upset and hated to leave you. A young man was carrying you," Ella recounted. "He seemed very concerned; would you know who I mean?"

"I remember a couple who made room for me . . ." Allison put a hand to her head. "But—" Memory stirred, struggled, and subsided.

"You said," Allison continued finally, "you *sewed me up?*"

"That's right. One has to be prepared to do a lot of things here on the prairie. The gash was just above the hairline, and it bled dreadfully. As you see, Dora and I removed your garments—Dora's been soaking them to get the blood out—and when I was through stitching your scalp, we bound you up and put you to bed. It's been several hours; I'd begun to wonder."

Ella paused, shaking her head, and Allison understood how helpless she had felt in the face of such an emergency. And how kind she had been to agree to keep her, tend her, mend her.

Ella tipped the cup of tea, now cooling slightly, and Allison drank gratefully.

"I'm afraid we have little or nothing to put on open wounds," Ella said with some concern. "We came with some medicine in case the baby got colic, liniment for burns and frostbite, tablets for sore throats, headache remedy, things like that. But the only thing I have for an open wound is Wire Cut Remedy—and it's a veterinarian concoction. It seems we are more prepared for our animals' injuries than for our own. Of course, there are no wire fences in sight nor will there be for ages, if ever.

"Wire Cut Remedy sounds fantastic if you can believe what they say about it, guaranteed to heal without leaving a scar—somehow I doubt that—destroying all germs and foul odors—"

"Foul odors?" Allison said weakly.

"Some sores turn bad. But not this one, I'm sure!" Ella sounded too positive, as though assuring not only Allison but herself. "Anyway, I was reluctant to use the Wire Cut medication. I think the best thing is to leave the wound open to the air. This good clean air should be a healer."

Thus saying, Ella carefully unbound the bandages, found the bleeding stanched, and left the puffy, purple wound open to the air.

"Hopefully it will soon form a scab," the good woman said. "I had to cut a little of the hair back, of course, but your hair is abundant, and you'll be able to pull it over the spot until it grows out again.

"Now I must help Dora fix some supper; the men will be in soon."

Thus saying, Ella Dabney rose from the side of the narrow bed, patted her patient, and went to the other end of the small space where her daughter was peeling vegetables and her small grandson was eating, occasionally giving a tentative *rat-a-tat-tat* on the tabletop with his spoon.

Allison's first thought: *It's time to take it all to the Lord in prayer.* Closing her eyes, lying back, she found comfort, and probably healing, in simple but earnest petitions lifted heavenward.

The wound healed rapidly. Ella was gratified with the sewing job and her decision to leave the wound open to the air. Allison was grateful to Ella, giving praise to the Lord for His healing and Ella's ministrations.

Sitting up in bed by the second day, then rising to play with small Petie and walk around the tar-paper shack, out to the sod barn and wire chicken run, Allison didn't take long in deciding the prairie was not for her; its huge spread, its vast spaces, overwhelmed her.

This place called Bliss—where was it? Was it another such as this wayside stop known as Dabney's Place?

"Bliss? Bliss?" the Dabneys and Goffs repeated when she inquired; they shook their heads. It wasn't until a creaking wagon of weary travelers came by to rest, to eat, to talk, that Allison learned that Bliss was in the heart of the bush country.

"Bush," the strangers said, describing the area to the north. "And thick bush, at that. Or at least that's the report we've had. Some people, defeated by the work of clearing it so's they can prove up their land, say it's too thick to take. Still, it's the place of our choice. We like green; we like the idea of lots of trees. We like the idea of bush. We're only sorry we have to plod through this flat land to get there." Here, in the face of their hosts' choice, drinking their water hauled many miles from a distant coulee, sitting in the shade of their tar-paper shack, their voices faded.

Bliss—whatever it was, wherever it was—was Allison's destination. That's where Georgina and David Abraham were, and they had extended a sincere invitation for her to join them. Surely such an invitation—considering all that had happened and was happening—had been prompted of the Lord.

She was eager to move on. She *needed* to move on for the sake of the Dabneys and Goffs. Having given her the bed in the small shack, Ella and Joe, whose bed it was, had joined Dora and Jerry and Petie in a tent in the yard. Allison was sure their provisions, which they shared with her generously, were scant, and the trip to replace them would take a day going and coming. Their cooking was done over a campfire in the yard, their supplies kept in boxes.

A sod house was in the offing, they explained to her; after showing her where it had been staked off, they led her to the prairie area where they were, as time allowed, cutting and stacking sod for its walls. Allison had seen inside the sod barn and shuddered, thinking of humans living in a duplicate of it—a burrow, in her estimation, fit only for rabbits or gophers or hibernating bears.

With some hesitation the travelers who had stopped at Dabney's Place offered Allison transportation. "You're welcome to go with us as far as we're going," they said. "If this Bliss is where you think it is, near Prince Albert, you'll be nearly at the end of civilization, at least for the time being. From there on it's Cree country—"

"Oh, thank you," she answered quickly. "But you see, I have a ticket, and surely I'll be allowed to finish the trip. After all, the train was responsible for the injuries I suffered."

She, the Dabneys, and the Goffs bade the visitors good-bye and watched the wagon, followed by a cow, trundle off across the prairie, growing smaller and smaller until it slipped over the curve of the earth and disappeared as surely as though the earth had opened and swallowed it. Once again Allison could look east and west, north and south, and see nothing but blowing grass.

The train tracks were a thin ribbon seemingly stretched from nowhere to nowhere. And yet, in a day or so, as soon as the bruising receded from her face, Allison would ride them to the horizon and beyond. Her heart, for some unaccountable reason, yearned for the beyond.

Ebenezer . . .

The sturdy oak-framed looking glass—hanging from a nail in the rough stud of a tar-paper shack after being transported west in lieu of the handsome but heavy French Pier mirror that was Ella Dabney's pride and joy—revealed a less-than-exquisitely dressed Allison.

Having worn borrowed clothes for a few days, she had now donned the clothes, the blood-stained garments, that had needed soaking in order to be wearable again. The white waist had fared well enough, the suit much less so. In spite of pulling and stretching, steaming and ironing, it showed sad signs of having shrunk, of being twisted out of shape. The skirt, of first-grade cheviot lined with taffeta treasured for its distinctive rustle and interlined with crinoline, and the bolero, trimmed all around with mohair-and-silk gimp and lined with "changeable" silk, simply were not intended to be submersed in water, let alone soaked and scrubbed.

With some dismay Allison pinched and pulled, stretched and smoothed, and still it bunched in strange places, bagged in others. If she hadn't lost weight throughout the days and weeks of her unconventional travels, it would never have fit at all.

Ella fussed around the young woman, with a yank here, a pat there, to say finally, with a sigh, "We did the best we could—"

"I know," Allison said quickly. "And I'm so grateful. I'll make out just fine. The West is not devoted to furbelows and finery, I've discovered that."

"We dress for utility, I suppose," Ella said, having worn nothing but cotton housedresses for weeks. A change to gingham or percale was the best she could hope for.

Allison turned from the mirror, satisfied that the bruising on her forehead had faded; the swelling was gone, and she had been able to pull her hair satisfactorily over the injury now well healed and of little or no concern.

She had tried to express her thanks to the Dabneys and Goffs, to Ella—a mother figure such as Allison had never known—in particular. She had tried to press payment upon them, half ashamed to do so, more ashamed not to. Perhaps suspecting her limited means, they had refused.

"We don't need money," Ella had insisted and added with a wry smile, "but if you have any marmalade in your trunk . . ."

Ella had a hankering for marmalade; sometimes, she admitted, it haunted her dreams. To savor once again a genuine English muffin liberally spread with marmalade—heavenly!

Of course there were no oranges, little sugar. "We think we'll find wild plums in the coulee," she said. "Plum jam will have to do, I guess. That is, if the sugar holds out."

Allison determined then and there to send a jar or two of marmalade to her hosts just as soon as she could. She had been impacted deeply by the sacrifices these folks were making to see their dream fulfilled. Life had held no such challenges for her.

To lose oneself in something meaningful, to see results, good ones, fulfilling ones. To rest at the end of the day with a sense of satisfaction in a task well done. To dream, and to work for the fruition of that dream. To serve . . .

Ebenezer...

Again the name—ephemeral, shadowy, fleeting—nudged her mind only to escape again.

Ebenezer. That it had something to do with someone on the train, someone who had unconsciously made a difference in the direction of her life, Allison now knew, but in a foggy way. Always the full memory of the man escaped her.

But now, constantly tugging at her mind, was the growing realization that life, after all, was not the proverbial bowl of cherries, that self was not the most important person in the world, that true satisfaction might be found in "doing unto others."

The influence of that sketchily remembered meeting on the train lingered on; those conversations, along with the kind ministry of Ella and her family, changed Allison forever.

Another thing—the teamwork of husband and wife here on the prairie homestead surprised and amazed her. Joe and Ella, Jerry and Dora—each couple was a unit. Neither could accomplish the task of wrenching a home out of the wilderness without the other. They were united in spirit, in purpose, in effort. Each had his or her own task to do and never counted it the less important contribution.

Allison recalled the pointless existence of the women of her mother's circle: A housekeeper ran the household, the husband ran the business, while the wife, a social butterfly, fluttered from one engagement to another, concerned more with the costume of the day than with the state of the empire or her next-door neighbor.

Surely there was more.

With her own future dim but promising, Allison's immediate goal was to meet up with Georgina and her husband, trusting it was the door to whatever else the Lord had in store for her. Surely it would not be to continue the meaningless existence she had known; surely a purposeful future awaited. It had become her hope and her prayer.

Whatever it was, it would not be defined by a perfect wardrobe! Knowing that the train, if on time, was due shortly, Allison tugged and straightened the shrunken clothes with a will and assured Ella and Dora they had done a good job on her behalf. More she found hard to say; words escaped her as she recognized the sacrifice these people had made for her, turning aside from the mountain of work that awaited them before winter set in on the prairie, sharing what they had with her, and doing it good-naturedly and generously.

Her appreciation was expressed in tearful embraces as the train appeared on the distant horizon and bore down on them. Jerry had taken a stance a few hundred yards up the track to signal that a stop was necessary.

With the iron monster vibrating, spewing steam, impatient to be on its way, and with their ears filled with noise, the time for words was past. Kisses and hugs were hastily given, hastily received, and Allison was assisted up the high steps into the car, hastening to a window where even now Dabney's Place was sliding past, a place poor in this world's goods but rich in all things that counted. And now, rich in memories.

Wee-sack-ka-chack—says the Cree version of Saskatchewan's history—built a raft and saved all the animals and birds from a great flood. He sent out a muskrat that returned with a fragment of dirt in its paw, and from it the land of today was created.

Ages and epochs passed, and settlers called the northern half the Canadian Shield, and the area to the south they called the Great Plains. Most of the Shield region was covered in boreal forest, the Plains in grass.

Where the Shield met the Plains there was a richly treed strip known as the park belt. Through it ran the Saskatchewan River, rising in the Columbia ice field, splitting into the North and South branches, flowing across the southern half, emptying eventually into Hudson Bay.

Homesteaders called it the bush. Although the frost-free season was, at best, one hundred days or so, the long summer days allowed for maximum hours of sunshine, and barring early frosts, grasshoppers, fire, and other deterrents, fine crops were possible.

The lure of this agricultural land as it became free for a ten-dollar filing fee was to draw hundreds of thousands of immigrants to the Northwest, eager to begin new lives, eventually to build a new society.

The trickle, soon to turn to a torrent, had just begun; Allison's train, snaking its lonely way across the plains to the bush, was filled with one wave of eager land-seekers.

Knowing nothing of the forces of nature—the pressure, heat, water, wind, and volcanic action that had shaped and formed the land over seemingly endless ages—Allison saw it as empty and echoing, and felt for the first time its pull, its attraction, its siren song.

But the song and the appeal arose in her heart only as the barren lands were left behind and the first scattering of bush appeared, enchanting her as it surrounded her and reached out to embrace her. The stretching prairie, in that moment, was forgotten.

It wasn't long until they pulled into Prince Albert, the end of the line. Named for Queen Victoria's beloved consort and founded by a Presbyterian minister in 1866, it was a vital community for homesteaders and settlers from the beginning. Now, just before the turn of the century, with the Lands Office established and doing a thriving business, it had become an important center for supplies and a jumping-off place for immigrants seeking a homestead.

With her baggage unloaded at her feet on the platform of the raw station, Allison's gaze took in the bustling town, and she felt the thrill of the pioneer.

Others, equally rapt and strongly focused, went their way with no thought, no glance, for the lone young woman.

Locating a hotel and obtaining a room was no problem; Allison was becoming an old hand at traveling. More tired than she knew, she collapsed on the bed, feeling a sense of arrival, of having completed her journey. Could such a thing be? Or was it possible there was farther to go—Kootenay and the remittance men's colony, for instance. She hoped not; passionately she hoped not.

A short rest, a scanty wash, a refreshing cup of tea, and Allison was ready, eager, to press on—to Bliss.

"Is there," she asked the waitress in the hotel's dining area, "a place by the name of Bliss around here somewhere?"

"Yes, indeed," the young woman replied. "It's about a dozen miles that way—" and her finger pointed in the general direction of east. "Fairway, Deer Hill, Regency—they're all out that way. Families with children move into an area, and a school comes into being. The community takes the name of the school, or vice versa. You got someone out that way?"

"I don't know; I hope so. Abraham is the name. Do you know anyone by that name? Georgina and David Abraham?"

"Sorry," the girl said regretfully.

"Well," Allison said, "I didn't expect to be that fortunate—to locate them that easily. They've just been here a short time, a few weeks, really."

"So what will you do about it?" the waitress said, beginning to gather up the dishes.

"Ask around, find a way to go out there, I suppose. Say, tell me—do they need any help here?" Allison was more than a little anxious now about the entire escapade (which made the elopement with Stephen Lusk seem like a romp), worried about her money running out, feeling very alone, very vulnerable, most unsure.

"Perhaps. You can always ask." The departing girl cast a skeptical look at Allison's clothes, fresh from the trunk and wrinkled but obviously well made, of excellent material, and stylish, insofar as she knew.

Allison took the remainder of the day to walk around, acquainting herself with the town, finding the energy exhilarating, captivated by the lack of fripperies and foofaraw, recognizing signs of certain small luxuries, catching a glimpse of the seriousness, and the excitement, of the homesteading of the West.

"You might inquire at the Creamery," the desk clerk at the hotel offered in response to her inquiry regarding Bliss. "No doubt someone has to bring the cream from Bliss farms to town regularly, perhaps daily, now that it's getting warm."

It was a good suggestion, and Allison, early the following day, did just that, making her way to the Creamery and asking if a delivery was due from Bliss.

"Yes, ma'am," a tall, rawboned man nodded. "Probably before noon."

"May I wait?" Allison asked, and who could refuse the big-eyed, anxious-browed young woman anything?

"Of course. And you may sit in the office, if you wish," the man offered. "In fact, I'll tell you when the wagon from Bliss arrives."

The man was as good as his word. Amid the clashing of unloading full cans and the loading of empties, he gave a jerk of the head and pointed with his nose toward a particular wagon being drawn up to the loading ramp.

Having waited three hours, Allison had lost all sense of propriety. Approaching the middle-aged man, she blurted, "Sir—I understand you are from Bliss, and I wonder if you can help me."

Angus Morrison—for it was he—turned his rugged, worn but still handsome face toward Allison and saw, with a father's eye, the taut grip of the hands as they clasped each other, the tense lines of the young, pretty face, and said gently, "Aye, lass. Tell me how I can help."

"I need," Allison said, ready to break down and weep now that the crucial moment had come, "I need to locate some . . . some friends of mine."

"An' are they livin' in Bliss?" Angus asked.

"I *think* so," the girl answered him.

"And what's the name?"

"Abraham. David and Georgina Abraham."

The Scotsman shook his head slowly, and Allison's heart plummeted. To have come so far . . . to have felt so *led*.

"Wait a minute; I'm remembering—"

"Oh, please—"

"Would they be churchgoers, d'ye think?"

Allison, actually knowing David not at all and Georgina just a little, nodded without a moment's hesitation. If there was one thing she was certain of from her short acquaintance with Georgie, it was that she was a church attender. If at all possible, Georgie would be in church. And she would have married a man of the same persuasion.

"I'm sure of it!" she said a trifle breathlessly.

"Well, then," the man said, "I think you may be in luck. There was a new young couple in church last Sunday. Seems as if I heard someone call him David. I was watching out for our pastor—he's still getting acquainted, learning names, and a' that. This other lad, the one I haven't met yet, is young, tall, big—"

"Oh, I'm sure it must be David! Well, you see, sir, I need transportation out there; I have a standing invitation to join them, and I need . . . I need—"

No further explanation was necessary. Angus Morrison introduced himself, learned the young woman's name, disposed of his load of cream, and drove her to the hotel to pick up her baggage.

Sitting on the high wagon seat, a heady experience for the gently bred English girl who was more acquainted with surreys and carriages, phaetons and hansoms, landaus and barouches, Allison was giddy with more than the elevation.

"Can it be," she asked tremulously, "that I'm really on my way to . . . Bliss?"

Angus, who himself had experienced the feeling—a mix of anticipation, unbelief, and satisfaction—said, "I found it so, m'self."

28

Having settled very nicely into the new parsonage and finding it comfortable and even attractive—picturesque to his eastern eyes, huddling as it did, low, whitewashed, a small gem in a green setting—the newly arrived pastor felt he was favored of God. He had been prepared to sacrifice, to suffer, to die if need be, for the sake of the "work." This piece of the wilderness wasn't as "wild" as his imagination had supposed. And its people were not the world's offscourings but men and women of spirit, determination, purpose. Having dared all, they were committed to making a go of it, however rugged that might be.

Ben Brown was immersed in study at the parsonage's round oak table, his books spread out before him, his hair in disarray from running his hands through it from time to time, when the first visitor of the day arrived. Rather reluctantly leaving his studies and the train of thought for next week's sermon, he went to the door.

"Good morning, Brother Brown."

It was . . . *who is it?* Still new to the district and the church and determined to be a good pastor, perhaps a superior one, Ben

Brown realized he'd have to do better in regard to remembering his congregation. His classes had emphasized the importance of knowing every member personally in order to be a true shepherd of the flock. The face of the woman peering up at him seemed familiar, but for the life of him he couldn't remember the name.

Struggling with his memory and sweating a little because of it, with the seconds ticking away while she waited, expectant, for his greeting, he did the best he could. "Good morning!" he responded in a too-hearty tone.

She was onto him; he could tell that. Her features took on a pinched, scornful look. This was not going well!

His options flickered through his mind: Make a guess? Ask her name? Apologize?

"Well," she said in a flat tone, obviously disappointed in him, recognizing and pointing out, without spoken words, his dereliction of duty, "I've brought you something from the garden—cucumbers, tomatoes, squash."

Ben Brown silenced a groan. Where, oh where, would he put the stuff? Never fond of squash, this green variety seemed rampant in Bliss gardens, and heaps and piles of it were arriving daily. He didn't know how to prepare it, and moreover, he did very little cooking, as hot as it was these summer days and receiving as many supper invitations as he did. The district, enthralled with the new pastor, had opened their hearts and tables . . . and gardens . . . to him without stint. And while he appreciated and responded to the love and the tables, he was having difficulty with the gardens.

"That's very kind of you, I'm sure," he said now, as enthusiastically as he could, adding lamely, as she seemed to wait and the silence lengthened, "Will you come in—"

The face was not only critical now but frosty. "Come in? That would be a most *improper* thing to do! Never let it be said that Thelma Bell didn't know her place!"

"I'm sorry," the harried pastor said, relieved to know her name now but wondering what was so improper about it and supposing young men shouldn't extend hospitality to middle-aged women. Why hadn't the class on ministerial protocol covered situations such as this! Better still, why didn't he have a wife to be the "helpmeet" a pastor obviously needed! Ben Brown, to date a contented bachelor, was finding his single blessedness far from being a blessing.

"I'm sorry," he repeated before the disapproval on her prim face. "I certainly didn't mean any insult. I wasn't suggesting anything, er, unacceptable."

Perhaps she believed him; perhaps she decided to put him out of his misery. Most likely she had accomplished what she had in mind: establishing her pure motives, lest it seem odd that she should show up on the pastor's doorstep with an excuse as flimsy as vegetables. Thelma Bell was a virtuous woman! And definitely not searching for a husband! Not by any means; let no one think it!

Whatever the reason, it seemed Thelma's heart softened toward him, and in spite of her age and recent widowhood, or perhaps because of it, she did an about-face. It was fine to be straightlaced, but it should only be carried so far.

"I can see you meant no harm," she said in a conciliatory tone. "So . . ."

With horror Ben Brown realized she was, indeed, going to come inside. What could he do but step back and allow her to precede him into the parsonage?

"We'll leave the door ajar," Thelma Bell said judiciously, "and that should silence criticism. I just want to see for myself that you're getting along all right. After all," she said playfully, "you are the church's responsibility, you know. And let it never be said that Thelma Bell didn't do her share of carrying the load."

Who was she! The wife of an elder? Chairwoman of a committee designated to see to his well-being?

At least he knew her name. "Will you have a seat, Mrs. Bell—"

"Widow Bell," she said, with a sigh of the proper magnitude. "But that was six months ago." Her tone managed to convey the

226

fact that she was fully recovered from her loss. "Now where would you like me to put—"

The inevitable had happened; her gaze had gone directly to the box overflowing with a vast supply of squash.

"I declare!" she muttered. "Why in the world didn't you say so!"

If Ben found it difficult to know what to say before, he was stricken dumb now. His mouth, he was sure, must be opening and closing like a fish's.

With a "Hmmmph!" she gathered up her offering and stumped out of the house.

"Maybe," he called after her desperately, "it could be canned."

"You don't can squash, *Reverend!*"

Ben Brown watched miserably from the doorway as Widow Bell flung her rejected vegetables into the buggy and followed them, as stiff as a poker if such a thing were possible when climbing into a tipping buggy.

After casting one dark look at the innocent box of squash, he returned to his studies.

Perhaps, he thought, in view of the many visitors he was receiving and the numerous invitations they extended, he should change his message to something other than Paul's warmly expressed desire to visit the Romans: "For I long to see you . . . that I may be comforted together with you by the mutual faith both of you and me" (Rom. 1:11a, 12). It had seemed an apt and timely thought as he and his congregation got to know one another.

But, he admitted now, the good people of Bliss needed no goad toward friendliness, no prompting toward hospitality; their invitations had been abundant.

That some of their interest in him was due to his state of bachelorhood he hadn't as yet suspicioned. "Unto the pure all things are pure" (Titus 1:15), another worthy statement by the apostle Paul, was true for Ben Brown and his innocence where the threatened female onset was concerned.

Innocent he may have been, but he was not stupid. And so, when another knock came and he opened the door and looked down into the upturned faces of two young women, understanding filtered through, though he scorned to give it much attention and certainly no permission.

At first there was silence—one girl was looking at him expectantly; the other wouldn't meet his eye. Ben took a deep breath, about to plunge into greeting unknown personages once again and doing it with diplomacy and tact, if possible. Thank goodness there didn't seem to be any squash in sight.

"Good morning," he said, supposing it was acceptable, if inadequate.

It was obvious the older of the two, a young woman, wasn't about to speak. Her face, in fact, looked mutinous. The other girl, younger and still childlike and shapeless, piped up, "We're the Dinwoody sisters—she's Eliza and I'm Victoria."

Ah, yes, the Dinwoody sisters. Daughters of Elder Adonijah Dinwoody. Standing expectantly on his doorstep. After the way Thelma Bell had so recently pointed out the poor taste of a female entering his male quarters unattended, Ben hesitated, not quite certain how to proceed.

The dreaded silence followed. Ben shifted his weight, cleared his throat, feeling his youth and his lack of experience keenly.

"Liza," Victoria hissed, nudging Eliza, who ignored her, having turned her attention to some distant bird on the wing across the yard. She followed its progress as though truly interested in its plan and purpose.

Victoria squirmed, turned red, and finally burst out with an invitation. "Papa . . . that is, Mama wants to know if you'll come for supper tonight."

She looked hopefully at him while Eliza, chin lifted, stared after a disappeared sparrow. But the stumbled words had revealed the true situation, the true source of the invitation: the Elder himself.

In the few weeks Ben Brown had been in Bliss, Brother Dinwoody had managed numerous innocent comments concerning the attributes of his daughter Eliza, of *marriageable age.* Now here she was, on display and the bearer of *his* invitation. And obviously not happy about it.

"Tonight?" the pastor repeated slowly, and Victoria nodded, again nudging her sister, whose expression never changed but remained cool and distant; clearly she was not happy with the situation.

"Tonight," Ben Brown explained with relief, "I have an invitation to eat with the Condons. Thank your father for me. And your mother," he added hastily.

"Eliza—" Victoria spoke crossly now, obviously tired of the responsibility of talking to their new preacher.

Eliza Dinwoody turned large, violet eyes on him, and with a look that could only be interpreted as reluctant, asked, "Tomorrow then?"

"Tomorrow," Ben stumbled, having no ready excuse. "Tomorrow will be fine."

The girls turned as one, stepped off the porch, and marched toward the road.

"Eliza!" On an impulse Ben called after them; they paused and the older girl turned. Raising his voice a little, Ben asked, "Would you mind coming back for a moment, Eliza?"

With only a brief hesitation the young woman walked woodenly back to him. Victoria stayed where she was as she supposed she should.

Ben Brown stifled a smile at Eliza Dinwoody's coldness; laughter would not be the best medicine at the moment.

"Eliza—" Ben said, looking at the closed expression, the tightened lips; here was one female who wasn't interested in the new pastor as husband material.

"Well?" she asked shortly.

"Would you rather I didn't come?" he asked.

The girl's face flamed. She was embarrassed; she was, possibly, ashamed.

"I won't, you know, if you'd rather I didn't," Ben said kindly. "There's no reason for me to come. No reason. None at all," he repeated.

Eliza raised her eyes to his. "It's Lars, you see," she muttered, tears very near the surface, held back by anger. "It's because of Lars Jurgenson."

And it was enough; her meaning was clear.

"Lars," Ben repeated, searching his memory and coming up with a picture of an energetic, rollicking sort of young man, blond, blue-eyed, full of life and laughter. "I see. And does Lars feel about you as you do about him?"

"Yes. But Papa; Papa—"

"I'm sure," Ben explained, "he believes he has your good at heart."

"I know that; he just cares too much! I'm old enough to make up my own mind! But Papa . . . Papa just drives me crazy! He'd make all my . . . our . . . decisions for us, if we'd let him. Fusspot!"

Ben threw back his head and laughed at her description of the fussy little man he knew as Brother Dinwoody. Eliza's threatened tears disappeared as she joined in.

"Perhaps," the pastor suggested at last, "when he finds out I'm not a possibility, he'll be willing to settle for Lars."

"Oh, thank you!" the girl breathed, her relief obvious. "And, and do come, Brother Brown. Do come tomorrow. I think," she said with an open face and true smile at last, "I'll enjoy it. Really enjoy it."

"It's settled then."

"Settled," she affirmed and walked to join her sister with a lightened step and, no doubt, a lightened heart.

Abandoning the sermon on visiting and having fellowship, Ben, new at sermonizing and searching his textbooks and theological tomes for another topic, settled on "Hypocrisies and Encouragements," Paul's warning to his disciples about the Pharisees. And wondered why, when Sunday morning came and he read his text, a ripple stirred through the congregation. And why

Brother Dinwoody sank in his seat until only the top of his thinning hair showed.

"Whatsoever ye have spoken in darkness shall be heard in the light; and that which ye have spoken in the ear . . . shall be proclaimed upon the housetops" (Luke 12:3).

29

It's beautiful ... so green! The birds! The sky!" Allison was captivated by the bush after the long and barren trek through the prairie. "And it's full of berries, I suppose—"

"There are berries," Angus confirmed, seeing through her eyes the beauty of the bush as he did at the first, before its crushing workload settled on him, never to leave nor lighten. "Berries of one sort or another during the spring and summer, hazelnuts in the fall. But it's the poplars we benefit from the most, I suppose—logs for building, wood for burning. What we clear from our land goes right back into the homestead one way or another. But," he said, knowing full well from experience, "we're talking about the good weather. Winter is another matter. These friends of yours, the Abrahams, will be working night and day to be ready for it."

"I can help," Allison said, but without the conviction she would have liked. Help—when her lily-white hands had never so much as washed a dish? Help—when her gardening experience had been limited to snipping flowers for the house?

Help—when her garments had been whisked away as soon as she disrobed, to be hung up by another, or washed, dried, and ironed before she saw them again, and all without any effort on her part? Help—when she had never so much as scrubbed a potato in her life, let alone boil it or mash it or cream it or scallop it or whatever else they do with potatoes?

"I'm terribly ignorant, I'm afraid," she admitted in a small voice. Playing the piano a little, singing a little, playing cards, serving tea—these graces seemed the most inconsequential of achievements when compared with milking cows, churning butter, baking bread, canning.

"But you're young, and you're healthy!" Angus said. "And you can learn. Many of us have had to do that; many of us are still doing that. That cream I left back there—I had never in my life collected cream, nor had I ever imagined living from its proceeds until the crop, good or bad, was harvested. We do what we have to do to survive; it becomes the source of our happiness, yielding enormous satisfaction. We learn to enjoy the little things— the first crocus in the spring, a new calf, fresh bread from our own grist, sunsets more glorious than any canvas in a king's palace—all for free."

Angus, in his rich Scot's burr, spoke eloquently and even passionately.

Allison recognized that here was a man of quality, probably well educated, yet a man who had forsaken everything he had known for the uncertain success of a Canadian homestead.

"These friends of yours," Angus said, "may be happy to have an extra pair of hands. You dinna know where their homestead is located, I take it."

"No," Allison admitted. "They just called out to me as they were leaving, separated from me by the crowd and the noise, and spoke the word 'Bliss.' We'll be in Bliss, my friend said, and though at first I thought she was describing her happiness, I knew it was a real place when she added that it was in Saskatchewan. Her last words urged me to keep in touch. I felt she really cared . . ."

Allison's voice trailed off. This fine man, this gentleman, knew nothing of her remittance girl status and would not. Born again, the child of the King, starting over in all ways, still Allison found herself ashamed of the remittance girl status.

She hadn't been in Canada long when she realized that many people strongly disliked remittance men. Educated but fit for nothing; ignorant of clearing land and farming, engaged in nothing productive, they were held in contempt. Having money and spending it foolishly when other immigrants lived on porridge and rabbits, they were envied even as they were despised. Staying to themselves, not taking part in Canadian society, they were unpopular. Their foolish behavior made them the butt of jokes; their uselessness was sneered at.

The fact that their culture would eventually have some good effect on the raw land was not yet foreseen. The fact that a few of them would forsake hunting and fishing and idleness for ranching and farming or other lucrative work had not yet become obvious. No, remittance men . . . and a remittance girl if there happened to be such a sorry creature . . . were not people to admire.

She realized that Angus Morrison and others, as she came to know them, would wonder what she, a girl and unchaperoned, was doing in the backwoods of Canada. A full explanation would be due Georgina and David; others would have to wonder. She could not, would not, admit to being a member of that graceless and feckless group—the remittance outcasts.

If Angus wondered about her hesitation to explain further, he said nothing. The West held many secrets, some better left that way.

Angus made the wise decision to ask about the Abrahams at the Bliss store. The general store supplied more than sugar and tea, nails and whitewash. It was the headquarters for news, the center for information both told and heard. It was as good as, or better than, a daily newspaper, some declared. No one wanted to drive ten miles to the store and ten miles back home and not have tidbits to share around the supper table with a family starved in more ways than one. Who in the district, for instance, had given up and moved away; who had been born; who had died or was likely to; who had married or was getting ready to, and much more.

And sure enough, the storekeeper, who was also the postmaster, knew exactly where the Abrahams had located.

"They've taken over the Mikovic place," he said in response to Angus's inquiry. "And you know where that is . . . just beyond Big Tiny's."

The Mikovic story had been a sad one, Angus told Allison as they moved on. "They were not prepared for the hardships," he said. "Not by any means. For one thing, they settled for living in a dugout—"

"Dugout?"

"Just a room scooped out of the side of a hill, dirt on three sides, logs or lumber across the front, and in this instance, not a single window in it. They were absolutely without funds when they arrived, but even so, they might have made it if they'd had a decent place to live. Winter in that dugout must have been like living in a rabbit hole. Mrs. Mikovic, I'm told, went mad. Raving mad. And who can blame her. We blame ourselves, in a way. Mary and I could have taken them in, made room for them until spring, if we'd known. But Mr. Mikovic put his wife on a sled and pulled out in a snowstorm, he was that desperate. We never heard," Angus said, shaking his head, "if they made it. At any rate, they lost the place."

In spite of the warmth of the day, Allison shivered. The beauty of the bush—it was deceptive. The dream—how quickly it could become a nightmare.

"Mary will be wondering where I am," Angus said, "and it's just aboot chore time. Would you consider staying the night with us, lass, and going on in the morning?"

And when Allison saw the snug home and met the gracious Mary and the sweet grandmother, Mam, who lived with them, her hesitation faded and she accepted the invitation happily. The supper was wholesome, the bath welcome, the bed comfortable.

Allison sank into it and into sleep as though settling into sheer bliss. Small amenities, small blessings, loomed large in the bush.

It was Mary, after all, who took Allison the remainder of the way in the morning; Angus, having been away one day, was pressured by the work awaiting his attention. Allison thanked him warmly for his care of her and his goodness.

"I don't know what I would have done," she said. "You made it into a pleasant experience. It was the first day I haven't been anxious for a long, long time. I think my heavenly Father had it planned—that you'd be there to help me. Do you believe in things like that?"

She knew he did when, at the close of the morning meal, Angus bowed his head and prayed. It was the prayer of someone on intimate terms with his God.

Strengthened, body and soul, Allison climbed into the buggy with Mary and drove off through the dewy morning down narrow roads through pressing greenery, serenaded by choirs of birds. Passing an occasional cabin or house where someone pulled back a curtain and waved, they jogged along, talking comfortably together, until they pulled into a small opening in the bush, and Mary said, "This, I believe, is the Mikovic place, or was."

The first thing Allison noticed was the smoke lifting from a stovepipe that seemed to be set directly into the hillside. The dugout.

30

If Allison had entertained any doubts about her welcome, they were laid to rest in those first few minutes.

As a dog barked a friendly greeting and the buggy creaked to a halt, a woman . . . girl . . . stepped from the dugout. At first Allison was unable to see the girl's face because she was bending her head to accommodate the low doorway, but as she raised it, Allison recognized her—Georgina!

Blinking against the morning light, Georgina took a moment to adjust her vision and another moment to accept what it told her: It was her shipboard acquaintance, often thought of, regularly prayed for—Allie Middleton.

With a glad cry Georgina was across the yard, stumbling over the dog, regaining her footing, flying to the side of the buggy.

Allison, having been unsure and uncertain—whether this was the right place, whether she would be welcome—tumbled from the buggy into the arms that were reaching for her. At long last her protective armor, having held her upright for so long and for so great a distance, shattered, fell, and was trampled underfoot as the girls embraced. Tears of relief and fulfillment ran down each pair of cheeks—Allison's thin, pale from travel and injury, Georgina's thin, brown from long hours of work in the Saskatchewan sun.

When Mary Morrison was confident that all was well, that Allison was in good hands and it was safe to leave, she turned back home. But not before she met Georgina and David, who came hurrying from the area of a small sod barn to add his welcome and to lift Allison's portmanteau from the buggy. Allison's steamer trunk, held in abeyance at the Morrison home, could be brought later.

But rather than taking the traveling bag to the dugout, David placed it inside a tent, which Allison, in the excitement of the first few moments and with so much to see, had not noticed.

Allison and Georgina stood face-to-face, hands joined, laughing, weeping, as they savored the moment, tried to believe the moment.

Allison could understand her own tears—a mix of fears fading, relief swelling in her heart, a knowledge of prayers answered. But Georgina? Why would she weep? For there was no pretense about Georgina's reaction; it was sincere.

Georgina's words were answer enough. "You'll never know the burden of prayer the Lord put on me for you! I declare, Allie, I believe I accompanied you across the continent, step-by-step, mile-by-mile, in prayer. No, don't thank me—I don't deserve any credit; it's what God laid on my heart, and I could only be obedient."

"I'm sure He put an extra burden on you the day this happened," Allison said as she lifted a tress of hair, revealing the still raw wound.

"So that was it," Georgina murmured with a note of awe, marveling at the all-seeing eye and the everlasting love.

"And it's what delayed me," Allison explained. "I was with these good people for several days, getting my strength back—I'd lost a lot of blood, they said. It took time to heal. You see, Georgie—"

"Come, Allie, and sit down. And then we can talk. Davie, would you build up the fire before you leave? I know you are anxious to get to work. I'll be sure and tell you all about our conversation."

David gave each girl a pat on the shoulder and, after a stop at the woodpile for an armload of wood, disappeared into the dugout, reappearing a few moments later and heading off across the clearing with a cheery wave.

In the shade of the poplars were several chairs, a table, some boxes—a comfortable camp arrangement—and it was here Georgina directed Allison.

Allison sank into a chair, surprised to note she was trembling, whether from physical weakness or the relief of the moment, she didn't know. Both, probably.

"You don't live in the . . . dugout?" Allison managed the unfamiliar word with hesitation, not certain it was a kind word to use. Perhaps "house" would have been less belittling.

"Oh, I couldn't!" Georgina said with a small shiver. "There's a very sad story about the lady who lived there before we came. And besides, it's as dark as midnight in there, unless the door is open. No, we stay out of there most of the time. We store things in there, and I cook in there. The Mikovics, poor things, left everything, desperate to get away and doing it in the middle of winter, and by cutter—a small conveyance with no room for household belongings. I feel dreadfully sorry for them, and someday we'll pay them for all the things they left—if we ever hear from them. In the meantime, it's given us a wonderful boost, supplying us with the things we need. There's the stove, a bed, kitchen utensils, some farm equipment, and of course a makeshift barn, and so on. It's like moving into a furnished place, in a way, except that it's so *dreadful* in the dugout. I can't imagine what it was like in the dead of winter; they must have crept around like moles. And think of the kerosene it would take to keep a lamp burning all the time!

"Mr. Mikovic," Georgina continued, "in the time he was here, managed to get logs cut and ready for a house—"

"Oh, Georgie, your own house!"

"And we need to get it up before winter. If we don't, it'll be the dugout for us. But David is digging the cellar, hauling the logs, assembling nails and shingles, and things like that. Soon now, we'll have a bee—"

"Bee—I've heard of quilting bees. Quaint idea, I always thought."

"Sensible idea! The men of the district, we're told, can put the house up in a day, probably get it roofed, windows in, floor down. We've already been to church and met some of them; others have come by to introduce themselves. Great people.

"But, oh, Allie," Georgina said, turning to her friend's story, "what are we doing talking about houses and bees and such when you are here, amazingly here, in the backwoods of Canada . . . in a tiny corner of the world called Bliss! Such a remote place, such a remote possibility. How did you find us?"

"You gave me the name before you and David disappeared, that day on the dock. I never forgot it—Bliss! Such an unusual name; more like a description than a location. Perhaps a portent of things to come, do you think?"

"I believe," Georgina explained, "it was named for the first settler. Still, I have no trouble with the thought that it might be a pledge of things to come. David and I consider it God's chosen place for us—our Canaan land, so to speak. Our Beulah land."

"Canaan, I understand. But Beulah?"

"Beulah. From the Bible. If this place weren't called Bliss, Beulah would be my choice. I'll ask David to read it to us tonight—the one Scripture that mentions it.

"Now unless I'm mistaken, the kettle will be boiling, and we'll have a cup of tea. Soon I'll need to start dinner. In this part of the world, the big meal, the main meal, comes at noon. But sometimes," Georgina said with an exaggerated sigh, "I think all meals are main meals with David."

"You love it; I can tell," Allison said, rising to follow Georgina. "You're happy; I can tell that, too."

Georgina's laugh was indeed a happy one. "And happier than ever," she said, "because you found us. Oh, Allie, I feel . . . I believe God has a plan and a purpose for you here."

Hand in hand the girls crossed the yard. Entering the dugout, Allison was taken aback by the smell, as of damp dirt; by the dimness, as of night even though it was midday. It was small, so small. Three sides were earth, as were the floor and the ceiling, though some effort had been made to fasten up a canvas to keep dirt from falling onto anything and everything. How chilling the thought of actually living in here, being shut in here.

With the door open there was sufficient light for Georgina to locate the pot and make the tea and set out cups and saucers; Allison sat on a stump at the side of a worktable and watched, absorbed; it was all so strange, so unreal, so foreign to anything she had experienced or known. Far, far away—in memory as in actuality—the silver service, the sugar tongs, the dainty sandwiches, the posturing, the proper teatime decorum.

"I can't believe it," she murmured, shaking her head with unbelief.

"It's unbelievable, that's why," Georgina said. "Hansel and Gretel wandering in a forest in the fairy tale was no harder to believe. But when you get bitten a few dozen times by mosquitoes, you'll believe it!"

Picking up the teapot now cradled in a cozy, she said, "If you'll bring the cups—"

Back under the tree, sipping tea, Georgina turned the conversation again to Allison. Why was Allison traveling this wild and lonesome land alone? Where was Theodora Figg?

Soberly Allison told of Theodora's perfidy as she had absconded with the funds intended to support Allison until her remittances began to arrive. "She left me high and dry," Allison said. "Absolutely alone in a strange land, and penniless, or almost so. She didn't even wait to see that I was safely in the company of Maybelle Dickey . . . you remember me telling you about Maybelle Dickey. Theodora took off, disappeared like a whiff of smoke in a high wind."

"This shocks me, truly shocks me! But she never did seem too concerned for your welfare, Allie. On the ship she went her way and let you go yours. But since it meant we could meet once in a while, I didn't complain. So what happened with this Maybelle Dickey?"

"Not a sign of her, Georgie. I don't know whether she never got my father's letter, or didn't care, or just what. I searched and waited and made inquiries, but it was a lost cause. I was absolutely desperate. Then, at the lowest point, who should appear but Binky—"

"Bertram Wallingford himself. And I imagine he extended an offer you couldn't resist."

"He meant it kindly. It was Gilly I was uncertain about."

"Gilly made an offer that wasn't . . . acceptable?"

"I could see it in his eyes. No thanks! So I went with them partway."

"And when did you make a change for points north?"

"I changed trains at Winnipeg, headed for Prince Albert . . . and Bliss."

"I love the way you say that. Bliss. True bliss, it seems, Allie, accompanies peace that passes understanding . . . joy unspeakable . . . rivers of living water."

Georgie hadn't changed. She was still a witness, still had a testimony.

"Georgie," Allie said, turning serious eyes on her friend, "more happened in Toronto than buying a ticket to Bliss, Saskatchewan. It was there, in a hotel room, alone and afraid and deserted, I started on my journey to the bliss you are talking about. The true bliss. In my despair I turned to the Lord—and Georgie, He was there! And," tearfully, "He hasn't forsaken me."

It is hard to say whose face shone the most—the teller or the hearer. Needless to say there were more hugs, more tears, words of praise.

"This is glorious news!" Georgina said. "The best you could have brought me. David will be so glad to hear it, for he's joined me in prayer for you."

The subject of Allison's salvation was not easily exhausted. Time flew by, and eventually Georgina decided, regretfully, it was time to fix dinner, the noon meal, and Allie accompanied her again to the dugout and had her first experience with paring potatoes. Scraping and scrubbing potatoes, actually, for these were new, generously shared from a neighbor's garden.

Never had potatoes tasted so good as they did that summer day—chunky boiled potatoes slathered in butter, sprinkled with salt and pepper, served on simple crockery under a poplar tree. Never had bread been so light and fragrant; never had milk, brought from the depths of the well, been so cool and refreshing.

The fact that supper would probably consist of the same things made no difference; it was all accepted as part and parcel of the new life, and the thanks, spoken over it by one pair of lips and three hearts, was sincere.

David lingered, hearing Allison's story. "Your injury," he said. "You haven't told us how you got that."

"It happened on the train," she began, and described, as best she could, the crowded conditions. "But you know all about that," she recalled, and they nodded.

"There was something about this part of the trip," she said thoughtfully, "something that got my attention, something I can't forget nor fully remember. Amid all the misery in our car, there was one person, a man, who wasn't too concerned with self to see to the welfare of others. A young man, I think, though he acted most maturely. Except for his grin . . ."

Allison paused, searching through her memory, remembering. Now, at last, the young, rugged, pleasant face smiled at her out of the fogginess that had surrounded the accident.

"A young man, with a grin, helping—" Georgina prompted.

"Yes, I remember quite clearly. He walked the aisle with crying babies, heated bottles on the stove at the end of the car, made tea and delivered it to elderly or ailing people." In a rush now she described the part the unknown man had played in the drama of that day on the train. "He stopped to speak to people, bending over them, perhaps encouraging them . . . played games with the

243

boys and girls. He gave up his seat to someone who didn't have one. And he did it all with such good humor, with this—"

"Grin?"

"I guess smile would describe it. A sort of self-deprecating—"

"Grin."

"A wry smile is a better way of saying it," Allison found herself explaining, feeling that *grin* was too limiting, too boyish, not descriptive of the feeling the facial expression had conveyed. "Sort of ironic, as though he were making light of himself and what he was doing."

David and Georgina glanced at one another, suspecting there was more to the story than Allison had told them.

"Was he an employee of the railway? Someone hired, perhaps, to see to the comfort of the passengers? If so, it would be his job; perhaps he was some sort of trained personnel."

"No," Allison said with conviction. "He was a passenger, heading, I don't know where he was heading. I was just beginning to know him . . ."

Allison paused, gone from them once again, digging into her memory bank, bringing up dim pictures but clearer than they had been. Georgina and David nodded wisely to each other.

"And then?" Georgina asked quietly, feeling she was treading on personal, private ground.

Allison started. "And then . . . and then the train stopped far too abruptly. Everyone screamed. I remember the screaming . . .

"The next thing I remember is being in the tar-paper shack of people by the name of Dabney, with a cut on my head that Ella, Mrs. Dabney, had sewed up."

"This," Georgina said gently, pulling back the abundant dark hair, showing it to David. "Had you fallen, Allie?"

"They told me that a wooden box fell from overhead, knocking me unconscious. The train stopped as soon as they came across a homestead with a woman on it. The man, the one I mentioned, carried me."

"The smiler. The smiling servant. Would that be a good way to describe him?"

Allison's face lit up. "Perfect!" she said. "He served and did it with a smile. I can't help but wonder—did he know the Lord? I think so; I can't help but think so. Well," she said regretfully, "I may never know." And she added, because her armor had fallen and she was truly among friends, "Though I've prayed . . ."

"His name, Allie? Do you remember his name?"

"Even in the worst moments, in the dark and dizzy places, I remembered his name. Oh, yes, I remember his name—

"Ebenezer."

That night, before they went to sleep and while the light of the long northern evening lingered, David read, at Georgina's request: "Thou shalt no more be termed Forsaken; neither shall thy land any more be termed Desolate: but thou shalt be called Hephzibah, and thy land Beulah: for the LORD delighteth in thee" (Isa. 62:4).

31

Although she refrained from saying so, Allison was taken aback by the size of the proposed log house. The small size.

But David explained, as he showed her the area marked out with the prepared logs lying nearby: "It's small for good reason. First, because of the logs already cut by Stanislas Mikovic; second, because of the heating problem—a big house demands more heaters and more wood, not an insignificant consideration. A small house is so much easier to keep warm."

"And third," Georgina said, "we don't have furnishings for a large house. As it is, we'll have to make do."

Make do. It was a term they all came to know and use. You made do when the butter ran out; bacon grease, or even cocoa thinned with a little milk, could be spread on bread. You made do when bread ran out and there was no more yeast; you made bannock. You made do when there were no clothespins; you spread the washing over the grass and low bushes. You made do when you didn't own a churn; you put the cream in a sealer or canning jar and shook it—no matter how long it took or how weary the arms became—until butter formed. You made do when you ran out of tea and there wasn't money for more—boiling water, poured into teacups with milk and sugar added to taste, gave you "Tea Kettle Tea." That is, if you had milk and sugar. If the teakettle bottom was blackened from sitting over the fire, you made do by taking it to the edge of the garden or plowed ground and turning it around and around until the earth scoured off the soot.

Standing beside the hole that David had scooped out, Allison looked down and imagined lowering herself into it, no doubt holding a lamp aloft with one hand and gripping a ladder with the other; she thought she'd feel like a gopher. Such a small hole, to hold supplies for a year or until the garden produced once again.

"There will be bins for the garden stuff," David explained, pointing here and there, "and shelves along the wall to hold the canning Georgie will do—"

Georgie took a deep breath and squared her shoulders in a gesture of pure bravado.

"I'll help," Allison said. "I plan to make other living arrangements for myself, but not too far away—probably in Prince Albert."

"Oh, Allie," Georgina answered, startled, "why in the world would you do that? You've just got here—"

"There will be a good boardinghouse in Prince Albert, I'm sure," Allison said as positively as possible. "I'll get along very well until money from home starts arriving. The first thing I must do is write my father. He has no idea where I am or where to send the . . . the remittance."

She used the word reluctantly, even to Georgina, to whom she had made an explanation of sorts on the ship.

"That's all behind you now," Georgie said. "This is a new beginning for you as it is for me, for David, for most everyone here."

"Yes, I know," Allison said. "That is, I know it with my head—"

"But you still feel . . . how do you feel, Allie?"

"Sorry, embarrassed, ashamed."

"As far as the east is from the west—listen to what the Bible says—so far has God removed our transgressions from us. That's good news, Allie, good news!"

"Yes, good news." Still, her foolish waywardness lay like an icicle in her heart.

"As for moving to P.A.—Allie, we want you to stay with us. Please stay here, at least this first winter!"

Allie blinked at the urgency in her friend's voice.

"You see, Allie," David put in, "I'm going to have to find work for the winter. We can't live all winter on our small supply of money and have any left over for seed and things like that in the spring. I hope I'll find work in P.A., perhaps at the grist mill or lumber mill, in which case I'll get home from time to time. But I'll not be the only man needing winter work, and I may end up going north to the woods. And that'll leave Georgie alone here for weeks at a time. We've yet to spend a winter here, but we've heard how hard it is, how cold, how long. The thought of Georgie being alone, facing everything alone, is more than I can bear. And yet we haven't known how to solve it. Until now, that is."

"And the house," Georgina said, "small though it may be, will have one end divided into bedrooms—one for us, one for you. So say you'll stay, Allie. Say you'll stay!"

Georgina's plea was difficult to resist. Especially when she added, "Perhaps that's one reason the Lord sent you to us—we need you!"

Never having been needed in her life, Allison was powerfully moved. Besides, she really had no other place to go, nothing to do, no one else to care.

"It sounds like a good solution for all of us, put that way," she said. "So let's think and pray about it." She knew her funds, once they began arriving, would be a tremendous help as she found ways to apply them on the homestead. Never in her life had she appreciated money; never had she been concerned about it or the lack of it.

Allison turned from the hole in the ground—cellar and storage place for their winter food—and felt an excitement, an expectation of things to come, things to *over*come.

"I'll go write my father," she said, turning away. "If you could let me have some paper?"

"And we'll get it to the post office and do a little shopping at the same time. Oh, Allie," Georgina said, changing the subject, "it's such an experience, shopping in Bliss's one store. It seems like a treasure trove when you need everything. I love browsing, dreaming of the things we'll get when we can. And when I make my purchases I pick and choose as though I were deciding between diamonds and rubies. Never have I been so careful, so selective. So thrifty! If red beans are cheaper than white beans, we eat red beans. And when it comes to buying flour, I get the hundred-pound sack and make sure it has the pattern I want so that eventually I'll have enough material to make something. It'll seem like getting something for nothing! We'll really feel like pioneers, Allie, when we wear flour-sack dresses."

Rather than being dismayed at the prospect, Allie found herself anticipating the new experiences, the simpler garb. Her own garments, removed from the trunk and shaken out, seemed pitifully inadequate for the tasks at hand. Hoeing in the garden, she hiked up a dress of french chelsea; kneading dough, she shoved up cuffs of foulard percale; a silk moire skirt, gathered up in her hands, served as a basket for eggs.

Her Creme Riviere, a "healing, cooling and penetrating ameliorative cleanser of the skin," and her Poudre Merveilleux, "this preparation gives the nails a splendid, lustrous and rosy appearance, which enhances so greatly the charms of a lovely and beautiful hand," were powerless to help her now. She got dusty and bathed in a zinc washtub; she got mosquito-bitten and uselessly dabbed on soda; she got sunburnt and applied kerosene.

Because of the sunburn, Allison decided against going to church, reluctant to meet the people of the district for the first time with a flaming nose.

It had been a week of firsts: first dishwashing, first baking, first chicken plucking, first bean stringing, first jelly making.

"I'll take the day to rest," she pronounced, "and recuperate. There'll be a busy week ahead, I'm sure. I'll try and use a little sense and protect myself from the sun. That way, I'll be fit to be seen next Sunday."

Georgina and David were anxious to go, eager to worship, looking forward to meeting their new friends. "And what's more," Georgina said, "David is hoping to approach the men of the church about raising the house."

"How exciting! I'll look forward to hearing all about it when you get home!" Allison said as she watched the wagon trundle off happily enough; there would be plenty of time for getting acquainted. She admitted to herself that she was showing unusual signs of reticence; she hesitated to think of it as shyness. Probably—she thought honestly—it was a reluctance to sit among blood-bought, born-again, heaven-bound people, contemplating her own unworthiness. A remittance girl! What would people think of her if they knew?

Allison squirmed uncomfortably. She knew she was forgiven; she didn't doubt it. But her humiliation at being thrust from home and hearth was profound. It was something she'd have to deal with, sooner or later.

It was a good time to wash her hair—she decided, turning her thoughts deliberately to other things—to sit in the sun and let it dry, to comb it and twist it and fasten it up.

Studying her shining head and her shinier nose in the mirror, she gaped at herself and hardly recognized the sunburnt face as the Allison Middleton—well-coifed, smooth-featured, self-assured—of a couple of months ago.

"If Mama could see me now—" she thought and almost shuddered for her poor mother's sake.

She managed to feed the range and keep the fire going, burning herself only once, which she counted an accomplishment. She managed to pull up the pail from the cold depths of the well, a well dug and lined by the absent Stanislas Mikovic, without tipping the bucket and losing the contents. She managed to combine the remains of last night's supper—a roast and potatoes and carrots—into a savory stew.

She managed, without any trouble at all, to burn it.

And didn't know it until Georgina and David were home, their clothes changed, and the three of them were sitting at the table in the shade of the poplar. Allison proudly filled three plates. Her first clue to the disaster was the grimace, quickly hidden, on David's face, and the warning signal flashed to him by Georgina, who, undaunted, took a bite and chewed valorously.

Tasting the concoction gingerly, and with difficulty swallowing it rather than spitting it out in disgust, Allison raised tragic eyes to her friends, to be met by their bursts of laughter.

"Don't look so miserable!" Georgina said. "It isn't a tragedy of major proportions!"

But to Allison, who knew the state of the cupboard, it seemed so. What else was there among the skimpy supplies that could be fixed quickly and easily—porridge took a long time; chickens took forever to chase down, butcher, pluck, and . . .

"We have plenty of bread," Georgina continued, "so we'll splurge and have bread and syrup. It'll be a treat."

Poor David, kind David. He gallantly ate most of a loaf of Georgina's good white bread, which was dripping with Rogers' Golden Syrup and accompanied by massive cups of tea, and declared himself "full as a tick" and just as happy.

Later, indulging in the ritual of the Sunday afternoon nap and realizing for the first time in her life how blessed it was, how necessary, how satisfying, Allison wisely counted the stew fiasco another learning experience and closed her eyes with a genuine feeling of satisfaction for a week's work accomplished.

At the table, David had announced that arrangements had been made: The men of the Bliss church would show up Tuesday for a log-raising bee.

32

"It seems we've been having a terrible lot of meetings lately," Brother Dinwoody complained as he settled himself into one of the school's desks. Outside, in the family wagon, waited his wife and children, impatient for their dinner. Alongside were the conveyances—buggies and wagons—of Angus Morrison and Bly Condon, their wives waiting with composure, satisfied the Lord's business was being transacted inside the church/school building. Herkimer, the bachelor, would find his rig hitched to the railing of the school fence and would make his lonely way homeward for his silent meal.

Herkimer, if he regretted his bachelor estate, never complained; in fact, it seemed he had given up seeking a wife. The single ladies of the district, always in short supply, were wooed by many another; Herkimer Pinkard found none to his taste. Or more likely, none of the available ladies found Herkimer Pinkard to their taste.

But no one could complain of his devotion to the church and its needs. Therefore, he and the other three members of the board gathered together as soon as the Sunday morning congregation had dispersed, the minister among them.

"This won't take long," Angus assured them, and they looked at him expectantly. What now? their expressions said. They had finally got the parsonage built, and the preacher here and in it. What could possibly need their attention now?

"Is there a problem, Angus?" Bly asked, checking his pocket watch and patting his rumbling stomach. "Was the offering down this morning?"

"No, not that. It has to do with the future of the church, particularly when it comes time for Ben Brown to leave—"

"Months away," scoffed Brother Dinwoody. "So what's the hurry?"

"Planning ahead," Herkimer offered, seldom in a hurry, "seems like a good thing. Remember, it wasn't raining when Noah built the ark."

Angus was accustomed to Herkimer's interjections and continued as though he hadn't been interrupted by the little exchange between two of his board members. "I've had a letter from Parker—"

"How are he and Molly getting along?"

"Fine. Just fine. Now if you'll give me your attention, brethren, we can conduct this business in proper manner and get on home."

"A hungry stomach cannot hear." Herkimer couldn't resist piping up one more time. The obscure quotation seemed to fit the occasion nicely.

Angus, usually the most patient of men, clenched his jaw and breathed deeply—it would be most surprising if he allowed his name to be presented for chairman of the church board another year.

"Go ahead, Angus," Bly Condon urged, while Brother Dinwoody frowned at Herkimer and clucked a disapproving *tsk*.

"Parker writes," Angus finally resumed, "that one of the teachers at Bible School of the Dominion has suffered a severe illness, and it will keep him from filling his position this year. At this late date, it's difficult to replace him—"

"Oh . . . oh."

"Oh, no, not that."

"I was afraid of something like this."

So responded the board members without ever hearing the remainder of the letter.

"Perhaps," Angus said, and who could blame him if he sounded a little testy, "one of you would like to take it from here?"

"Sorry . . ."

"Sorry . . ."

"Aw, you go ahead."

"You seem to be ahead of me, as usual," Angus said dryly. "Now where was I? As you have suspected, they've asked Parker to fill the position. It will be a one-year commitment. Since he had already arranged to be absent from us for about half that time, he asked that we consider giving him the extra time away, still with the option of returning to the Bliss pulpit at the end of the school year."

There was silence for a moment, but no one seemed too surprised; they had felt from the beginning that Parker Jones was meant for bigger things, better places than Bliss.

"How does Molly feel about this?" Bly Condon asked. "She seemed dead set against leaving Bliss at one time."

"She's agreeable to the one-year commitment. After that, she, as well as all of us, will need to make some decisions. Well, gentlemen?"

"Lucky we have Ben Brown already here—"

"Would he stay on, do you think? And are we agreed on asking him?"

There followed a lively discussion concerning the abilities of the young man to lead the church an entire year. His preaching ability was not in question; they were enjoying his lively spirit, his refreshing manner of speaking, his honest joy in the Lord.

"You're the one to lead the church, Angus," Bly pointed out. "With you at the head of the board, what fear do we have for that part of it? The kid—that is, Brother Ben—is doing a great job of preaching, and you're doing a great job as chairman. I say let's give Parker the permission he wants and then approach Ben about extending his time with us. If I'm not mistaken, he's enjoying himself."

"I certainly don't want to go through more weeks and months of waiting for another pastor," Herkimer spoke decidedly.

"It would mean we'd have to fill the pulpit again," Brother Dinwoody noted, and he was off and dreaming, scheming how he might expound on "Wives, be in subjection to your own husbands." A twittering mouse at home, Brother Dinwoody was a roaring lion in the pulpit.

"I agree with Herk. Let's ask Ben to do it," Bly said hastily, noting the speculative look in Brother Dinwoody's eyes and wanting to avoid any further harangues from the pulpit.

"I understand now why you didn't want him in on this meeting, Angus," Herkimer said. "I had thought, at first, that he should be here."

"I felt we'd be more free to express ourselves—"

"Well, I move we ask Ben Brown to fill out the year," Bly Condon persisted, amiable but hungry.

"I second it," Herkimer said immediately.

"How about you, Brother Dinwoody?" Angus asked, and all eyes turned on this unpredictable member of the board.

Brother Dinwoody lingered over his answer, savoring the moment. Perhaps his eventual "It's all right with me" reflected his disappointment concerning the night Ben Brown had eaten supper at his house and showed not a whit of interest in Eliza. Never one to give up easily, he could see that this new arrangement would give him time to resume his campaign for a husband for his daughter. He hadn't given up on the preacher.

But he had heard there was a new girl in the area—a prospective threat where a young, unmarried man like the preacher was concerned. Already Brother Dinwoody's devious mind was at work.

"I suppose," he said with an innocence so overdone that they were all immediately alert, "we'll all try to spend some of the day Tuesday at the log-raising for those new people, the Abrahams?"

and got a chorus of assurances, somewhat hesitant, it's true, since his intentions were suspect.

"I understand they have a girl living with them," he said, adding craftily, "an unmarried girl."

"Oh, yeah?" Just as Brother Dinwoody had hoped, the shaggy red head of Herkimer Pinkard turned toward the speaker. But so did the heads of Bly Condon and Angus Morrison, both happily married men.

"You love sayings so much, Herk," Brother Dinwoody said, quirking an eyebrow toward the district's number one bachelor, "you should know the old one, 'First come, first served.'" It would solve things if Herkimer engaged the attentions of the new girl, leaving the appealing pastor free for . . . for someone else.

Angus's face was a study; he obviously felt it was not fitting for an elder of the church to speak thus.

"She's a child, Herk, half your age," he said, and Herkimer, relieved of the expectations of one and all that he get himself a wife, relaxed visibly.

Foiled again! Brother Dinwoody sighed and wondered how he could develop and deliver a sermon on "Children, obey your parents in the Lord; for this is right."

J ust think," Georgina said at the breakfast table, a very early breakfast table, "this is the last day I'll cook a meal in the dugout!"

Her emphasis revealed the struggle and misery it had been and the pleasure and satisfaction she was anticipating.

"Whoa!" David cautioned, stirring his porridge. "We may not have the furnishings in the house by tonight. It probably won't be finished. Logs raised, yes; roofed, yes; floor in, I think so. How far we get depends on how many men show up. Some will be roofing while others will be flooring, I expect. Perhaps the women and girls will work away at the chinking at the same time—"

"Busy as bees! Isn't it good of these folks to do this for people they really don't know? I'm so very, very grateful." Again Georgina's voice betrayed her emotions. It was going to be a moving day, in more ways than one.

"I believe that some of them," David said, "feel a sense of guilt over the Mikovics and the sad conclusion to their stay in Bliss— there's one instance when the experience was far from blissful.

Folks wonder, I'm told, if they might have done more to help. But it was wintertime, and winter separates people, keeps them to themselves, even more than the work does in summer. Blizzards keep them hibernated in their own home, just trying to survive. Your neighbor could starve or freeze, and you might not know it—it's happened more times than one would like to think. That's one reason, Allie, we want you to stay over winter, to be company for Georgie. I know it's selfish—"

"Not a bit!" Allison said. "I'm the one who is grateful, thankful—to you and to God." Tears threatened. "I look around me and can hardly believe all that has happened. That I'm where I am, with the expectations, hopes, that I have."

"And what are those?" Georgina asked gently.

"Of course I can't know exactly, at this stage—it's all so new, so promising. I only know that somewhere along the way I've come to the realization that I'll only be happy and fulfilled if I do something for others. Quit being selfish and self-centered, and, well . . ." Allison hesitated, reluctant to expose her feelings, perhaps unable to express them satisfactorily, "serving."

There was silence at the breakfast table, broken only by the sweet song of a nearby bird.

"Is it like a . . . calling?" Georgina asked.

"It's like," Allison said simply, "a stake driven down in my heart. Just a knowing, a certainty, even a . . . a burning desire."

Georgina's hand, work-roughened but expressive, was laid over Allison's. "I think we understand," she said. "And I'd call that a calling."

All three laughed at the alliteration of her words, and the serious moment passed, for the time being.

David and Georgina had set up what they called "the family altar," and now, before they separated for the day, David read a passage of Scripture and prayed. God's blessing was requested on the day's activities and on all who participated; Allison's "call" was voiced, along with a request for enlightenment and fulfillment. "Help her understand it more fully, Lord," David prayed, "and, in Your time and way, bring it to pass."

At the amen David rose from the table and headed off to chores. Soon the wagons of the district would be pulling in, the men equipped with axes, saws, hammers, levels, mauls, ready to go to work, and David needed to have all things in readiness.

Allison lingered at the table; her face, which had been eager, had darkened, as though a cloud had passed over the sun.

"What is it, Allie?" Georgie asked, concerned, pausing in her task of clearing the table.

"It's, it's me," Allison said miserably. "I find myself dreaming, making all these grand plans, and then, and then I remember—"

"Remember?" Georgie prompted.

"Remember that, after all, I'm a . . . remittance girl." There was deep, deep hurt, even shame, in Allison's voice, and Georgie, about to make light of the problem, recognized it as a serious one.

"Did you ever think, Allie, that Jesus knows exactly how you feel? In a way, he was a remittance man."

"Whoa!" Allison unconsciously found use for David's word and found it a good one. "Jesus? Whatever do you mean, Georgie? He wasn't guilty of anything."

"He was stricken, smitten of God, and afflicted. He was oppressed. He was despised and rejected of men. Does that sound familiar, Allie?"

"Yes," Allie said uncertainly.

"Do you know what the word *remittance* means, Allie?" Georgina was intent now, earnest.

"To send money, a payment."

Breathing a prayer, Georgie set aside the dishes she held, sat down, fixed her eyes on Allison's, and said, *"Remit* has more than one meaning. As well as payment of money, remit means to release from guilt or the penalty of sin."

Allison looked up, a glimmer of hope in her eyes.

"The Bible has many references to the remission of sins," Georgina continued, "and remission is the act or process of remitting. Do you see the connection?"

"I'm trying . . ."

"Here, let me read it to you." Georgie picked up the Bible so recently laid aside by David. "It's right here in Romans 3:23. It's all about righteousness through Jesus Christ. Listen: 'All have sinned, and come short of the glory of God.' And sin would mean separation from the Father, right?"

"Right," acknowledged the separated one.

"Let me read the next few verses: 'being justified freely by his grace through the redemption that is in Christ Jesus: whom God hath set forth to be a propitiation'—that means an atoning sacrifice—'through faith in his blood, to declare his righteousness for the remission of sins that are past.' Did you hear that, Allie? *Sins that are past!*"

A wondrous light was kindling in Allison's eyes, replacing the darkness. "My sin—gone, remitted through Christ."

"He made the payment, Allie; He paid the price."

It was cause for tears, tears of happiness; it was cause for tremulous praise; it was grounds for victory.

"Now," said Georgina, with mock severity, rising to her feet and once again gathering up the dirty dishes, "never let me hear you fret because of the past again. You've gone from remittance girl to daughter of the King, all in a moment."

Allison, helping, reached for the drying toast scraps, feeding on the true bread from heaven; she picked up the greasy butter dish and, like Job in his good days, felt her steps were washed with butter; the sticky syrup container was honey in the rock to her.

"They'll be arriving soon," Georgina reminded, and the girls fell to with a will, getting the "housekeeping" jobs out of the way. They had baked and cooked the day before, and the dugout table was stacked with goodies awaiting the meal that would be served in the middle of the day, covered with tea towels against a horde of flies or any dirt that might happen to fall from the ceiling.

It had felt good to Allison, since arriving in Bliss, to use her young muscles, to be engaged in physical effort, and she looked forward to helping with the building. Whatever this "chinking" was, she could do it if other women could, she determined.

In preparation she had dressed in the plainest gown she owned, having first, with Georgina's help, ripped away as much of its trimming as possible. Still, if she'd only known it, its rosy coloring did ravishing things to her dark eyes and hair and the caramel cream of her skin from which the sunburn had receded. Fully recovered from both the sunburn and the scalp injury, she looked the picture of vibrant young womanhood. What's more, the joy of the Lord, so recently released, brightened her features like sunrise . . . Sonrise.

Down the road they came, appearing through an opening in the bush—the buggies and wagons of Bliss. Men, women, numerous children, waving, calling greetings, pulling into the Mikovic—Abraham—yard, ready to give of their time and strength to help a neighbor.

<hr />

Brother Dinwoody, preparing to go to the bee, gave instructions to his sons concerning the work to be accomplished that day. Vesta, his wife, who would accompany him, admonished Victoria about her tendency to dream and dally and reminded her of the cream to be churned, the weeds to be pulled.

Brother Dinwoody climbed into the wagon, into which the boys had tossed the tools he would be using at the log-raising. Vesta, and Eliza who would accompany them, placed the basket of food in the rig and climbed up, taking their places alongside Brother Dinwoody on the spring seat.

"In the cupboard are samples of everything I'm taking," the loving mother said, looking down at the children left behind, and four young faces brightened.

"But don't go in there and gobble it down now; wait until noon to eat it," the wise mother warned, and four faces fell.

"Well," the compassionate mother added, "eat a doughnut now, and save the rest for later," and four faces shone. Good-byes were barely over and the wagon down the driveway before the children scrambled for the kitchen and the doughnut plate.

It was good, and pleasant, riding along with one's wife at one's side, and one's daughter, too. So thought Brother Dinwoody. It was at that moment of contentment he heard Vesta clear her throat; it wasn't a normal sound. Having been married to the same woman for more than a quarter of a century, Brother Dinwoody figured he knew a normal sound when he heard it; he also figured he knew an ominous sound when he heard it.

Alert now, Brother Dinwoody, glancing at his wife to see if he could determine the cause of the ominous sound, intercepted a meaningful glance passing between his wife and his oldest daughter.

Alarm bells rang in the bosom of Adonijah Dinwoody.

"Beautiful day," he offered . . . quavered, for he dreaded confrontations with his nimble-witted wife. And she'd been far too docile about her upswept hair for too long; Brother Dinwoody felt certain this was about to change.

If he wasn't mistaken, the corner of his eye caught the movement of Eliza's elbow as she nudged her mother.

"Adonijah—" Vesta began, and Brother Dinwoody's heart sank.

Vesta called him by his given name only in the most portentous moments. It had begun with "I take thee, Adonijah" and had continued through all the solemn occasions of their married life. Otherwise it was "Ijah."

"Adonijah, do you think you might pull off and stop for a bit?"

"We'll be late—" he began desperately, feeling the net tightening around him.

"Eliza and I," Vesta said, "have aught against thee."

Without a doubt, she had his attention. Aught? *Aught?* Brother Dinwoody was far from ignorant of the Scriptures and recognized the word. But to have used it in everyday speech, or to have heard it used . . .

"Aught?" he asked rather feebly. This was more serious than he had supposed. Finding a wide spot in the road, he pulled off, stopped the team, turned with dread toward the adult females of his family. "Aught?" he repeated.

"It's Scripture," Vesta reminded him. "You're very free at giving out Scripture, Adonijah—topknot come down, indeed! We'll see if you're as good at taking it as you are at giving it out."

"Well, of course—" he began defensively.

"Now, Adonijah," Vesta began, with Eliza nodding at her elbow, "we, Eliza and I, want you to know that we've had enough, more than enough."

"Enough?" he quavered, his eyes going from one accusing face to the other.

"Enough of this interfering with our personal lives. We love you for caring, but you care too much! We want you to be head of the family and give us guidance, but leave our footsteps up to us!"

"Head . . . footsteps . . ." Brother Dinwoody was perspiring, and the sun was barely up.

"This hairdo," Vesta was continuing. "I'm sick and tired of wearing it up like this, but I can't take it down if you are going to gloat victoriously because of it. I want to take it down and wear it in any way that I choose."

Vesta was taking out the hairpins, shaking down her hair, gathering it into a bun, and fastening it to the nape of her neck in the old style. "I'm doing this because of my own free will, not because of your misguided opinion. Will you henceforth kindly leave my hairstyles up to me, whether up or down?"

More than ready, Brother Dinwoody had no trouble giving that assurance.

"And, Papa," Eliza said, bravely, beseechingly, "provoke not your children to wrath!"

Nailed to the wall, the busybody father could only acknowledge his interference in his daughter's life, foolishly so, unnecessarily so.

Brother Dinwoody, his eyes closed, admitted to himself that he had been a meddler. Vesta had always shown good sense in all that she did; Eliza had been an obedient daughter in all ways. Whatever had possessed him!

But he knew. A small man in stature, insignificant in most ways, or so he always felt, he had allowed pride to creep in, giving him a feeling of exaltation, a false sense of importance. Speaking from the pulpit—the glorious awareness of people listening to him raptly, the sensation of power and position, the feeling of authority—had been his downfall. The exultation of that experience flickered to life for one final moment before he snuffed it out.

Where, he wondered in the honesty of the moment, had been his acknowledgment of God's leading? Where the recognition that to God be the glory? Brother Dinwoody groaned and, not reluctantly, laid aside his fleeting moments of importance in favor of his old, usual self, inadequate as it might be.

But Vesta was saying, "Ijah, please just be your old, sweet self. That's the man I fell in love with, and that's the man I'm happy to live with."

And Eliza was adding, "You can trust me, Papa, not to be wayward, not to do anything to disappoint you and Mama. But please go back to being my dear papa once again! I love you, Papa!"

In losing we win, Brother Dinwoody thought dimly as he promised to be himself—his *dear* self—once again, and he was amply rewarded by a few tears, tender smiles, warm kisses.

Vesta never looked prettier than she did that summer morning with her hair pinned rather precariously to the back of her head. And when they pulled into the Abraham yard and lanky Lars Jurgenson came bounding to the side of the wagon to help a rosy-cheeked Eliza down, Brother Dinwoody gave the lad, very freely, a warm greeting.

Such excitement! Georgina greeted each wagon and buggy, each rider, and David helped secure the horses and rigs. The men of the district swung down, tools in hand or belt, and went to work with a will; most of them knew what they were doing. A few greenhorns were instructed and supervised, put to work notching logs, lifting them into place, assisting in numerous ways.

Four stakes had been joined by twine to outline the size and shape of the house. A trench lowered the first logs for an ideal base; soil would be piled around it by wintertime to add warmth. The corners were fitted as closely as possible for the same reason. The doorsill meant skilled labor, and the windowsills, but experienced hands made short work of them.

Girls stood by, ready to stuff moss and mud mixed with straw between the logs as soon as the men gave the go-ahead signal. Eventually the walls would be plastered with clay and whitewashed.

It would be a simple, snug building, a warm, beloved first home.

Georgina and the Bliss ladies were busy setting up for noon dinner. The fire was kept going in the range to keep the kettles of food hot, either on top of the stove or in the oven. Boards were laid across sawhorses, cloths stretched over them, and dishes set out in preparation of the feast to come; bread was cut; butter, jam, jelly, and pickles were ready. Radishes gleamed like jewels; sliced tomatoes and cucumbers and onions tantalized appetites jaded by winter's limited cupboard and titillated by summer's bounty.

Allison never knew she could be so happy, so released. She never knew she could feel kinship with people of the earth. Filling a pitcher with water from the well, she delighted in taking refreshing drinks to the perspiring builders. When it was time for them to come down and eat, she handed out fresh toweling for dank and damp male bodies as the shirtless men splashed water on themselves at the basins set out for them. She filled plates for the children and helped settle them on grass or stumps or wagon tongues to eat. With a knife clutched awkwardly in her hand, she helped with the unaccustomed task of slicing cakes and pies and bread.

Helping, serving, never had she felt more fulfilled; never more contented.

Once and once only she murmured, "Isn't this fun?" only to be met with puzzled glances. These women, she realized humbly, still had to go home to backbreaking labor and unrelenting responsibilities.

"You're right, of course," Mary Morrison said, and a few others nodded belated agreement. "The change, the being together—of course it's fun. It gives us pleasure to see another home go up. It's pleasant to eat together, to talk things over."

"I know I need to learn to relax," one mother harried with three small children admitted. "To enjoy time off without feeling guilty about it."

"So don't give in and give up," women of experience admonished, perhaps determining to go home giving thanks for blessings rather than bowing under burdens. Both were abundant.

Getting acquainted, working, the day was half gone and the men back to work before Allison realized it. She, with the other women, gathered around tables mostly denuded of food and looked ruefully at the scraps remaining. They hadn't eaten, and it didn't look promising.

"Cheer up!" Georgie said. "I set aside a couple of pies, a pot of baked beans, and a plate of garden stuff."

"Smart woman!" Praises for Georgina's foresight abounded.

"The workman . . . woman . . . is worthy of her hire," someone misquoted and heard no correction.

Gathered around, filling their plates, settling down comfortably, someone glanced down the road and remarked, "Say, isn't that the preacher?"

Those who had met him and might know, shaded their eyes. "Sure looks like it. He said he might show up; he had to check on Grandma Jurgenson first. She's under the weather, the boys said when they rode up."

Allison righted the cup of a careless child and refilled it with milk.

"Whoa!" The plodding horse pulled up and came to a stop, and someone hurried over to greet the pastor as he dismounted, to ask him if he'd eaten, to urge him toward the table.

Allison, napkin in hand, was cleaning the face of the youngest Polchek when Georgina, with the pastor in tow, stepped to her side, called for her attention.

"Allison, I want you to meet our preacher, Ben Brown."

Allison looked up. And up. And blinked into the sun shining behind the tall man's head, giving him a halo of sorts, an otherworldly appearance, as though from a different time and place.

"It's you!"

There was, in the preacher's voice, a ring of exultation such as a prospector might use when he struck gold, holding it aloft and publishing his find to the world. A ring such as a father might use when he holds in his arms his first child. A sound that a shepherd might make rejoicing over a lost sheep.

A hand, two hands, reached out to Allison. Two warm hands gripped the ones she automatically, numbly extended. Two hands drew her close.

"It's you," the voice said again, exultant, fraught with feeling, rich with emotion. "I've prayed; God alone knows how I've prayed . . ."

It was unreal; it was wonderfully, marvelously real. By the grip of the hands, holding hers and not about to let her go, Allison counted it real.

For a brief moment she had the sensation of yesterday falling away as though it had never bound her; of tomorrow stretching out to the horizon and promising fulfillment with blessings and bliss beyond measure; of today, and happiness held—sure and secure—in the palm of her hand . . .

Ebenezer.

Ruth Glover was born and raised in the Saskatchewan bush country of Canada. She has written many poems and books, including the Wildrose series for Beacon Hill. Ruth and her husband, Hal, live in The Dalles, Oregon.

Each novel in Ruth Glover's Saskatchewan Saga is filled with enchanting characters, surprising plots, and fascinating historical detail. Set in the late 1800s, the stories introduce Scottish and English emigrants who bravely journey to the wild Canadian frontier.

Book 1

Book 2

AVAILABLE AT YOUR
LOCAL BOOKSTORE

Book 3

The Saskatchewan Saga

Journey to Bliss

RUTH GLOVER

The Saskatchewan Saga

Seasons of Bliss

RUTH GLOVER

Book 4

The Saskatchewan Saga

Bittersweet Bliss

RUTH GLOVER

Book 5